MW01204136

RED HOT

STEELE

A Daggers & Steele Mystery

ALEX P. BERG

BATDOG PRESS
KNOXVILLE, TN

To Sara, who wouldn't let me quit without giving it my all

Batdog Press
www.batdogpress.com

Publisher's Note: This is a work of fiction. Names, characters, places, and incidents portrayed in this novel are a product of the author's imagination.

Editor: Brittiany Koren
Cover Art: Damon Za
Book Layout: ©2013 BookDesignTemplates.com

Red Hot Steele/ Alex P. Berg — 1st ed.
ISBN 978-1-942274-03-2

1

"**G**ods, this place is depressing." A dilapidated flophouse loomed over me. Four stories of faded brick and crumbling mortar. Four stories of blood, sweat, and tears, built on the backs of indentured half-breeds and destitute immigrants seeking refuge from their misery. Four stories of grim memories and heartbreak, smack dab in the middle of the Erming—the worst slum New Welwic had to offer.

It was just the sort of place I expected to find a gang of murderous goblin cannibals. Sadly, I'd dealt with their ilk before.

I dug my fingers into the crop of short, umber-colored hair that roosted upon my head and scratched. "I know we're talking about rat-poor degenerates here," I said to Griggs, "but you'd think the tenants could liven the place up a bit. What do you think, old man? Use the decaying bricks to jury rig some planters for flowers? Or maybe have someone spray a touch of graffiti onto the walls?"

Griggs glanced up at me out of the corner of his eyes with a look most people reserved for mental patients. "You, uhh...sure this is the place, Jake?"

That's me, Jake Daggers—six feet, three inches, and 220 pounds of sausage- and donut-fueled crime fighting brilliance. Everyone else at the precinct calls me Daggers. It's an unspoken code. No self-respecting homicide detective ever goes by anything but his surname unless it's so damned long and complicated it ties people's tongues into knots just thinking about it. But Griggs was a little long in the tooth, and by a little, I mean his teeth were darn near dragging on the floor. He was far past the age of caring what anyone else thought, so he called me by my given name and I let him.

I took a step toward the battered bricks. Once upon a time they'd probably shone a deep cinnamon, but centuries of the gods' heat and tears had turned the bricks a pale amber. A worn sign that was mostly splinters held together by grime hung from the front of the building. I gave it a wipe with the edge of my coat sleeve. Faint numbers peeked from underneath the sludge.

301 E. 57th.

"Yeah, this is the place," I said. "Apartment 407."

Griggs grimaced, probably as he envisioned the number of stairs awaiting him inside.

I took a look up the side of the flophouse. A set of eyeballs stared at me from between boarded up windows, and I could feel the heat of more sets of peepers burrowing into me from behind. I glanced back and spotted a couple of bearded uglies in an alley across the street. They looked none too friendly.

Griggs noticed them, too. "I knew we shouldn't have let our rickshaw driver run off."

"What, you think he would've stood around waiting for us?" I said. "In the Erming? Fat chance, pops."

Griggs glared at me. "Shouldn't we wait for backup, at least?"

"I sent a runner for Rodgers and Quinto before we left. They should be here any minute. In the meantime, we need to get our asses up those stairs. Every second those disgusting, degenerate greenies run free is a second too many."

I probably shouldn't have said greenies, but the filthy goblins we'd been following for the past week had me seriously steamed. The word 'greenies' carried centuries of hateful racial overtones with it, and considering the neighborhood, if any goblins had overheard me we could've faced a rising tide of angry race riots. Fires, looting, the works. Captain would've been pissed.

Luckily, Griggs was the only one who heard my slur. He grumbled, but I think it was only because he was still dreading the stairs.

I pushed into the hovel and mounted the staircase with Griggs in tow. The warped boards underfoot cried out with each of our steps like banshees announcing an impending death. Hopefully it wouldn't be Griggs. With him, natural causes were as big a threat as goblins.

"Well, so much for the element of surprise," I said. "If the baddies are here, they'll know we are, too."

Griggs grumbled again. I was starting to think he'd come down with a debilitating case of lockjaw.

We successfully reached the fourth floor without Griggs coughing up a lung, which I considered a victory. I sidled my way over to the seventh and final door on the left. A window unit. *Nice*. Apparently the goblins had splurged for the penthouse suite.

My partner gestured toward the door. "Looks like someone beat us here."

The lockjaw had abated. Good. That meant Griggs wasn't at risk for immediate death. Captain would've been pissed if I let the old buzzard croak while on the job, but having him pass into the spirit realm from a simple mouth spasm? That would've earned me a demerit for sure.

I glanced down to see what Griggs was talking about. The door stood ajar, and a splintered hole had replaced the padlock.

I slipped my right hand into my coat pocket and grabbed Daisy.

Daisy is the worst kind of woman, a heartbreaker and a home wrecker, but in the literal sense not the figurative. She's a foot and a half of steely eyes and cold shoulders, and she's got the meanest slap in the seven boroughs. She's my nightstick.

Griggs pulled out his own, some poor girl who'd never been christened. I think Griggs still pined for the days when a cop could carry an executioner's sword around and not raise any eyebrows, but nowadays the only head-knockers who were allowed blades were the army boys.

The regulations didn't bother me any. Daisy was my girl. My affair with her was the longest, most satisfying

relationship I'd ever had with a woman, an
cluded the three years I spent married to my e

Though part of me longed to barge into ... apartment foot first, discretion won out over my intrinsic
desire to break things. I eased the door open and
slipped into the penthouse, Daisy at the ready.

The apartment was as well lit as a hog's bowels and
smelled just as nice. It took a few moments for my eyes
and nose to adjust. Thick drapes hung over the windows, drowning out all natural light, and a pungent
smell of dried blood and offal permeated the space.
Most flophouse apartments, especially those as filthy
and decrepit as this one, were studios, but much to my
surprise this pad was a three-room affair. Not only that,
but the rooms were divided by real, honest-to-goodness
wooden doors. Truly this flat represented the crème de
la crème of flophouse living.

In the center of the apartment, a couple dozen waxy
candles emitted a pale, flickering light. Candles that
were arranged neatly, almost ritualistically, in a tight
spiral. Candles that surrounded a very attractive, and
very naked, young woman.

I rushed to her side, partly to ogle, but mostly to
help. Or at least that's what I told myself. How much
ogling would be involved would depend on just how
dead she was. I pressed two fingers to her throat. A
faint pulse pushed back against my brawny digits.

"Get over here," I hissed to Griggs. "She's still
alive."

Griggs obliged. "Gods, that's a lot of blood."

Below the woman, the floorboards were stained
black with the sticky stuff, whether human or goblin I

couldn't tell. Griggs was right though. There sure was a lot of it. Luckily for the girl, none of it appeared to be hers. Not yet, anyway.

A faint creak sounded behind me, and I swung my head around in response. The doors stood tightly shut in their frames, but my ears had already uncovered the gambit. The question, however, was whether my goblin friends were hiding behind door number one or door number two.

I stretched. I swung my arm. I gripped Daisy tight. I chose door number two.

2

I unleashed the full force of my foot's gods-given talent into the flimsy door, tearing it from its hinges. The crash of wood on wood mingled with high-pitched shrieking, similar to the sound a tabby makes when it slips and falls into an ice-cold river. Two goblins—three and a half feet tall, dark green skin, mouths full of double rows of pointed yellow teeth—turned to face me. One wore a tattered red shirt and no pants, and the other wore rope-drawn cutoffs fashioned from the finest remnants of a potato sack. Though the goons had spared no expense on the swanky digs, apparently their extravagance had its limits.

Behind me, I heard the other door thrown open, and the pitter-patter of small, clawed feet racing for the exit soon followed. I swore as I considered my options, but my new friends didn't allow me much time for introspection.

The goblins came at me in a hot whirlwind of crazy. I barely had enough time to belt out a strangled warning to Griggs before the first green terror hit me. The lunatic with the cutoffs ordered a sampler platter of Jake Daggers' signature calf and thigh meats, but I introduced his face to Daisy before his chompers could do any real damage. That's when Pants-free McGee torpedoed me in the giblets.

Pain exploded around my nether regions. I fell back as Pants-free McGee clawed at my face with his poorly manicured paws. I barely held him off with my free arm as I sucked in air to help stop the burning. The pant-less wonder inflicted some cursory damage to my arm in the scrum, but eventually Daisy and I convinced him to take a nap.

I stumbled back into the foyer, holding my tenders, to find Griggs writhing around on his backside next to the naked girl. I rushed over as fast as my swollen baby makers would allow.

"Griggs! Good gods man, are you all right? How bad did they get you?"

"It wasn't the goblins. My damn back gave out." Griggs groaned and waved me off. "I'll be fine. Go catch those murdering pieces of trash."

I nodded, and ignoring the distinct possibility of third degree chafing, I took off. I burst out the door and raced down the stairs like a prize-winning thorough-bred. At least that's how I envisioned myself. To the unbiased observer I probably looked more like a recently gelded draft horse. I'm thick and meaty, and I've never been known for my speed.

As much as I pushed myself, I knew I chased a lost cause. Pants-free McGee and his loony bin cell-mate had held me up just long enough for the other green devils to hightail it out of there and vamoose. Griggs and I would gather the psycho brothers, of course. We'd take them back to the precinct to interrogate them, but I already knew what they'd tell us.

A whole lot of nothing.

Headcases like those two were invariably never more than hangers-on. The real brains behind the operation must've been behind the other door, and so the goblins' murder spree would undoubtedly continue. I thought about the poor girl upstairs who'd misplaced her clothes. Well, at least we'd saved one.

I shook my head as I reached level ground. I had to stay focused. Maybe they'd still be on the street. My eyes were sharp. I could pick them out of a crowd. I hadn't laid eyes on them, of course, but how many maniacal, bloodthirsty goblins could there be roaming the streets at dusk? Heck, maybe some of them wouldn't be wearing pants, either.

I burst through the flophouse's front door and nearly collided with a man mountain, one that happened to have two squirming goblins clutched in his massive hands.

"You don't look so good, Daggers," he rumbled. "These little guys get the best of you?"

I realized I was bent over, breathing hard and grabbing my jimmies again. I straightened as much as was feasible, given the circumstances.

"Quinto," I said. "Nearly perfect timing. I could've used your help a few minutes ago."

Hypothetically, if I happened to start a bar fight and could only choose one friend to have my back, I'd probably choose Quinto, all six feet and seven inches of him. He was built like the proverbial brick outhouse.

His face looked like it'd been used to break rocks, and I wouldn't be surprised if he'd been gainfully employed in the past doing just that. The big guy had it pretty rough growing up—even rougher than me. I guess it's to be expected when you're part troll.

Allegedly, I should say. Quinto had dropped some hints to that effect over the years. The grayish hue to his skin supported the notion, but no one at the precinct had ever been dumb enough to press him on the issue. Of course, some criminals *had* been that dumb. One brainiac once insinuated Quinto got his troll blood from his mother's side. Quinto put the guy through a wall.

Quinto smiled, showing off his full assortment of mismatched buckteeth. "Actually, Daggers, I think we showed up at just the right time, don't you?" He hoisted the goblins higher as a point of emphasis.

The 'we' part meant him and Rodgers, who had a third goblin pinned to the ground. Rodgers and Quinto made quite the pair. Quinto with a face ugly enough to curdle milk, and Rodgers with his sandy blonde hair, blue eyes, and boyish good looks.

Rodgers cuffed his struggling captive and wrestled him to his feet.

"You sure you're all right, Daggers?" Rodgers flashed a perfect, white smile. "You're looking greener than these guys."

Rodgers tried to produce a quip for every occasion, but they fell flat more often than not. I gave the guy credit for trying, but everyone at the precinct agreed I was the undisputed king of quips.

I gave Rodgers a nod. "Yeah, I'm fine. Fertility is overrated. What took you guys so long, anyway?"

Rodgers jerked a thumb over his shoulder. "Had to call in some backup."

Now that Rodgers mentioned it, I noticed we weren't alone. A good half-dozen bluecoats from downtown had shown up, and they'd brought a horse-drawn paddy wagon with them.

Horse-drawn carriages were common in my infancy, but as the city grew, so did manure problems. High traffic areas became almost impassable to anyone without a good set of galoshes and a wicked case of nasal congestion.

In response, the city banned horse-drawn carriages except for use by armed forces and police. Other than cleaner streets, the result was a massive boom in the rickshaw industry, which ended up creating huge numbers of jobs for the city's less fortunate. Since poor people were cheaper and more abundant than horses, rickshaw rides became affordable. Ultimately, everybody won. Well, except for the horses—but I'm sure the black market beef business thrived for a while.

Regardless, it was good thinking on the part of Rodgers and Quinto to request the wagon. We'd need to get all the goblins back to HQ, and I sure as heck wasn't going to carry Pants-free McGee or No-shirt Norbert all the way back there. I had no intention of letting them attempt to turn me in a walking delicatessen again.

Quinto's detainees were getting feisty, so he cracked their skulls together and tossed them to the boys in blue.

"Say...where's Griggs?" Quinto raised his bushy eyebrows at me. "Is he still upstairs?"

Leave it to the part-troll to subtly point out the obvious: that a detective always has his partner's back, that a detective never leaves a partner behind, and that both of those things apply doubly when the partner's birthday predates the known origins of the universe. Of course, Griggs had told me to go, but what if Daisy's magic fairy dust had already worn off? Griggs wouldn't enjoy the psycho brothers' company.

All my internal philosophizing came out as a grunt. "Yeah, I should probably check on the old guy, shouldn't I? I'll be back."

3

Griggs' situation had improved. He'd progressed from writhing on the ground to writhing while sitting up. The number of curses streaming from his lips had also increased. That meant he was feeling better.

"Hey, old man. Did I beat the Reaper?"

Griggs gave me the fisheye. "Save your attempts at wit for someone who cares. Did you catch those damn goblins?"

"Yes. Well, no, actually. Quinto and Rodgers did. They met me at the bottom of the stairs. Probably best for the goblins, to be honest. Daisy was itching to get hot and heavy again."

Griggs frowned. "So to answer my question...no, you didn't."

I shrugged. "They got caught. It's the same functional result. I don't see why it matters."

"It matters because they could've—heck, they *should've*—gotten away. And it wouldn't have happened if at least one of us was in decent enough shape to catch them."

"True," I said. "You should hit the gym. I hate to break it to you, but you're getting a bit flabby."

"I wasn't talking about me."

"Hey, you don't have to tell me twice. I'll be right behind you, old-timer. Just let me snag a beer first."

Griggs sighed.

I returned to the scene of the scrum. My friends, the wardrobe-impaired goblins, continued to saw logs. They looked so peaceful. You'd never know they'd lost a battle with an eighteen-inch piece of steel except for the lovely purple bruises blossoming across their faces.

I tsked. The resulting color clashed horribly with their natural skin tone. The hardened fashionistas at the local poke would give them hell about it for sure.

I waltzed back to Griggs, who sat on the floor next to the naked girl. She seemed no worse for wear, though she still rocked her birthday suit. Her chest expanded and contracted rhythmically with her breathing, but she'd yet to crack open her eyes. I wondered if she might be in a coma.

Griggs barked at me. "You going to stand there staring, or are you going to do something?"

"You have to admit, standing and staring is *something*." And I could stare for a while. Whoever she was, she was easy on the eyes.

"Smartass."

"I don't see you jumping up to help her," I said.

"I'm not sure I can even stand, much less jump," said Griggs.

"Fine, I'll cover her up. If only to keep your lecherous, old eyes off her."

The drapes would do the trick. I pulled a set off the nearest window, letting in the waning light of dusk, and lay the thick cloth over the mystery woman's private areas. As I did so, I heard sharp creaks approaching from the stairs. Bluecoats, coming to clean up our mess. Good timing, too. Badge or no badge, I didn't want to get caught in the Erming long after dark. The lamplighters guild refused to service the slum for safety reasons, and city officials agreed that was probably best for all parties. Well, except for the poor saps who lived in the Erming, but who cared about them?

"C'mon old-timer," I said. "Let's leave the mop up duty to the grunts. I'm pretty sure I saw a medic or two among the nightstick swingers. They'll take care of our lady friend."

I gave Griggs a hand and pulled him up.

He grimaced and clutched his back. "Give me some support, youngblood."

My eyebrows might've jumped off my face. Griggs never admitted weakness. His back must've been hurting him worse than he let on.

With Griggs' arm over my shoulder, we hobbled out past the blues and down the stairs. Griggs started to wax philosophical to me by about the second landing.

"You know, Jake, I've got to be honest with you. I don't know how much longer I can do this."

I chuckled. Griggs had been threatening to hang up his coat and boots since the day I joined the force a little over a decade ago.

"Tell me about it. You've probably only got another twenty good years left in you. A score and a half, if you're lucky."

Griggs shook his head. "No, I'm serious. I mean it this time. I'm too old for this crap. I let you down in there and we both know it. You'd be better off with someone else at your side. Someone with a fresh set of legs. I'm going to retire."

I'd heard that line a million times before, too. I nodded and made a noncommittal grunt of acknowledgement. "Come on, partner. Let's see if we can catch a ride back to HQ on that paddy wagon."

4

As it turned out, my unshakable confidence in Griggs had been misplaced. The old buzzard hadn't been crying wolf after all.

He came into the precinct the following morning, walked right into the Captain's office, and slapped his badge on the desk. Said he was done. Said it was his time to go and wished everyone the best. No long goodbyes or tearful farewells.

Or at least that's how Quinto related it to me later—I'm not exactly one of the first employees into the office. It's not that I hate mornings, it's that they always come at such an inconvenient time of the day.

Blissfully unaware, I followed my typical mid-morning routine, walking up Schumacher Avenue and onto 5th Street where I greeted the precinct's imposing façade—a solid wall of granite featuring wide, iron-banded double doors and a massive bas-relief carving of the seal of justice which displayed a soaring eagle holding a pair of scales in its razor-sharp claws. I breathed in deeply at the sight of it, goose bumps rippling across my arms.

When I arrived at my desk, I found Griggs surrounded by our office staff, all of them taking turns giving the old timer a hearty pat on the back. I figured the higher-ups were trying to cut back on healthcare costs again by indulging in some home-brewed chiropractic experiments. Then I realized what was happening.

At first I couldn't believe it. Griggs? Retiring? I sank into my chair and sat there in a dull stupor. I'd been on the force for a solid twelve years, and during that entire time the old buzzard had always stuck by my side. He wasn't the most agreeable partner to be sure. His scowl could draw rainclouds, he was about as chatty as an oak tree, and his brand of compassion was strictly of the 'suck it up and shut it' variety. But Griggs was my partner. The only partner I'd ever had.

As I sat there in shock in the hard-backed excuse for a seat the city hall penny-pinchers determined was suitable for all public servants, I reflected on how little I actually knew about my partner. Despite his occasional month-long vows of silence, we did talk on occasion. I knew once upon a time Griggs, like me, had made the mistake of getting married, and he had a daughter and two grandkids to boot. I knew he'd served in the army back when most of us were still evolving to walk on two legs instead of four. I knew he liked to play dominos and go fishing in the summer. But beyond that? Who was the man behind the dried leather mask? In twelve long years, I'd never taken the time to find out. I guess I never would.

While I stewed in my emotional soup, the Captain negotiated for a farewell bash with Griggs, much to the buzzard's chagrin. As some sort of cruel practical joke, the Captain sent Quinto out to get party hats and a cake. I envisioned Quinto at the party store, ordering a couple dozen conical hats and a frosted gateau from a terrified clerk—a clerk who probably couldn't imagine anyone as ugly and intimidating as Quinto having any friends at all, much less two dozen. I then thought of Quinto sitting alone in a room, cramming fluffy white cake into his gaping maw with a two-and-a-half foot stack of party hats strapped to his egg-shaped melon.

I smiled, but it was short-lived. I wasn't in the mood.

The party itself felt awkward, as all farewell parties do. I didn't have much to say to Griggs, and he seemed intent on keeping the meaning of life to himself, so I sulked in a corner and filled the hole in my gut with frosted sugary grief.

Before I knew it, the party was over and Griggs had left—for good. A strange knotting sensation filled the pit of my stomach. Even though the cake had been sweet enough to give me heart palpitations, I didn't think it was the culprit.

Captain saw me squirming and aimed a manly head nod my way. It was his way of showing concern, as if to say 'Buck up kid, you'll be fine.' And I would be. *Heck*, I'd have to be. Our medical plan didn't cover depression, and I couldn't exactly be depressed about losing an old buzzard like Griggs. Could I?

That night, I confronted my feelings of confusion and despondency head on like any other red-blooded male—by self-medicating myself with copious amounts of beer. I drank. A lot. I ranted. I ripped. I roared. I got thrown out of the bar. Well, not so much thrown out as escorted home. Luckily, I had the sense to fill myself with the nectar of the gods at Jjade's, and by lucky, I mean it's the only place I ever drink. I'm practically an institution there.

Jolliet Jjade is the sole proprietor of the aptly named Jjade's, a watering hole far nicer than it has any right to be, given its clientele. Jjade's an interesting cat. With long, chestnut brown hair split right down the middle, caramel-colored skin, and an impeccable fashion sense, you'd think she'd have suitors lining up around the block.

Only problem is she's a he.

At least I think she is. I've never asked to see the goods. Regardless of what's going on downstairs, I consider Jjade a good friend, and I'm fairly certain she was the one who helped me home that night—though my recollection is fuzzy.

The next day, the gods took pity on me. As a tribute to my stupidity they granted me an overcast morning as a boon, though their benevolence ended there. My head throbbed as if Daisy had pounded it during a bout of infidelity, and when I arrived at the precinct, I felt like nothing in the world would please me more than sharing some of my alcohol-induced misery with the rest of the sad saps in the city. Pounding heads and taking out my rage on poorly hinged doors would do the trick, but the Captain was having none of it. He took one look at my face and stuck me on paperwork detail.

I thought my newfound assignment as a pencil pusher would only last until the end of the day, but the following morning I found a stack of old case files on my desk even Quinto would've had a hard time seeing over. The Captain was giving me a subtle hint—he didn't think I was emotionally ready to hit the mean streets again anytime soon.

Well if he wanted to play hardball, fine by me. I knew how to win the game he played, and it had nothing to do with how quickly I could scrawl my pencil across the mammoth-sized stack of files on my desk. The key to victory lay in how big of a pain in the ass I could make myself around the office.

I re-acquainted myself with the coffee pot and got to work.

5

I sorely underestimated the Captain. No matter how much crap I flung around the precinct, none of it stuck to the pack leader's office. I should've known better, but my hubris got the better of me.

To be fair, I'd turned orneriness into an art form. Few men could put up with me at my worst, but the Captain was one of them. He was an old jarhead—even though he was balding, he still sported a high and tight. Being ex-marine, he was uniquely qualified to deal with rabble-rousers like myself, and he tended to do so with unmatched vocal ferocity, by which I mean he was a master at chewing people out. That, and not his flapping jowls, was what earned the Captain his nickname—the bulldog.

My first day of paperwork detail I was a model of inefficiency. I stopped by the break room and commandeered the entire coffee pot, office ethics be damned. I hovered over every desk I could find, chatting up everyone from Rodgers and Quinto to joes I barely knew. Rodgers got so bored he ran out of zingers. Even the poor runners hanging around outside the front of the precinct got to hear my life story.

I barely moved a quarter inch of paper before it was time to punch out. The bulldog gave me a murderous glare from behind his office windows as I left, but he kept his mouth shut.

The next morning, a second Quinto-sized stack of papers awaited me on the opposite side of my desk, and my trusty hard-backed butt-supporter had been replaced with a three-legged stool. The Captain's message was clear. *Get your ass to work.*

I ignored the suggestion and moseyed off toward the break room to romance my mistress, the coffee pot. On the way I stopped by Rodgers' desk to chat, but he scowled at me and told me to get to work. Apparently, the Captain had rallied the troops in my absence. My efforts at loafing were already meeting heavy resistance.

Undeterred from my goal of turning the office into a churning morass of inactivity, I surged onward, but much to my surprise, the ever-present pot of coffee had disappeared. In its place was a handwritten note:

Dear Officers of the Law,

Coffee is a privilege to be consumed by productive members of the force only. Let it be known that I've confiscated the pot until such a point as Detective Daggers clears the stack of unfinished paperwork from his desk.

—The Captain

I gulped. The bulldog was pulling on his old marine training. Don't punish the agitator. Punish his squad mates until they force him back in line.

After I got over the initial shock, I realized the Captain's plan might actually work to my advantage. A few days without coffee, and the entire precinct would revolt. Of course, my fellow detectives might kill me in the process, but at least my goal of spreading discord would be achieved.

As I waltzed back to my workspace, several members of the squad shot me ugly glares. I responded with a collection of my most winning smiles, secretly thinking they could all go suck eggs.

I settled onto my stool and into the chasm created by the Captain's paperwork. Griggs' empty desk glared at me like a sullen, silent sentinel. We entered into a brief staring competition. The desk won.

Behind Griggs' empty spot, Rodgers and Quinto's desks sat face to face. Quinto scribbled away at some papers, oblivious to my recent defeat.

"Hey Quinto," I said. "You're not much of a coffee person, are you?"

He turned his big ugly mug around. "No. Why?"

"No reason."

The rest of the office I could handle, but I didn't want to piss Quinto off. I cast a quick glance toward the Captain's office. The bulldog spotted me and looked pleased with himself. I smiled and waved.

I started doodling. I'd half-finished a fairly decent sketch of a scantily clad water nymph when I heard the Captain's door wrenched from its frame.

"Daggers!" the Captain barked. "If you don't get to work in the next millisecond, you're going to find yourself on janitorial duty for the rest of the week. And if that doesn't sound like your cup of coffee, then you might as well start packing your things now, because you're headed for an extended unpaid vacation."

It's amazing what the threat of starvation can do.

I got to work on the pile in front of me. I'd figured I could wear the Captain down given enough time, but I was sorely mistaken. After about a week of butting heads, I started to despair that even I wasn't hard-headed enough to out-stubborn the guy. Though I'd gradually waded my way through all of the paperwork, the old bulldog kept finding new mundane tasks for me, none of which included anything that resembled actual detective work.

I became desperate. I pleaded with Rodgers to let me tag along with him and Quinto on a case. He took pity on me and agreed, but the Captain nixed that idea as soon as I'd taken two steps toward the door. I checked and rechecked my mail slot, to see if anyone needed my keen deductive skills. I even thumbed through old cold case files to get a fix.

In only a week of inactivity, the Captain had turned me into a shaky mess. I'd blame the coffee, but the Captain was still strictly rationing the supply.

The only good thing about my incarceration at the precinct was that I'd developed such an intense case of cabin fever it'd driven all thoughts of my old pal, Griggs, from my mind.

In retrospect, I'm certain that had been the Captain's plan all along. He's a clever old goat. But as Griggs once told me, the only certain thing in life is change, and a whole bucketful was headed my way.

6

The sun beat down on my neck as I strode up Schumacher Avenue. Sweat beaded on my scalp, threatening to make a break for my collar. I sent a quiet prayer to the gods that the day would turn out cooler than advertised. Quinto emitted a unique and wholly unpleasant funk on hot days.

As I turned onto 5th Street, I spotted my friend Tolek and his push broom-like mustache by the street corner and wandered over. Tolek was an immigrant of the human variety who operated a mobile kolache cart. He often propped it up under an awning across the street from the precinct. It was the worst of stereotypes, but the guy made a killing selling doughnuts to us gumshoes.

Tolek waved at me as he saw me approach. "Mr. Daggers," he said in his lilting accent. "Good to see you today. Your usual?"

The guy knew me too well. I couldn't say no to his apricot kolaches.

"Make it two, Tolek. I have a feeling I've got another long day ahead of me."

As Tolek fished out the pastries, a gang of pre-teen ragamuffins begged me for coins. They tended to hang out around the precinct in the hopes that some of our regular runners wouldn't show, but if that opportunity never materialized, they had no qualms about getting underfoot and being general pains in the rear.

I shooed them away. They annoyed me to no end, probably because they reminded me of myself when I was their age. And even worse, they reminded me of my son—although at five, he was still a fair bit younger than the thieving rapscallions that surrounded me.

Yes, I'm a father, but not a particularly good one. One would think with my childlike exuberance I'd be a great parent, but historical evidence has disproved that, I'm afraid. Really, my relationship with my boy never had a chance. By the time he was old enough to inter-act, my relationship with my ex, Nicole, had already fallen off the deep end. The infighting between us poi-soned the interactions I got with my son, which were few and far between given the long hours I was putting in at work.

Normally, I tried to avoid thinking about my failings as a father. I found it was easier to ignore problems than try to solve them, but Nicole insisted I could still salvage my relationship with my boy. For gods' sakes, he was five. All he wanted was to toss a ball and run around and talk to me about his day. I could do that. The only problem was, due to the custody agreement, to spend time with my boy I also had to do the same with Nicole. Dealing with my guilt over poor parenting was one thing, but dealing with the simultaneous feelings of affection and loathing that wrestled through my brain every time I reunited with Nicole was something else—something I still wasn't ready for.

I headed through the station's massive iron doors, under the seal of justice, and into the precinct, all the while thinking I needed to tighten my belt straps and give my little squirt a visit. I was so engrossed in my thoughts it wasn't until I practically tripped over it that I realized my hard-backed lumbar supporter had returned to its rightful home. Before I had a chance to reintroduce my posterior to the seat, the Captain barked at me from his office.

"Daggers! In my office, now."

I brought a kolache with me. No telling how long the old bulldog would chew on my hide.

"Captain?" I asked.

"Close the door. Have a seat."

I plopped my butt down in one of the no-frills government surplus guest chairs. I eyed the Captain's padded leather throne, telling myself that with a few more decades of hard work and perseverance, I too might acquire that level of opulence.

The Captain crossed his arms and leaned back, levying me with his steely gaze. His jowls quivered, and I prepared for a Grade A reaming.

None came.

The Captain just stared at me. Call me crazy, but I think I sensed a modicum of concern lurking beneath his hardened leather exterior. Little chance of it seeping into whatever he planned on discussing with me, though.

My stomach rumbled. I tore a chunk out of my kolache. "So..."

"So," said the Captain, frowning at me. "You're a giant pain in the ass, you know that?"

I sensed this was not the time for playful banter. "Yes, sir, I do."

"Well, then. Glad you acknowledge it. You going to keep being a pain in my ass?"

"I'll stop being a pain in the ass when you give me something useful to do," I said.

"And I'll put you back on assignment when you stop being a pain in my ass."

"It appears we find ourselves at an impasse," I said. "How about we call off the dogs on both sides? You put me back on patrol, and I'll stop being a thorn in everyone's side? You know you need me out there. Quinto and Rodgers are looking a little worn around the edges."

It was true. Both of them were burning holes in their shoes with all the extra legwork the Captain was tossing their way.

The Captain stared at me some more and added an extra bit of downward curl to his frown. Then he remixed his concoction yet again by adding some grunting. I passed the time by wolfing down the rest of my kolache.

Finally, the Captain made an articulate noise. "As much as I'd like to let you continue to storm around the office like a bull with his nuts in a vice, you're right. I need you on the streets. Not because I know you'll actually get work done out there, but because it might finally let the rest of us get some work done around here. But before I allow you to do anything, there's the issue of your partner..."

I shrugged. "I'm over it. Griggs is ancient history. Just send me out with Rodgers or Quinto, and I'll be back to filling the cells with foul-smelling punks in no time."

"Are you kidding?" The Captain's eyebrows shot up. "Rodgers and Quinto would kill me if I stuck them with you full time."

"Not a problem. I work better alone anyway."

The Captain shook his head. "Not happening. You know everyone needs a partner."

"What then? Are you promoting someone? Is it Elmswood or Drake from upstairs? Don't tell me you're thinking about sticking me with that weasel-faced guy. What's his name? Ferndale?"

"Fernandez. And no—to all of your questions."

"Well?" I gave the old codger the inquisitive eye. "What then?"

I think the Captain grinned, but I couldn't be sure because I'd never seen him do it before. "You'll see."

Someone knocked on the door.

"Speak of the devil," said the Captain. "Come in."

7

The door swung open and in walked one of the finer creatures I'd ever seen step foot into the precinct. A woman—nearly six feet tall, with bright azure eyes that stood out like warning beacons—stepped into the Captain's office full of muted browns and grays. Her dark brown hair swept into a pompadour before falling into a long ponytail. Based on her sharp nose, arched eyebrows, and slightly pointed earlobes, I guessed she carried elf blood in her veins, but she wasn't a pure breed by any measure. A coffee-colored pantsuit hugged her waist and flared out over her narrow hips down to her pointed dark leather boots. While the suit's color matched her hair, the lecherous part of me couldn't help but think her bare skin might be a much better complement to her eyes.

"Daggers," said the Captain. "Meet Shay Steele. Steele, Jake Daggers."

I gave the elf-lady a wink and a smile. "Nice to meet you, sweetheart. So you know, I like my coffee black with a hint of sugar."

Her pretty mouth contorted into a confused frown. "Um, excuse me?"

"Oh, and I tend to like fried snacks. Tolek's kolaches from across the street are the bee's knees. Apricot's my favorite." I turned to the Captain. "About time the higher-ups pitched in for a secretary."

The Captain laid into me with a vicious glare. "No, you idiot," he said. "This is *Detective* Steele. Your new partner."

I could feel the heat radiating off the new girl's cheeks before I turned back to look at her. Faced with the possibility of her as a partner, she suddenly seemed less of a sexpot and more of a liability. Her suit jacket couldn't hide her skinny waiflike arms, and judging by her smooth cheeks and straight nose, the only fights she'd ever taken part in were with her dear old daddy over how much she could spend on a new pair of shoes. She was rawer than my jimmies had been following my fight with the goblin lunatics. The Captain couldn't honesty expect to pair me with this girl, could he?

Little Miss Indignant and her hot cheeks looked at me with ill-restrained furor. I smiled, giving her a knowing wink, and turned back to the old bulldog.

"Ohhhhh...I get it," I said. "Very funny. Let's pull one over on old Jake Daggers."

I heard a piqued voice from behind. "Um, pardon me but—"

"You know, if you wanted to punish me you could've stuck me with Ferndale."

"You realize I'm right here don't—"

"*But this?*" I said. "This is a low blow, even for you Captain. I mean to make me babysit this farm-fresh chick while you laugh it up—"

The elf-girl went into full on teakettle mode. "I'LL HAVE YOU KNOW I'M HIGHLY QUALIFIED FOR THIS POSITION. I HAVE RECOMMENDATIONS FROM THE BEST PROFESSORS IN CRIMINAL JUS-TICE, AND—"

"ENOUGH!" bellowed the Captain. "Detective Steele, please have a seat. Daggers, if I so much as hear a peep out of that fat mouth of yours, I'm going to make sure you develop a fat lip to go with it."

Miss Steele sat, her face a brilliant crimson. I kept my yapper shut.

"Detective Steele," the Captain said. "I'd like to apologize for Detective Daggers. His cognitive abilities have suffered from taking too many blows to the head over the years."

I frowned. That was uncalled for, even if my head was lumpier now than it had been when I'd joined the force.

"Now Detective Steele, if you could try to do so in a more subdued tone, why don't you share a little of your background with Detective Daggers."

The elf girl had trained her eyes on the floor during the Captain's short address. She took several measured breaths, lifted her head, and turned to face me. Her cheeks had faded to a dull pink, but her brilliant azure eyes burned with a fierce fire.

Hmm. Perhaps I'd underestimated her.

She launched into a pre-prepared speech. "As the Captain informed you, my name is Shay Steele. I have a degree in Paranatural Ocular Postsensitivity from H. G. Morton's school for—"

I couldn't help myself. "Wait, what the who now? A degree in what from where?"

Elf girl pressed her lips together and raised her eyebrows at me in a way that either indicated she was coming on to me, or she thought I was about as sharp as the edge of a toddler's spoon. I assumed the former.

"As I was saying...from H. G. Morton's school for the Exceptionally Gifted and Talented."

"Gifted and talented how, exactly?" I asked.

"We all exhibit some form of supernatural or paranatural abilities."

The mouse that manned the wheel in my head was taking a break. I couldn't quite connect the dots. "So..."

"I'm a clairvoyant," said Miss Steele.

"You like to spy on people while they get it on? Kinky. I like it. But I don't see how that's relevant here."

Steam puffed from elf girl's ears, but Captain took her off the fire before her teakettle started whistling again.

"No, you dolt," the bulldog said. "That's a voyeur. A clairvoyant is someone who can see into the past. A psychic, if you will."

The mouse wheel finally made a full turn.

"I see." I didn't really though. "So...what then? You can walk into a crime scene and figure out exactly what happened? See a dead body and know who the killer is with a snap of your fingers? Where does that put me? Am I getting demoted to bodyguard detail?"

Elf girl shook her head. "It doesn't exactly work like that."

"So, how exactly *does* it work?" I asked. "Enlighten me."

"Well, you know how a tapestry is made of woven threads?"

"Of course I do. I'm a master of the loom. Don't patronize me."

That solicited a steely gaze and a pair of puckered lips, but Miss Steele went on. "Well, I think of time as a tapestry, one most people, like you, can't see. Me? I can't see the whole tapestry either, but I can make out a few threads. What I do is pick at those threads until the rest of the tapestry falls into place."

I scratched my head. "So...you're only marginally useful, then. Well, that's a relief. I guess this means I've still got a job."

Miss Steele threw her hands in the air with an exasperated sigh. "You're incorrigible! Do you even know the meaning of the word 'manners'?"

"Hey, that's not fair. Just because I confused a clairvoyant for a sex addict—"

The Captain chose that moment to butt in. "Alright, enough Daggers. Detective Steele, please feel free to set your things up at the empty desk across from Detective Daggers'. And you—" The Captain stabbed a finger in my direction. "Stay here in my office. I need a word."

I gulped.

8

Elf girl closed the door behind her as she left. I started to sputter, but the Captain quieted me with a vigorous shushing.

"Don't start with me, Daggers," he said. "I've put up with more of your crap than you have any right to expect. The only reason I do it is because you get results. You and Griggs had the best case closure rate of any partners in the precinct, and as much as I hate to inflate your already bloated ego, I'll be the first to admit your success wasn't because of Griggs. Trust me, he was my partner long before you showed up, and he was average at best."

I think a fly flew into my mouth. Maybe a whole swarm. I'd expected the Captain to hold me back so he could chew me into pieces not heap me with praise.

He kept going.

"Look Daggers, I know this is unorthodox. She's not a typical recruit. She didn't work her way up the ranks like you did. And she's a little green around the edges—"

"A *little?*"

"Let me finish. She's a work in progress to be sure, but she's a once in a lifetime find. Morton's hasn't had a clairvoyant emerge from their ranks in years, and the fact that she's willing to put her skills on the line for the greater good is both shocking and commendable. As if that wasn't enough, she wasn't lying about her resume. She graduated at the top of her class, with high honors. Her recommendations are outstanding. Oh, and she even interned here a couple years ago. Impressed a lot of people."

I raised an eyebrow. "Really? I don't remember seeing her. And she wouldn't be easy to forget." She was a whole lot easier on the eyes than Quinto.

"She worked with a couple guys over in narcotics for the summer. I think she spent time in white collar, too. Regardless, she's the real deal Daggers. And you're the perfect partner for her."

I gave the Captain my best fisheye. "Oh, what, and Griggs' departure had nothing to do with this pairing?"

"Opportunity is only part of the reasoning behind my decision. You may be a numbskull, but your skills will complement hers perfectly."

By which I'm pretty sure the Captain meant I could absorb any punches that came our way while Miss Steele could do the heavy mental lifting. "Gee, thanks."

"Look," said the Captain. "If you both work together as well as I think you can, you just might become the best pair of scumbag hunters this city has seen in a long time. I know you take pride in your badge, Jake. This is a real opportunity to make a difference. Don't blow it."

Apparently I'd underestimated the Captain yet again. He knew when to retire the rabid dog routine and break out the honey.

"Alright," I said. "I'll give her a fair shot. Just answer me one question. Has she ever even seen a dead body?"

The Captain shrugged. "I'm not sure, but I'll tell you this. I interviewed her before bringing her on, and she's tough. A lot tougher than you're giving her credit for. Don't underestimate her."

Tough, huh? We'd see about that. If she ended up spewing chunks all over our first stiff then I'd know how tough she really was, but I'd give her the benefit of the doubt for now. At least she wasn't meek. Her fiery repartee with me had proven that.

Tough or not, I had no intention of sparing her my razor sharp wit and biting social commentary. Even if the Captain thought a fancy degree allowed Miss Steele to cut forward several spots in line, she wasn't about to earn my respect so easily. For her sake, I hoped her special powers included the ability to grow thick skin at a moment's notice.

Although, I have to admit, I liked her skin just fine the way it was. I took a peek at her from through the Captain's windows and wondered if I might get to see more of it in the future.

9

I sauntered over to my desk and plopped down in old faithful. Elf girl made a point of ignoring me as she unpacked a box full of curios.

Behind her, Quinto, Rodgers, and a few other office fixtures peered my way—or more accurately, Shay's way. The girl was a looker, though I couldn't tell if the other cops were giving her an eyeball shakedown or trying to see what delicious new hijinks would break out between the two of us following the eruption of Mt. Steele in the Captain's office. I'm sure everyone had heard. Dogs down the street were probably still howling in pain.

Rodgers tried to flash Shay his pearly whites, but she'd yet to look his way. I'm not sure why he insisted on trying to charm every pair of breasts that walked by. He was happily married with a couple of kids—cute little buggers, too. I think he just enjoyed playing the game. I tried to send him a subliminal message with a nod and got a similar one in return, as if to say, *Good luck with this one, bud.*

I glanced back at the farm-fresh new recruit. She'd placed a frame in one corner of her desk, probably holding a painting drawn by one of those street vendors that whipped out six portraits an hour. From my side of the desk, I couldn't see who the portrait depicted. Was it her? I doubted it. She didn't seem particularly narcissistic. That meant it was either a picture of her parents, her kids, or her significant other. My bet was on parents. Given her obvious desire to dive head first into a burgeoning career as one of the city's finest, kids or a boy toy would've only gotten in her way. Besides, her slim hips held no traces of the aftereffects of pregnancy.

At the other far corner of the desk she placed a springy little green plant with a half dozen unopened violet buds. Not tulips, but something similar. A plant would mean she was a nurturer, something I wouldn't have guessed based on first impressions. Perhaps her fiery demeanor was a front, intended to protect her from the cold, hard world of crime she'd willingly decided to embrace. The plant would keep her grounded, reminding her of her obligations. Regardless, she'd need to nurture the dickens out of that plant if she wanted to prevent it from dying a slow death. We didn't get near enough natural light from the windows in the Captain's office to support much of anything green in the pit.

She also placed a wooden carving of a mythical creature in the center of her desk. From my vantage point, it looked to be some sort of elephant-lion hybrid. Was it a symbol? And if so, for what? Power? Strength? I couldn't discern the meaning behind that one.

The few documents she'd received from the Captain she placed in a neat stack at the front, right-hand corner of her workspace. She made a point of tapping the edges of the pages together with her fingernails so they all lay in perfect alignment with one another. Then she made sure to orient the pages with the desk itself. Clearly, I had a perfectionist on my hands—perhaps an obsessive-compulsive.

Of course, she might've also been nervous. I've found people who are uneasy often pour their energy into inconsequential minutiae instead of facing whatever's bothering them head on. Which in this case was likely me.

I couldn't help but analyze her. It's what I do. I'm a detective. Give me clues and I'll try to figure out what they mean, whether it be at a crime scene or on a first date—not that I date that often. Of course, sometimes my imagination gets the best of me and my analyzing turns into overanalyzing. That usually doesn't end well. It may have contributed to the end of my marriage. Or my wife might've left me because I'm a jackass.

Eyes still on her mementos, Miss Steele broke the silence with a frigid joust. "Can I help you with something, Detective Daggers?"

I gave her my best witty riposte. "Huh? What?"

"You've been staring at me and my desk for like five minutes."

I never said I was the quickest draw when it came to processing information, but I'll get the job done eventually. "Just checking out your desk."

She eyed my workspace, covered in worn pencil nubs, food wrappers, and files that had been thrown haphazardly across its surface—not to mention my un-eaten kolache, which languished uneaten on a pile of requisition forms.

"Don't even think about it," I said.

Now it was her turn to provide a witty counter. "What?"

"My kolache." I grabbed it and tore a chunk out with my teeth. "I saw you eyeing it. If you want one, buy your own."

"I wasn't eyeing your donut."

"I think your stomach is in league with your eyes, but your brain hasn't realized it yet."

Shay's eyebrows furrowed as she tried to figure out exactly what I meant. She shook her head and sighed. "Look," she said in a voice that had lost some of its ice, "I think we may have gotten off on the wrong foot. I'll be the first to admit it was wrong of me to raise my voice the way I did as long as *you* admit some of your—how should I put this—*playful banter* was out of line. So, what do you say?"

I gave her a blank stare. "What do I say to what?"

"Just apologize, won't you? That's all I ask."

One of the runners from out front burst in and ran to the Captain's office. As I considered Shay's request, I saw the runner bend over and whisper something into the Captain's ear. I took a calculated risk.

I gave Shay a cheesy smile. "I'll file your request with management, sweetheart."

Before Miss Steele could verbally explode all over me again, the Captain stuck his head out of his office and bellowed at the two of us.

"Daggers! Steele! We've got a body in a service corridor of a fancy hotel. The Lawrence. It's on the corner of 3rd and West. Go check it out. Take Rodgers and Quinto with you. This one sounds fun."

Before elf girl could regroup, I hopped out of my chair and grabbed my coat. As warm as it was, it was the best way to keep prying eyes off Daisy, and I couldn't very well leave her. She might get lonely.

"What luck, partner! First day on the job and already you're on a case. Just try not to soil your smallclothes when you see the stiff, ok?"

Shay gave me an evil glare, but she couldn't prevent a bit of color from creeping into her cheeks. I couldn't tell if it was from anger or if my jibe hit too close to home. I suspected the latter.

"I'll be fine," she said around clenched teeth.

"Of course you will," I said. "You'll be with me. Rodgers! Quinto! C'mon, let's hoof it."

10

The Lawrence Hotel wasn't too far from the precinct, maybe a half-hour's walk. It was situated on the waterfront of the Earl Fulcinet Ferdinand River, more commonly known as 'the Earl.' I never paid much attention in history class, but if my memory serves me correctly it was named after some stuffy aristocrat whose primary achievement in life involved paying a cartographer to slap his name on a river discovered by the poor saps from which he extorted taxes. Seems a fitting tribute that everyone referred to the river by his title only and not his name.

The Lawrence made its home on the west side of the river—the good side, same side as the precinct—though the hotel lay in a much swankier district than the workplace of us gumshoes. People referred to the neighborhood as the Pearl district, or 'the Pearl' for short, due to the fact that the banks of the Earl used to be teeming with pearl-bearing mussels before overzealous fishermen nearly wiped them out.

The main draw of the Pearl was Magister Hall, the most renowned theater in the city. The place hosted two shows a day—a matinee and a nightcap—three hundred and sixty-five days a year. With over two thousand seats, a sell-out crowd all but guaranteed at every show, and ticket prices that would make a public servant like myself weep, the place generated more revenue than most small municipalities. But Magister Hall wasn't the only place in the Pearl making the tax collectors smile. Travelers came from far and wide to experience the Hall's shows, and they had to rest their heads somewhere—somewhere like the Lawrence Hotel.

I picked the Lawrence out of a lineup of other swanky hotels as soon as it popped into view. I'm not entirely sure what gave it away. It might've been the massive columns running up and down all eight stories of the building's façade. Perhaps it was the elaborately painted red and gold embellishments that peeked out from within the lobby and screamed of glitz and glamour. Or perhaps it was the giant sign outside that read 'The Lawrence Hotel.'

I'm nothing if not observant.

Rodgers had been chatting young Miss Steele's ear off the entire trek over from the precinct. Even now he prattled on about some old case he and Quinto had gotten mixed up in.

"So anyway," he said, "the next body we found was barely recognizable. It was so mangled it looked like rabid dogs had gotten at it. It was nasty. You know how organ meat looks when—"

"Give it a rest, Rodgers," I said. "She's green enough without you messing with her hue. Besides, we're almost there."

Though I joked about her queasiness, she looked far more relaxed than when we'd left the precinct. During the walk, she'd initially ignored me. As her rage subsided, I noticed her peering my way on more than one occasion. The brain between my legs tried to convince me the glances were born from lustful desire, but the brain between my ears saw things differently. Her glances had been deliberate. Calculating. I could practically hear the gears churning inside her head. A scheme was underway, and I'd have to wait to find out what it was.

A doorman wearing a red and gold frock coat and with a ring of sweat around his cap opened the door for us as we approached. Once inside, I flashed my badge to a hotel clerk working the front desk. She hustled off and returned with a tall, bespectacled maître d' in tow. His dark hair was highly styled with thick mousse, and he wore a dark suit and tie. He dabbed at his forehead with a white kerchief, the fabric damp with sweat.

"Detectives. Thank you for coming," he said in a strained voice. "My goodness, when the morning crew arrived and found that man dead I nearly fainted, and in such a manner as well, and who would've guessed that after such an event as last night's, why in all my years I've never seen such a thing, and to think it happened here at the Lawrence, no sir, we certainly can't have that sort of thing, and—"

The maître d' must've moonlighted as an auctioneer. I had to interrupt him before the body at our crime scene crumbled into dust. "Hold on there, pal. Why don't you take a deep breath and tell me what you know. And keep in mind most of us prefer sentences over stream-of-consciousness word vomit."

The maître d' stiffened and pulled back, but he got the message.

"Very well," he said. "Last night we held a charity event in the grand ballroom. A benefit for children of wounded war veterans. Often these events last long into the night, sometimes until three or four. As such, we leave the cleanup until the following morning. It's not fair to the workers to expect them to stay that late, you see. Anyway, one of my duties here at the Lawrence is to oversee that all daily functions are performed according to schedule. So you can imagine my dismay when the cleaning crew came to me this morning and informed me there was man lying *dead* in one of the service corridors of our hotel. The workers were visibly distraught, and I don't blame them. Why, when I saw it..." The man shuddered and lost a little color. "Well, perhaps you should see it for yourselves."

"Sounds like a plan," I said. "Lead the way."

As the maître d' turned, I gave my new partner a friendly elbow in the shoulder. "You hear that? Sounds like a good one. You didn't eat too much for breakfast, did you?"

Shay gave me one of those calculating looks again and followed it with a smirk. "Are you kidding? You wouldn't share your kolaches with me, remember? I guess you'll just have to settle for dry heaves."

Wait, what? Had the raw little rookie just tried to out quip me? Was that part of her recently hatched plan?

I hitched up my trousers. Nobody out quips Jake Daggers. *Nobody*.

11

The maître d' ushered us through the grand ballroom, onto a raised stage at the back, and into a
corridor full of ropes and pulleys and other
mechanisms for controlling curtains and lighting. A
traffic jam of dining carts lined the hall, each crammed
with dirty plates, half-filled glasses of sparkling wine,
and leftover slices of sheet cake. Amid this backdrop, we
found our formerly-breathing leading man.

He lay face up on the floor in the middle of the corridor. His smooth skin and high cheekbones brought to
mind the she-elf standing next to me, but a darker hue
colored his face than that of young Miss Shay's. I haz-
arded a guess that the stiff was the not-so-proud owner
of dark elf blood.

Dark elves had been getting a bad rap for centuries.
Most of the other races viewed their dark skin as a
brand of immorality, but the simple fact was dark elf
civilizations had arisen in jungles. Their greenish-
brown skin camouflaged them in thick underbrush.

Of course, the average joe didn't let something as simple as genetics stop him from hurling insults at them. People labeled dark elves as charlatans, thieves, and nexuses of vile diseases that afflicted a man in his nether regions. As with all stereotypes though, some actually had legs. Partly because of workplace discrimination and partly because of their natural, sultry good looks, many dark elves fell into the sex trade where they tended to pick up all sorts of nasty ailments.

Based upon his attire, our dead friend had risen quite a bit higher than his natural station in life. A black tuxedo with a white cummerbund and necktie hugged his frame. His close-cropped ebony hair flowed up and over to the side, giving him a rather dashing, debonair look. He'd probably made ladies swoon in droves. You know, before he acquired the massive, gaping hole in his chest.

Rodgers whistled. Quinto grunted. The maître d' swallowed hard, excused himself, and backed away. I took a few steps toward the dead guy to get a closer look.

I'm no spring chicken. I'd seen dead guys with holes in them before. Spears, swords—heck, even pickaxes could do the trick. But the hole in this particular dead guy was unique. For one, the hole was big, maybe the size of one of Quinto's fists. More interestingly though, the hole didn't cut through him. It'd *burned* through him, and not just the fleshy parts. Skin, muscle, bone. All gone. Vaporized.

I peered straight through his chest cavity to a blackened scorch mark on the floor beneath him. Not only had whatever killed him been powerful, it'd been violent. Tiny charred holes pockmarked his suit, as if a massive shower of sparks had exploded upon him in an orgy of fire. Only one thing came to mind that could cause damage like that.

I turned to Rodgers and Quinto. "Now I see why the Captain had you guys come along. Unless I'm mistaken, boys, I think we've got us someone who's been murdered...by *magic*."

Quinto snorted. "Well, I'll go ahead and check the—"

He paused as he noticed the same thing I did—my new partner acting extremely odd. While I'd been looking forward to seeing how long it would take her to add her intestinal fluids to the crime scene, the show I observed was of an entirely different variety.

Shay stretched her arms out to the sides, as if petitioning for silence, and extended her fingers into the air. Her digits flicked, grasping at a nonexistent breeze. Her eyes glossed over and began to flit back and forth like those of a woman caught in the throes of deep sleep.

I stretched my wit and tried to shed some light on the situation. "Hey, uh...are you ok?"

Shay spoke oddly, as if her voice traveled through water. "The tapestry...it beckons."

Tapestry? Oh, right. She meant she was communing with the dead or having visions of yesteryear imparted to her by the ancients or something as equally ludicrous.

She continued to wave her fingers and tilt her head about at weird angles. I walked around behind her so I could observe her and the stiff simultaneously. As strange as Shay's hand gestures and head movements were, the truly unnerving part about my new partner's physical state was her eyes. They cut through me as if I were made of glass.

Me? Invisible to the female eye? With my charm and good looks? I soothed my ego with the notion that she wasn't ignoring me but rather seeing into the past. A past in which my smiling mug didn't exist.

After a few long moments, the storm passed from Shay's clouded eyes. Her arms floated back to her sides, and her gaze refocused into the material world.

"Well?" I asked.

Quinto and Rodgers, quiet as mice during the ordeal, leaned forward, eager to hear what Miss Steele had gleaned from the spirit realm.

"It wasn't magic," she said.

"What?" I asked.

"How this man died. It wasn't by magic."

"How do you know that?"

Shay raised an eyebrow at me and tilted her head to one side. "Really, Detective Daggers? Do I have to explain this again? Did you have kolaches stuffed in your ears back at the precinct when I explained how this works?"

Rodgers sniggered. Quinto cracked a small smile and shook his head.

Back when I was married, my wife had come by and spent some time at the precinct once. She came away shocked—mortified, really—at how Quinto, Rodgers, and I could make light of something as serious as murder. She never understood.

We had to.

The alternative was to let the awful truth that the world was full of heartless, murdering bastards fully seep in, and that wasn't a healthy thing for the mind to dwell upon. No, the best guys in the business all had a sense of humor—which, I realized, boded well for Shay.

Unfortunately, it didn't bode well for me. Rodgers and Quinto often peppered me with lighthearted ribbing, but they rarely got the best of me. The skinny half-elf, on the other hand, had done it in less than an hour.

"I remember your discourse on paranatural hoodonkery quite clearly," I retorted. "There's a tapestry. You pick at it, like a supernatural booger, and then the crusty bits dry up and fall off."

That line earned a snigger from Rodgers, but not Quinto. At least I'd earned one half of the pair back.

"That's not exactly how I related it," Shay said with a hint of disgust.

"Whatever. So who killed the guy? And if the killer didn't off him with magic, then how?"

Shay shook her head in a condescending manner. "It doesn't work like that, Detective Daggers. Threads, remember? I only see threads. And as it turns out, the tapestry here is complex. The only thread I was able to pull free involved the murder itself, and there's no scent of magic on the thread at all."

"You can *smell* magic?"

"Look, it wasn't magic. Trust me. I may not be a weaver, but I know what the threads mean."

I shot her my best quizzical look, but Shay didn't elaborate.

I harrumphed and stuck my hands in my coat pockets. "Well, I guess we'll have to figure this murder out the old-fashioned way."

While part of me was dismayed that my fresh-faced new partner's supernatural talents didn't include plucking murderers from thin air, another part of me was glad to retain talents of use to the city. Homelessness didn't particularly suit my lifestyle.

I kneeled and checked the dead guy's pockets.

"Well, I think we can rule out a mugging," I said. "Not much chance of that happening here in the hotel. Besides, he's still got his cash on him."

He did. Quite a bit, in fact. Not to mention a deftly engraved gold pocket watch attached to one of his belt loops by a fine chain. Unfortunately, what the guy didn't carry was any sort of documents, bills, or paperwork that identified him.

That wasn't particularly surprising. Several years ago, the city had levied a rule mandating all city residents obtain a government-issued identification card, but the cards were mainly for tax collection purposes. Few people carried them around. Sometimes I wished the lawmakers would force everyone to carry the cards at all times, but I doubt it would make my job much easier. Most of the city's poor would ignore the law, and criminals would be smart enough to get fake cards.

I straightened and beckoned to my pals.

"Quinto, why don't you help me cordon off this crime scene? And Rodgers, can you track down that maître d'? See if he can find a doorman or a clerk or someone who can help identify this stiff."

As Rodgers shuffled off, I gave my new partner a sly grin.

"What are you smirking at?" she said.

"Well," I said, "I was thinking. Now that I've seen your talent, so to speak, it's time to see if you have any real ability, by which I mean—"

"Deductive reasoning?"

My face must've betrayed my surprise. Already the young whelp was finishing my sentences? It took Griggs years to do that.

Shay leaned in close over the dead body. "You're wondering how I knew you were going to say that, aren't you? Is it my 'talent,' as you called it? Or did I use my deductive ability? I'll let you deduce that one by yourself."

Shay inspected the body. I grumbled. I may have underestimated how much moxie the fresh-faced pup had, and I hadn't yet figured out whether or not I liked it.

12

poked the dead guy in his flabby bits until Rodgers found his way back to the scene of the crime. With him, he brought an elderly woman in a black cocktail dress. As soon as she drew within eyeshot of the dead guy, she wilted. Rodgers helped steady her. She cast a look in the dark elf's direction and exchanged a few hushed words with Rodgers before retreating back up the corridor. There, she leaned against a doorframe to help still her chattering knees.

I could understand. I'd been there before. My adolescence had been far from a dream. I'd seen bodies, and not at funerals where people milled about, drank punch, and ate lousy cake, either. I'd seen bodies on the streets. People who'd set foot in the wrong place at the wrong time.

But it was a different story when the dead person at your feet was someone you knew. Someone you had a connection with. Someone you cared for deeply. Someone like, say, your own mother.

It happened when I was thirteen. The police officers in charge of the case told us it was a mugging gone wrong. Perhaps my mother had fought back—she'd always been scrappy—or perhaps she'd recognized one of her assailants. Either way, it didn't matter. The detectives in charge never discovered anything that resembled a motive in the case, nor did they ever track down the murderers.

And that made me furious.

It was that lack of closure, and the agony associated with it, that drove me into police work. I swore I'd never let another little boy suffer the same pain I had. It wasn't until years later, after a decade spent working the beat, that I realized the pain hadn't come from my lack of closure. It'd come from my loss, and nothing could ever change that. But try to explain that to a kid armed only with a stack of detective novels and a towering pile of his own grief and insecurities.

I wondered if my history of loss—the death of my mother, my divorce from my wife, and my craptastic relationship with my son—in any way affected how I'd dealt with Griggs' departure. On the surface, it didn't seem like it would've. I cared deeply about all of the former individuals, and I would've traded Griggs for a can of beans and some spare change. But maybe it was simpler than that. Maybe Griggs' departure hit me so hard because he was one of the only people I had left.

Rodgers tapped me on the shoulder. "Hey. You alright Daggers?"

"Hmm? Yeah, of course."

"You sure? Because you seem a little out of it."

I shook my head. "Just thinking, that's all."

Rodgers gave me his trademark grin. "Oh. Well, that explains the vacant stare then."

Apparently, someone at the precinct had designated it as the official rip on Jake Daggers day without notifying me. I'd have to talk to management.

"Are you going to tell me who that old broad is or not?"

"Her name is Constance Drude," said Rodgers. "She's the one who organized the charity ball held here last night. Based on those wobbly knees and the prayers she was whispering to me, she knows the dearly departed. I figured I'd let you handle her."

"Thanks."

I dismissed Rodgers with a nod before turning to Miss Steele. "I'm going to interview the witness. Why don't you tag along to see how someone with actual working experience handles things?"

Shay had been dragging her eyeballs across everything in the corridor from the rafters to the floorboards. She shrugged and nodded. "Sure. I'm anxious to see what clever insights you can draw out of her. Like, say, her name."

"Joke's on you." I grinned. "I already know her name."

"Yeah. I know. So do I."

I raised an eyebrow at her. "Oh, really? And how do you figure that? Did you see it in your mystical web of past events?"

"Um, no," said Shay. "I overheard you and Rodgers. Seriously, I was like five feet away."

I grumbled. I didn't like being played for a fool, but Shay's comments rang true. I needed to focus. I had paranormal activity on the brain. With Miss Steele and her snappy retorts nipping at my heels, I made my way over to the old matron.

Her eyes bore into the ground, and I could see a slight tremor in her legs. "Excuse me, Ms. Drude?"

She looked up at me with watery green eyes.

"Detective Jake Daggers, homicide. Mind if I have a few words?"

"Oh, um...yes, of course." She tucked her hands under her arms close to her body, as if giving herself a hug. "I'll try to help however I can."

As she looked at me, I realized once upon a time Ms. Drude must've been quite a head turner. With prominent cheekbones, a slim jaw line, and fierce emerald eyes, she radiated a feline sleekness. The ravages of time had taken their toll however, as battalions of wrinkles had marched across her face and taken up fighting positions on her forehead and underneath her eyes. She tried to hide them with concealer, but the makeup only masked so much, just as black paint couldn't completely hide the underlying gray in her hair.

Based on her attire, Miss Drude had yet to realize she rode the wrong end of the bell curve. Her cocktail dress would've looked ravishing on a woman half her age, but with Miss Drude as the coat rack, I found myself awash in a monsoon of sagging skin and liver spots.

"Ms. Drude, I understand you're the charity event organizer?"

She took a deep breath to steady her nerves. "Yes, that's right. I work with the Veteran's Legacy Project. We're a charity that provides food, shelter, and medical care to the families of those who fall in the defense of our nation. We were hosting a charity ball here at the hotel last night. We raised quite a lot of money, enough to help hundreds of families, and one of the most generous pledges of the night came from poor Mr....Mr...."

Ms. Drude glanced at the tuxedo-clad dead man and broke into tears. I prodded her—verbally, not physically. I had no interest in touching the woman. "So, I take it you know the deceased?"

"Yes," she said between sobs. "His name is Reginald. Reginald Powers. The poor, sweet young man. What could he have done to deserve this?"

"Reginald Powers?" I suppressed a sudden urge to punch the dead guy in the face. "You've got to be kidding me, right?"

My discourteous remark sobered the old matron up. "What? No. Why? I'm certain that was his name. Miss Talent introduced us last night."

Shay spoke up. "What reason do you have to suspect that wasn't his real name, Daggers?"

"Seriously?" I said. "Reginald Powers? That's the kind of name for a guy who's the captain of a sailing team at a yacht club. The kind of guy who wears monogrammed sweater vests and enjoys discussing the finer points of polo."

"I like polo..." said Ms. Drude.

We both ignored her.

"So?" said Shay. "He's wearing a tuxedo and was attending a charity ball. Why can't those things apply to him?"

"Don't be so naïve. The guy's a dark elf." I turned back to Ms. Drude who'd been following our conversation closely. "Is the dead guy new money or old money?"

She understood the question. "I'm not sure. Perhaps you should ask his fiancé. She'd know better than I. I only met him last night."

"His fiancé...would that be this Miss Talent you mentioned earlier?"

"Yes," said Ms. Drude. "Miss Felicity Talent. I believe she lives in Brentford. I can find the address for you if you wish. The Talents have a long history of charitable donations to our organization. I should have their information in my travel journal. It's in my room."

"You're staying here at the hotel?" I asked.

"Yes," she said. "I know from experience these galas tend to go long. Many of our guests didn't leave until past four. I've found it's much easier to rest at the hotel and head home in the morning. Besides, the hotels are usually happy to offer a complimentary suite for the night. It tends to encourage future business."

Well, that explained the cocktail dress. Ms. Drude likely hadn't packed a change of clothes. Of course, that didn't excuse the cocktail dress's length...but I digress.

"Alright," I said. "Mind if we escort you back to your room, Ms. Drude? My partner and I could use that address, if you have it."

"Of course, detectives. It's on the fourth floor. I'll show you the way."

As Constance pried herself off the wall, I delivered a set of detailed instructions to Quinto and Rodgers. "Can you two handle this mess?"

Quinto shot me a hand sign. His thumb and index finger joined together in a circle while his three other digits splayed out radially—the international signal for 'you got it'.

"Great," I said. "When you're done, head back to HQ and see if you can dig up anything on a Felicity Talent. We're going to talk to her, but I want you guys to be able to tell us everything she doesn't."

I cracked my knuckles. Interrogations—I mean, interviews—were always fun.

13

Four flights of stairs later, after fifteen minutes of small talk and at least two unsuccessful pass attempts directed at me by Ms. Drude, Shay and I left suite 408 with an address in hand.

Shay sniggered. "I guess I had you pegged all wrong. You really are a charmer."

I shuddered. Apparently Ms. Drude was actually *Miss* Drude, and I was the lucky recipient of her trauma-fueled advances. *Oh happy day.* I could've appreciated her sentiments if they'd come about forty years earlier.

"Could we agree not to talk about what happened in there?"

A look of mock seriousness crept across Shay's face. "Oh, I don't know about that, Detective Daggers. It might be pertinent to our case. I think Detectives Rodgers and Quinto should be informed."

"Look," I said. "Ms. Drude was clearly residing in a fragile emotional state after the death of her dear friend Mr. Reginald Sweatervest. She was seeking comfort and—"

"And you were just the one to provide that comfort, weren't you?" Shay grinned an evil grin. "Don't worry, Detective Daggers. I understand."

I groaned. "I'm making this worse, aren't I?"

Miss Steele nodded.

"Right. I'm going to shut up."

Together, we headed back down the stairs, out the Lawrence's wide double doors, and onto the streets of the Pearl. The address Constance had provided was indeed in the Brentford neighborhood, only about a half-hour's walk away. All the city's best shopping and entertainment resided in the Pearl, so many of the city's more affluent neighborhoods pressed up as close as possible.

Brentford was one of the swankiest.

As a kid, I often fantasized about what it would be like to live in splendor. Then I grew up and took a government job. Soon all my fantasies died slow miserable deaths.

Homicide could be a heck of a thrill ride at times, but lucrative it was not. A financial advisor once told me if I played my cards right, scrimped and saved and invested my earnings properly, I might be able to afford a small cottage *near* Brentford in retirement—at the ripe old age of five-hundred and twelve.

I glanced at Shay's pointy leather boots. "You good to keep walking in those things?"

"Just because a pair of boots is stylish and attractive doesn't mean they can't also be comfortable. I'm fine."

Years of interaction with the fairer sex told me Shay's claim was a pile of bull feathers, but who was I to argue? If she wanted a chance to show off her plantar fortitude, I certainly wasn't going to coddle her.

"Alright then," I said. "Time to wear out some leather."

Our feet carried us across the northern half of the Pearl, past high rise hotels, overpriced boutiques, and bistros that featured bite-sized portions tailored for pompous epicureans. Most of the restaurants had patios that spilled into the streets where patrons could gather to laugh and smoke and flaunt their money. Given the day's unseasonable heat I figured we'd avoid the worst of the patio crew, but clouds had rolled in while we'd poked and prodded our new victim at the Lawrence. The incessant jabbering of haughty foodies hounded us on the first half of our walk.

As we passed Mercantile Street, the shops and cafes disappeared. Two and three story estates with mani-cured lawns populated by hydrangeas and daylilies took their places. Rent-a-cops stood watch on street corners, eying us as they fingered their nightsticks. I flashed one my badge, more out of pride than necessity. The hired goons had made us from the moment we set foot in Brentford.

The farther we walked, the ritzier the houses be-came. Topiary gardens replaced tightly-trimmed lawns, and gleaming porcelain fountains sprouted like weeds. I half expected to stumble across a house with a moat and trained attack alligators.

Shay and I arrived at our destination after a trek up a small hill. To call the place a house would be a disserv-ice. It was more of a castle, complete with cylindrical turrets at the corners and honest-to-goodness stone battlements. No moat, though. Or alligators, thankfully.

The sight of the place sent alarm bells ringing through my head. Such a home, in Brentford of all places, would quite literally be worth a fortune. I'd been around the block enough times to know when money and murder found themselves in close proximity, there was often an obvious reason why.

A security guard stopped us at the gate to the estate.

I pulled out my badge. "Hi. I'm Detective Daggers. This is my partner—"

"Detective Steele. Yeah, I know," said the watchman. "Miss Talent is expecting you. The butler'll take you to her."

"Wait, what?" I said. "She's expecting us?"

The guard gave me a quizzical look, though to be fair it may have been his regular face. "A runner came with the news. Maybe half an hour ago. We were expecting you sooner."

Right. Runners—the method by which virtually all time-sensitive information in the city was delivered. I tended to forget the vast majority of them worked free-lance. When word got out about Reggie Sweatervest, I'm sure a whole pile of street urchins would've been clamoring to get word to his well-to-do fiancé as fast as their little feet could carry them.

Shay chimed in. "We would've arrived sooner, but Detective Daggers was indisposed. He was attacked by a cougar."

That elicited another confused stare from the guard. Miss Steele grinned in response. I was starting to wonder who'd abducted the indignant little elf girl from the precinct and replaced her with someone with sass. I suspected the change in behavior was a ruse to try to gain my favor.

"Yes, well, thankfully the cougar was on its last legs," I said. "I was able to fend it off."

"Might've been faster if you'd offered it some meat." Her grin widened.

Did she mean what I thought she meant?

I glared at my partner. "C'mon. Let's go find Miss Talent."

14

The butler at the door ushered us in and offered to take our coats. I opted to keep mine. Daisy gets lonely when left in a closet. He then escorted us out of the foyer, across an expansive glass-ceilinged atrium and into a sitting room with a trio of overstuffed sofa chairs upholstered with supple brown leather.

A number of portraits adorned the walls, some as tall as me and about three times as wide. One depicted a stern-faced, gray-haired geezer in a three-piece suit as he leaned against a hardwood desk. Another depicted the same old geezer next to a young woman—a woman with close-set eyes and wild red hair who wore a bright lemon sundress. The third portrait showed the same geezer at a much younger age, with firmer skin and hair the color of rust. In the last portrait, he stood alongside another young woman—a woman with flowing cinnamon hair but the same close-set eyes as the girl in the yellow dress. My brain started to piece the puzzle together.

Having been shown to the sitting room, the butler bowed and excused himself, promising to bring the Talent girl. As he left, I plopped my posterior down in the nearest sofa and propped my feet up on an oval-shaped coffee table whose surface had been polished to a reflective shine.

My partner shot me a look of disdain. "Wow. You sure made yourself comfortable, didn't you?"

I shrugged. "What? It's a sitting room. I'm sitting."

She eyed my feet. "Yes, it's a sitting room. Not a sitting-and-defiling-the-furniture room."

If my partner's new social strategy involved hurling large quantities of insults, she'd quickly find out that wasn't going to work very well. Quips I like. Verbal abuse, not so much.

"Hey, I'm trying to help out my fellow man," I said. "I'm a job creator. Without me, the poor sap whose job it is to rub layers of grime off this coffee table would be out on the streets. Do you want that kind of guilt hanging over you? Besides, my shoes aren't *that* filthy."

Shay only had a moment to chew on my impromptu capitalist discourse before shrill sobbing broke the silence. The butler arrived with a pair of young ladies in tow.

Both were crying, one more so than the other. The worst offender wore a pale saffron-colored gown that stuck out awkwardly over her too-wide hips. Her shock of scarlet hair badly needed to be introduced to a comb, and her puffy, bloodshot eyes were too close together for comfort. Based on the portraits in the sitting room, I identified her as Felicity Talent.

With one hand clasped tightly in Miss Talent's, the other woman dabbed at her cheeks with a white handkerchief. Tears welled in her eyes, but I barely noticed. Other features fought for my attention.

The girl was a straight-up bombshell—slim and busty with bronze-colored hair that fell to her shoulders in waves. A low-cut white shirt hugged her ample bosom, and brown pants wrapped themselves around her rear as tightly as a kraken squeezing a pirate ship. If she'd wished it, she could've set an entire room of wolves to howling with a wink and a smile. I pressed a hand to my thigh to keep my own back legs from thumping. I had no idea who she was, but I wanted to find out.

I'd started to deposit a trail of drool upon the couch. I think Shay noticed. She took the initiative.

"Excuse me...Miss Felicity Talent?" she said. "I'm Detective Shay Steele, and this is Detective Jake Daggers. We're very sorry for your loss."

Shay glanced at me. I was still trying to locate my tongue, so she continued. "I know this is a difficult time for you, but do you mind if we ask you some questions regarding your fiancé?"

Felicity sniffled and nodded as she tried to stem her tide of tears.

"Y-y-yes detective, of...of course. I'll...I'll do my best."

The bombshell guided Felicity to an open sofa chair, easing her down onto the puffy cushions with care. Kneeling beside her on the couch, she spoke to her in a strained voice.

"Oh, Felicity. Dear sweet Felicity. My heart breaks for you. No one should have to suffer through the loss you've experienced. Know that if you need anything—anything at all—I'll be here for you."

Felicity looked into her friend's eyes with a mild look of panic. "Wait...Gretchen, are you leaving? No, please don't. I need you!"

I scrunched my face. Gretchen seemed like a dowdy name for such a jaw-dropping young woman. Misty or Jasmine would've suited my fantasy better.

"I know. I'm sorry, sweetheart," Gretchen said. "But I don't want to interfere with the detectives' work. We may not be able to bring Reginald back, but at least the detectives can bring his killer to justice."

Gretchen glanced at me. I thought I caught a wink, but I might've been suffering from testosterone-fueled hallucinations.

"Besides, I should tell my family the news. They'd want to know. I'll be back as soon as I can, Felicity. I promise."

Felicity nodded glumly. "Yes, I suppose that's true. But please...hurry back."

Gretchen put Felicity's hand over her heart. "Of course, my love."

The bombshell turned to us. "Excuse me detectives. I should go. Please, be gentle with Felicity. She's a wounded bird, and her skies are stormy."

With that she left, taking with her the heat of a thousand suns and plunging the room into an icy quagmire, devoid of purpose or meaning. Well...perhaps that was an exaggeration. But the room sure did seem less bright without her.

I blinked to clear the fog from my eyes and turned to the teary-eyed redhead. With her busty friend gone, perhaps we could all focus on the important matter at hand—the violent murder of her fiancé.

15

"So, um, Miss Talent," I said. "Do you mind if I call you Felicity?"

Red took a deep, labored breath and nodded through her tears.

"Well then, Felicity, as my partner already mentioned, I'm Detective Jake Daggers. We need to ask you a few questions regarding your fiancé. How about you start with his name and a physical description?"

"His name is Reginald. Reginald Powers," she said. "Or I guess I should say his name *was* Reginald. He went by Reg. I still can't believe he's gone..."

Her voice cracked and fresh tears sprung from her eyes. Her damsel in distress routine was the only thing preventing me from making another crack about her fiancé's ridiculous name.

Red composed herself and continued. "He was a little over six feet tall with dark hair and dark eyes. He had some dark elf ancestry. But it's not what they say. They're not all bad, you know? Reg surely wasn't. He was the sweetest man I'd ever met..."

More tears ensued. I started to wonder how deep Felicity's reservoir reached. While she cried herself out, I compared Miss Talent's description to my mental record of the dead guy. It was a match.

I pulled out a spiral-bound notepad and pencil from an interior pocket of my coat. My old noggin could only hold onto so much new information before some of it would get displaced by thoughts of busty women or booze or juggling circus animals.

"Can you tell us some personal information about Reginald? Who was he? What did he do for a living? That sort of thing."

"Well," said Felicity. "He was a contractor."

I raised an eyebrow. "Really? He built houses for a living? I wouldn't have picked him for that."

Felicity blushed. "Oh, no. Sorry. That's not what I meant. I mean he was good at negotiating contracts between parties. He worked for Drury Arms, an arms manufacturer. They supply weapons to the local infantry division, but Reg helped negotiate a number of big new deals with overseas commonwealths."

Interesting. I scribbled a note in my pad.

Not content to sit and listen to my pencil rub against paper, Shay jumped into the fray.

"Do you know if Reginald had any enemies?" she asked. "Had he been involved with anything dangerous lately?"

I chuckled under my breath. It's not that Shay asked poor questions, but the style in which she phrased them made it sound as if she'd plucked them straight from a police-issue how-to handbook on witness interrogation.

Felicity shook her head. "No, not that I know of. Honestly, Reg was a saint. I have no idea why anyone would want to hurt him."

"Had he been acting strange lately?" Shay asked.

"No..." Felicity paused. "Well, he had been a little nervous."

I raised my head from my pad. "Nervous? About what?"

"About our wedding. We were set to get married just two weeks from tomorrow." Felicity had composed herself admirably since the start of our interview, but the thought of her impending nuptials brought more fresh tears running down her cheeks. "Even though we were so close to the date of the wedding, he asked me last week if I wanted to elope."

Shay beat me to the obvious question. "Elope? Why?"

"As I said, he was nervous. All the pomp and circumstance. The months upon months of wedding planning. I've been stressed out, too. I've tried to hide it, but I think it was getting to be too much for Reg. Maybe if my mother were here to run interference it might've been easier, but my father can be a little imposing on his own."

I let Miss Talent hold to the notion her fiancé had just been experiencing pre-wedding jitters. My experience told me otherwise.

"And your father—what does he do?" I asked.

"Oh, he's in the metals business. He owns a couple manufactories. We've been blessed with success, but if you ask father he'll tell you blessings have far less to do with success than hard work."

"I see," I said. "Your fiancé, Reg—did he have his own place or did he stay here?"

Felicity blushed again. "Oh, no. He didn't stay here. Father wouldn't allow that. Not before marriage."

"Alright. So can you show us to his home?"

"Well, I've never been there personally, but—"

"Hold on," I said. "You were to be married in a couple weeks, and you've never been to his place?"

"Well, as I said, Daddy is very protective," Felicity said. "He didn't want me in a suitor's company unattended, even after Reg and I became engaged."

Dear old Daddy Talent was sounding like a real hard ass. Then again, if I had a young daughter I'd probably chain her to the pipes in my bathroom while I was away at work. The city can be rough on young girls who lose their way.

"But I do know his address," Felicity said. "415 West 7th. Apartment 405."

I made a note in my pad. The information Red provided would act as a starting block for us to push off from. Now came the hard part of the interview—the part I always dreaded.

"I don't mean to be blunt," I said. "But we'll need you to head to the precinct to identify your fiancé's body. We have to be sure it's really him."

Red's tear ducts had run themselves dry. She merely nodded as she stared off into oblivion. "Of course."

"One more thing before we leave. Do you mind if I ask you about your friend?"

Shay gave me a sidelong look only women can give—a mixture of jealousy, disgust, and contempt all rolled into one piercing glance. All women have the ability to generate such a look, but most can only do so when in the temporal and spatial vicinity of a woman substantially more attractive than them.

I shrugged it off. I've received my fair share of evil glares in my lifetime.

Felicity looked confused. "What friend? You mean Gretchen?"

"Yes," I said.

"Oh. What about her?"

"Who is she? What's her relation to you?"

Felicity held a hand to her heart. "Oh. Well, her name is Gretchen Winters. She's my best friend. We do everything together. Shopping, dinners at the country club, shows at Magister Hall. She was even helping me plan my wedding..." I was wrong about Felicity's supply of tears. More of them rolled across her cheeks and splashed onto the increasingly sodden lap of her dress. "Why do you ask, Detective? Is this relevant to the case?"

Shay raised an eyebrow. "Yes, Detective Daggers. *Is it* relevant to the case?"

I loosened my collar. Suddenly the room felt warmer. Luckily, I could cover my tracks with the best of them.

"Miss Talent, it's our job to gather as much information as possible when we're investigating a crime. You never know what may or may not turn out to be pertinent."

"Oh. Of course," said Felicity. "I see."

I stood and tucked away my notepad. "Thanks for your assistance, Miss Talent. We'll be sure to contact you if we have any more questions or find any leads.

And don't forget to visit the precinct when you get a chance." I motioned to my partner that it was time to leave.

As we approached the front door, Shay spoke in a mocking tone. "*It's our job to gather as much information as possible...* Very convincing, Detective Daggers. I almost believed it. Or I would've, if I hadn't seen your tongue lolling at the sight of Chesty St. Clair."

Chesty St. Clair? I thought I was the only one who made up creative nicknames for nobodies. Apparently, young Miss Steele only needed a little external motivation to get her creative juices flowing.

"Hey, as I said, you never know what information will be relevant. Besides, it's not like I asked for a personal introduction or anything."

Shay rolled her eyes.

"C'mon," I said. "Let's go check out the dead guy's place."

16

After another half hour of walking, our feet brought us to Reggie's apartment building. It sat roughly four or five blocks west of the edge of the Pearl. Based on the affluence of his fiancé and her assertions of his deft financial acumen, I'd expected an extravagant residential tower, complete with gilded door handles, walls of glass, and a sharply dressed doorman who knew every resident's name. Instead, an average four-story apartment building loomed over me.

I glanced at Shay. She looked nonplussed.

"Well?" I said.

"Well, what?"

"Doesn't this seem a little odd to you?" I asked. "Is this really the place our wheeling and dealing, tuxedo wearing, cash-laden dead guy lived?"

"It's not that bad. I'll bet it puts your apartment to shame."

"That's not a fair comparison," I said. "My apartment had a herd of stray cats squatting in it when I moved in. The lingering aroma was the only reason I was able to haggle the rent down to a reasonable level. Sometimes I swear I can still smell the funk."

Shay gave me a look that indicated I'd shared too much information.

"Don't judge me," I said. "I'm divorced. I've had to make concessions. My point is, don't you think this place is a little bland for a guy like Reggie Mortis?"

"Reggie Mortis?"

I sighed. Clearly that quip fell flat. "It was a joke. You know, like rigor mort—"

"I got it," Shay said, holding up a hand to get me to stop talking. "Look, you're the one who brought up his dark elf background. Maybe the ritzy apartments wouldn't rent to him because of his race?"

It was a plausible theory, but the seasoned veteran within me suspected an ulterior motive.

I led the way to the fourth floor and into a hallway lined with muted green paisley wallpaper. I found the apartment about a dozen paces from the end of the steps on the right.

I stretched to limber up. "Too bad old Reggie Sweatervest didn't have his keys on him. Guess I'll have to do what I do best."

I backed up to the other side of the hallway and readied my trusty kicking foot.

"Wait," Shay said. "Aren't you going to try the knob first? It might not be locked."

I lost my balance and nearly fell.

Shay sniggered.

"Don't do that," I said. "Never interrupt a man when he's getting ready to show a lock who's boss. And no, I wasn't going to try the door. I mean, this isn't what I'd call a rough neighborhood, but what kind of idiot would leave their apartment—"

Shay turned the door knob and pushed on through.

"—door unlocked." I eyed the padlock in the door-frame. "You got off easy. Better hope I don't have to come back here."

I followed my partner into the dead guy's living quarters only to find her in the throes of another spiritual encounter. Her arms floated at her sides, fingers tickling the air as they had back at the Lawrence when we first found the stiff. Rather than standing still, she was rotating slowly in a circle. As she completed a rotation, I noticed her darting eyes had the same faraway, milky quality I'd seen the first time, as if she were peering far into the future or the past. Or simply studying the paint flecks on the walls.

I didn't want to risk a paranormal reprimand for interrupting her, but after a minute or so I got restless. Shay blocked the path further into the apartment, and I wanted to flex my deductive muscles.

Just as I was about to say something, she lowered her arms and stopped spinning.

"Get anything useful this time?" I ventured.

She ignored the dig.

"I found two threads," she said. "One was from an older tapestry. I saw bad men. Troubled men. Short, with beards and tattoos. They were here to see Mr. Powers, but I don't think he was here."

I pursed my lips. That piece of information was rather concrete. I'd been expecting another dubious insight along the lines of 'it wasn't magic,' but perhaps Shay's ability wasn't quite as useless as non-alcoholic beer. Assuming it could be trusted, of course. I still had my doubts about her first thread. Reggie Sweatervest's chest cavity still screamed 'magic attack' to me.

"Alright," I said. "What about the second thread?"

"The second thread had an aura of freshness. It was recent. I felt someone. Alone. Here. Not Reginald, but someone else. They were on fire."

I wiggled a finger in my ear. "I'm sorry. Did you say 'on fire?'"

"Yes," Shay said. "But you have to understand how the threads work. Just because the individual was on fire in my vision doesn't mean it actually happened. It only means the fire and the individual are closely related."

My trust in Miss Steele's supernatural abilities fell back down a precipice. A man on fire? *Really?*

"Well, I'm sure that's a very prescient insight. Now why don't we see what a good old-fashioned pair of eyeballs can tell us."

I pushed past Shay into the apartment, a three-room affair. The entryway led straight into an all-purpose living room containing a wooden desk, a small dining table with two chairs, and a raggedy loveseat probably rescued from an errant street corner. A door on the right led to what I assumed would be the bedroom, and an alcove to the left contained either a kitchen or a washroom.

Exploration would have to wait. The riches before me beckoned. A glimmer of something shiny sneaked out from within a long cardboard box at the edge of the moth-eaten loveseat. I stepped forward and peeked inside. Weapons stared back at me. A knife, two daggers, a pair of hatchets, a studded mace, and the pièce de résistance—a full length sword. All were military grade. As an officer, I wasn't even allowed to own these sorts of weapons, much less a regular schmuck like Reginald.

I turned my attention to the desk, which tried to hide from me from under a mountain of paper. Stacks of records and files littered it, but there were other types of printed documents, too. I noticed calligraphed designs on small placards. Some looked tribal in nature. Small boxes, stationary, and stencils added to the clutter.

As I approached the desk to take a closer look, something triggered alarm bells in my head.

I smelled smoke.

17

Mommy and Daddy Daggers didn't raise a fool. Smoke comes from fires, and fires tend to treat people poorly. As dodgy as my profession can be, the dangers I faced on a regular basis paled in comparison to the sorts of things the city's firefighters tackled headfirst.

Instead of fleeing the building however, I stayed put. The smell of smoke was faint. Tired. The smell of a fire that had burned itself out.

I followed my nose to a metal wastebasket at the side of the desk. Within it, wispy gray embers floated around lazily. Someone had burned a stack of papers— and recently, by the looks of it. I thought I spotted a faint ember that still held some color at its core. It faded from view as the charred piece caught a breeze and drifted out of the trashcan.

A breeze? From where?

I looked up. A window at the side of the room stood half open, letting in a trickle of fresh air. I ran over and pulled the window up the rest of the way. A rickety fire escape snaked its way down the apartment building's side. I scanned the confines of the alley beneath but saw no trace of anyone—not even so much as a wine-soaked hobo.

"I told you."

I turned around at the sound of Shay's voice. "Huh?"

"I told you. About the fire. You didn't believe me."

"I never said that." But I did sound defensive. Why? I didn't need to explain myself to her.

"You didn't have to say it. It's plastered all over your face, Daggers."

I couldn't argue. I had doubted her. But her predications hadn't been particularly prophetic thus far, so I hadn't put much stock in them. "Right now you're batting one for three," I said. "Don't get cocky."

I walked back over to the wastebasket and kneeled. I sifted through the charred wisps, hoping to find a scrap that still contained script on it or anything that could offer a clue as to what had been burned. Unfortunately, whatever had been torched had given up its secrets. The paper could only serve as fertilizer now.

Shay was busy searching through the items on the desk. I joined her. "Find anything interesting?"

"Plenty," she said. "Take a look at this."

She handed me a couple of the small boxes I'd noticed earlier. Inside one was a fine, cream-colored powder. Within the other was a block of a dark solid material. I rubbed my thumb against it. It gave easily under pressure, and my thumb came away black.

"This is—"

"Makeup," Shay finished. She flourished a little appliqué brush she'd also found. "And check these out."

She handed me a small stack of cards. The first one was a government tax identification card. It listed the owner as Reginald Powers. Reggie's elaborate signature sprawled across the bottom half of the card, and an official, embossed seal of the city engulfed the lower right corner.

The second card was also an official identification card, as were the third and the fourth. Different names were listed on each card. Maxwell Fortnight. Henry Pool. Bradley Snood. A different signature embellished each one, and each gleamed with the same official seal.

I scanned the desk for more identifying documents, and one in particular drew my eye—a small black leather billfold similar to the one I carried with me on the job. I opened it. A soaring eagle holding a pair of scales in its claws stared at me from the face of a shiny golden shield.

To anyone who didn't walk into work day after day under a giant rendition of the seal of justice, the badge would've been quite convincing. But I knew better. The angle of one of the eagle's claws was off. The badge was a fake.

I scratched my chin. "Makeup. Fake IDs. Forged documents... This guy's a professional con artist. What do you want to bet we'll find disguises and wigs in the bedroom?"

"It gets even more interesting," Shay said. "Look at this."

She offered a couple syringes and a vial full of an oozing caramel-colored liquid. I took the bottle and held it to one side. The liquid moved as slowly as molasses.

"Crank," I said. "Low grade stuff, too. Interesting...very interesting."

I left the desk and performed a quick walkthrough of the apartment. The kitchen held nothing of interest, but the bedroom yielded a few more secrets. Disparate outfits filled the dead guy's closet, from suits to denim coats to weatherworn work clothes. I even spotted a police officer's blue coat. *Surprise, surprise.*

On the floor of the closet, a number of wigs adorned severed mannequin heads. Short, tousled brown hair. Medium length black hair. Enough styles for an assortment of guises. One particular wig stood out with its long, feathery blond locks. Paired with his dusky skin, Reginald must've looked like a majestic god while wearing it. Either that or a cheap gigolo.

A backpack hid behind the disembodied mannequin heads. I unzipped the top and looked inside. Fat stacks of cash languished inside like wine-soaked hedonists. The plot continued to thicken.

Back in the living room, I reexamined the cardboard box filled with implements of murder. Possession of any one of them would've landed Reginald in the joint. I turned the sword over in my hands. Felicity had mentioned Reggie was a successful broker for an arms dealer, but why had he filched some of the goods and stuffed them in his apartment?

Shay continued to sift through the piles of stuff on our dead friend's desk.

"I found wigs and disguises in the bedroom," I said. "Not to mention a backpack full of cash. You?"

"There's tons of documents here," Shay said. "It's going to take a while to get through them all. We should probably box it all up and take it to the precinct."

I made a noncommittal sound of agreement. We'd need to gather up the arms, files, disguises, and other contraband. It sounded like a lot of work. "Why don't we head back to the street and see if we can flag down a couple of beat cops to help? Lugging crap around town is beneath my pay grade."

Shay didn't disagree. I doubted her slight frame could support more than a couple daggers at a time.

I led the way out of the apartment. "So, what's your take on the situation?"

Shay stumbled as she pulled the door shut behind her. "Seriously? You're asking me?"

"I want to see if you can do more than paint tapestries."

"Tapestries are woven, genius. And I don't weave them, I pluck at them."

"Yeah, whatever," I said. "I'm not good with metaphors."

"What are you good with, then?"

"Quit stalling. Show me if your fancy schooling was worth the money somebody else shelled out for it."

Shay took a deep breath. "Um. Ok. Well...the forged documents and disguises are a dead giveaway. Reginald—if that is his real name—was a con artist. And if he had a sack of cash in his bedroom, he must've been a successful one. We know about his relationship with Miss Talent. Based on the family portraits we saw in her sitting room, I'd wager Felicity is an only child. That means she stands to inherit her father's entire fortune. I can only imagine Reg was attempting to marry her for her wealth."

"Go on," I said.

"We know someone came by the apartment. Recently. I saw it in my vision, and you found those charred remains in the wastebasket. But whoever came by didn't trash the place, and they left the cash. So they must've come by for other reasons. Like, say, to eliminate evidence. There's only one logical person who would've done that."

"Reginald's murderer," I said. "We'll get the boys to dust for prints. Anything else you'd like to add?"

"Yes," she said. "There's one more thing that's bothering me. That backpack. Felicity said Reginald had proposed eloping with her. The rucksack backs that up. If he wanted to leave in a hurry, he'd need cash. But if Reginald were marrying Felicity for money, why take off with a single sack of dough?"

"Maybe because he knew someone was coming after him and he wanted to skip town. But you're right. That part doesn't jive with everything else."

I pursed my lips. I was reasonably impressed, but I'd never admit as much. Rookies are like steaks. They need seasoning before they become palatable. Telling my little elf partner she'd met the required minimum level of observational prowess to call herself a detective would only serve to inflate her ego, and our partnership only had room for one bloated sense of self. Mine.

We reached the bottom of the stairs and headed back onto the street.

"Not terrible," I said. "But you forgot something. Something that doesn't fit the narrative. The weapons and drugs. Crime is a war, and weapons traffickers and drug peddlers are the grunts in the trenches roughing it up. White-collar swindlers like Reggie are the captains. They stand back, keep their hands clean, and politely let everyone else get stabbed. The two don't often intermingle."

"Hmm." Shay's eyebrows furrowed. "If that's the case, who are the generals?"

"Are you kidding?" I said. "The guys with the real money and power. Politicians and businessmen. Guys like, well...Felicity Talent's father, probably."

"And here I thought you weren't any good with metaphors."

I flashed a grin. "Sometimes inspiration strikes."

I spotted a bluecoat and flagged him down. I explained the situation and made sure he understood we needed everything of interest in Reginald's apartment boxed up and transported to the precinct. I also keenly pointed out how I was aware of the sack of cash in the closet and expected it to be among the items delivered. With the money still in it.

He had the decency to at least feign outrage at my insinuation. Good man. He'd probably only steal a few coins.

18

As we neared the precinct, my stomach informed me with a vicious growl that it was nearing lunchtime. I coerced Miss Steele into stopping at a corner eatery about two blocks away from our command post, at a place called Noodles and More.

An elderly gnome couple ran the place, and their driving passion in life was their love for making noodles. They'd show up at the restaurant at about four in the morning, mixing water, salt, and flour into dough, and kneading it until it achieved a nice springy texture. Then the real work began. The gnomes would pull the noodles by hand, stretching the dough out as far as their little arms would allow and twirling it around itself until it twisted tightly like a pretzel. They'd pull on the ends, rinse, and repeat until the dough reached the right consistency. They'd keep working on the noodles for hours, all the way until opening right before the big lunch rush.

They first opened the shop about the time I started my job as a gumshoe. At that point, the shop was just called Noodles. But there was one small problem.

The poor gnomes' noodles were terrible.

You'd think handmade noodles would be hard to mess up, but the old gnomes figured out a way. Business dried up faster than a water droplet on a hot wok. The little shop nearly closed down. After that, the Noodles eatery became Noodles and More, and luckily for the gnomes, the 'More' part was worth the price of admission.

Shay eyeballed the cafe as we stepped underneath the awning in front. "You sure about this place?"

"Of course I am," I said. "They're fantastic. And they've yet to fail a health inspection that wasn't due to mold. Just don't get the noodles."

Shay gave me that too much information look again.

"Honestly, I know I gave you a hard time about them earlier, but we could get a kolache or something instead."

"Don't be silly," I said. "Kolaches are purely for breakfast. Besides, I need something a little healthier to keep me on my toes."

I hollered at Grandpa Gnome and ordered a cheesesteak.

Shay ordered some sort of salad that reminded me of rabbit food, except no self-respecting rabbit would've eaten the wilted greens and root vegetables in question. Then again, Shay's look of disgust upon receiving her plate indicated she wasn't going to eat it either. Maybe that's how she stayed so skinny.

Noodles and More had never bothered to splurge on anything as fancy as tables or chairs for patrons, so I commandeered a spot at a standing bar and chowed down. Shay picked at her sad-looking salad with a look of distrust. I thought I heard her stomach rumble, but she seemed more concerned with the possibility of contracting salmonella than the dangers of hunger pangs.

After devouring roughly half of my cheesesteak in mutually shared silence, I realized this could be an ideal time to establish a connection with my partner, who, in contrast to my initial gut reaction, might not be a completely terrible detective.

I swallowed a steaming mouthful of beef and cheddar and attempted to break the ice with a witty opener.

"So..." I said.

Shay looked up from her pitiful plate of mixed greens. "Yeah?"

"Thought you might like to take this opportunity to share a bit about yourself."

"Yeah, well, I tried that when we first met, remember? You weren't particularly receptive to it."

"To be fair, I thought you were the new secretary."

Shay's cheeks flared. "Right, because a little half-elf girl couldn't possibly be any good at detective work. That's a *man's* domain, right?"

The conversation wasn't going exactly as I'd planned. Shay was mortaring a wall around herself with alarming speed.

"Look, it's not like you can blame me," I said. "You're new. Inexperienced. I figured, if anything, Captain would promote from within for Griggs' old job."

Shay stared at her lettuce. "You don't trust me."

"Darn right I don't. Not yet, anyway."

Clap. The last brick settled into place.

I tried to chat while I finished my sandwich, but Miss Steele had retreated into one-word answer mode. Was she from the city? Yes. Did she have any siblings? Yes. What kind? Brothers. Older or younger? Older. After a few questions I gave up.

As I wiped beef drippings from my chin with a paper napkin, I contemplated the inner workings of my new partner. Although I'd only known her for a few measly hours, already I'd had the pleasure of experiencing her in five different varieties: calm and collected, explosive and fiery, biting and witty, deductive and thoughtful, and now detached and emotionally unavailable. Which state, if any, best represented the real Shay? And did her emotional rollercoaster have anything to do with her strange supernatural abilities, or was it simply due to an estrogen imbalance?

I tossed my napkin in a waste bin and snapped at Shay to get a move on, possibly more harshly than I should've. I instantly regretted it, but I reasoned I could apologize later.

19

My beat cop underlings were nothing if not efficient. In the time it took us to walk to the noodle shop, have lunch, and stroll back to HQ, the boys in blue had boxed up all of the dark elf's belongings, loaded everything onto a cart, and wheeled the entire kit and caboodle back to the precinct doors.

Quinto had been enrolled to help unload stuff. He was turning the shiny broadsword we'd recovered over in his hands when he noticed us approaching.

"Daggers. Detective Steele." He followed that last part with a nod of his head in Shay's direction. He'd never offered me the same simple courtesy. Jerk... "You sure have a knack for finding interesting toys in strange places."

"What?" I said. "Don't tell me you didn't see the whole 'wealthy philanthropist is secretly a sword-swinging dope fiend' thing coming?" I added some wacky arms for comedic effect.

Quinto chuckled and shook his head. "Rodgers wants to talk to you. He did some legwork on the victim and on that Talent woman. Said he found something you might find interesting."

"Thanks. We'll track him down."

Rodgers wasn't at his desk. After a few minutes of wandering, we found him in the most logical hiding place—the break room.

"There you are," I said.

Rodgers leaned against the counter, a steaming mug of joe gripped in one hand and a battered tubular stick of meat in the other. I wondered where it had come from. Was Tolek selling corndogs now, too? If so, I might have to reconsider my devotion to Noodles and More.

Rodgers swallowed a mouthful of coffee. "Daggers. Steele." He gave Shay a nod and a smile.

I frowned. Nobody ever gave me a nod, but introduce a pretty little thing like Miss Steele into the work environment, and suddenly everyone was losing control of their neck muscles.

Rodgers turned his eyes back to me. "You ok, Daggers? You look like you swallowed a grapefruit."

"I'm fine," I grumped. "Quinto said you had something for us?"

"Sure do," he said as he bit into his fried meat log. "And it's juicy."

I couldn't tell if Rodgers was referring to the findings or his corndog. His failed quips had a way of engendering confusion.

Rodgers swallowed. "I talked to our friends down at Taxation and Revenue, and it turns out Miss Felicity Talent is totally loaded."

I recalled the palatial estate she called home. "Yeah, we figured that one out already."

"Where the wealth comes from is the interesting part," said Rodgers. "Her father, Charles Blaze Talent, the third, owns a consortium of foundries in the industrial park east of the river."

Shay perked up. "Foundries? Interesting that Felicity didn't mention that."

"She told us her dad was in the metals business," I said. Felicity hadn't exactly lied, but she'd omitted information. I made a mental note of it.

"It gets better," said Rodgers. "Her father often goes by a nickname. Perspicacious Blaze."

"Perspiwhaticus?" I said. The mouse in my brain was on sabbatical again. I wasn't getting whatever Rodgers hinted at.

"He's a fire mage."

Oh. Right. Mages had a long-standing tradition of taking on ridiculous, complicated pseudonyms to make themselves seem more fearsome and imposing. To me, it made them sound like racehorses.

The implications dawned on me.

"Did you say *fire mage*?" I asked. I turned to my partner with a sly grin. "Now, I don't suppose a fire mage might know anything about his dead son-in-law-to-be who happened to have a hole burned into his chest? Or about a mysterious fire we found in said future son-in-law's apartment?"

Shay raised a condescending eyebrow at me. "Yes, Daggers. I made that connection, too. But I'm telling you, Reginald wasn't murdered by magic. I know what the threads tell me, and they're never wrong."

"Nonetheless, I think it's time we go have a chat with dear old Perspi...Perspi..." I turned to Rodgers. "What was it again?"

"Perspicacious."

I threw my index finger in the air with a flourish. "Perspicacious Blaze!"

The crippling condescending eyebrow epidemic had spread to Rodgers. "You done now?"

"Yeah," I said. "You want to come with us?"

Rodgers shook his head. "I think Quinto would kill me if I left him by himself to go through all that wagon crap you guys sent back. I'd better stay."

"Guess it's just you and me then," I said to my partner. I eyed her boots. "You want to walk?"

"I'm fine if you are," she said.

I'm an expert at female doublespeak. My failed marriage can attest to that. "Why don't we get a rickshaw?"

20

The guard at the Talent's estate gave us a sour, confused look when we rolled up to the gates. I didn't take it personally. I'd concluded his furrowed eyebrows and jutting lip were a permanent fixture of his ugly mug.

I flashed my badge again in case lemon-face had forgotten who we were. He grunted and waved us through.

The butler reacted with substantially more grace than the muscle out front. He gave us a low bow, offering pleasantries as he ushered us indoors. After informing him we needed to speak with the master of the house, he led us on a circuitous path through the villa. We traipsed across the cavernous glass-ceilinged atrium and out onto a meandering breezeway that fed into a tower separate from the main house. Neatly manicured topiaries lined the path, trimmed into alternating cubes and spheres.

I snorted. The idea of spending time and energy in the temporary mastery of something a dog would relieve himself on was absurd to me.

Inside the tower, Shay and I followed the butler up a winding stone staircase to the top level. Daddy Talent's study. The place practically oozed money. Mahogany bookshelves, custom built to match the curvature of the tower, overflowed with leather-wrapped tomes. An ancient hand-drawn map of what had constituted the nine kingdoms before a fit of democracy had broken out hung over a window, and a bearskin rug sprawled across the floor. The bear's mouth gaped, its teeth glistening in the afternoon sun. If I were a rabbit, I would've been terrified.

In the middle of the room, behind a mahogany desk plucked from the same mold as the bookshelves, the old Talent geezer sat. In person, he seemed less of a codger and more of a retired hard-ass. His hair sprouted silver rather than gray, and though the creases that lined his face indicated his age, they resembled carved granite more than squishy, folded flesh.

Despite his hard visage, I was disappointed. I'd expected more from someone with his unique skill set. Perhaps flames shooting out of his eyeballs or fire motes rippling across his skin.

As we entered, Talent's eyes turned up from a stack of paperwork to examine us over the rims of his blocky spectacles. Something deep within the eyes smoldered, giving off a cool heat.

Ahh. So there *was* a fire.

"Sir," said the butler. "Some detectives from the constabulary are here to speak with you."

Constabulary? Apparently Jeeves held a master's degree in linguistics. Is that what our society was coming to? Guys with university degrees taking on jobs as valets?

"Yes. Come in," said Mr. Talent, waving off the butler. His voice, hard and lean, matched his exterior. I sensed my patented quip-heavy approach would be wasted on him, so I decided to play it straight and cut to the meat.

"Perspicacious Blaze?" I asked. "I'm Detective Daggers. This is my partner, um...Detective Steele."

The words felt fuzzy as they left my lips. I realized I'd never referred to her as a detective. Had that been an intentional slight on my part? Did saying the words add legitimacy to her position? I stowed the thoughts in my cheek for me to chew on later.

"Call me Charles Talent," said the graybeard. "I only use the moniker Perspicacious Blaze as my public persona. In matters of business, I use my given name."

"Very well, Mr. Talent," I said. "We're here regarding the murder of your soon to be son-in-law, Reginald Powers."

Charles Talent exhaled and ran a weathered hand through his hair. "Yes. What a disaster. Poor Felicity is inconsolable. As if she hasn't had to deal with enough personal tragedy in her life already. If her mother were here perhaps she'd be able to guide her through this, but I've always been terrible at providing support in matters of the heart. And as if dealing with my disconsolate daughter weren't hard enough, I also have to deal with this mess of a cancelled wedding. Do you have any idea how many people I have to notify and how many deposits I'm going to lose?"

The old man removed his glasses and pressed his fingers to the bridge of his nose. After the brief moment of weakness, he blinked and replaced his glasses. "I hope you're here to inform me of some leads in your investigation, at least?"

Shay jumped into the fray. "Actually, Mr. Talent, we were wondering if you could tell us about Reginald."

"Very well," he said. "What do you want to know?"

"What were your impressions of him?"

"He was a nice enough young man. Had a good head on his shoulders. Knew how to strike a deal. I liked that. Most youths lack a keen business sense these days."

"And did you approve of his engagement to your daughter?" asked Shay.

"Yes. He was honest and forthright with me, and he treated my daughter with love and respect. I fully supported their union. Or at least I supported the endeavor as much as any father can be expected to when he's about to lose his daughter."

"So," I asked. "You didn't have any suspicions about him or his devotion to Felicity?"

The old guy chuckled. "Detective, suspicion is a quality that develops naturally for every father of a young woman. When you're as wealthy as I am, that suspicion is magnified tenfold. I can't tell you how many suitors of Felicity's I've had my doubts about, but Reginald wasn't one of them. He loved Felicity. Plain as day." His eyes narrowed. "Why do you ask? What are you getting at?"

I glanced at Shay before turning my eyes back on the old man. "Mr. Talent, I don't know how to tell you this, but we have reason to believe your future son-in-law was a Grade A confidence man."

21

The eyebrows on old granite-face rose in what appeared to be genuine surprise. Either the geezer was a seasoned actor, or he truly didn't know.

"Really?" he said. "Are you sure?"

"We found numerous forged documents in his apartment," said Shay. "Identification cards. Bank records. You name it. Not to mention wigs, makeup, and disguises. He also may have been involved in a number of other illegal activities, including both drug and weapons trafficking."

Mr. Talent leaned back in his chair, silent in thought. I sensed an opening, so I attacked. "Mr. Talent, could you tell us what exactly you do for a living?"

"I'm the head of a consortium that owns a number of foundries here in the city. I'd assumed you were aware of that fact."

"I was," I said. "But what exactly qualified you to lead such a consortium?"

"I'm what a layman would call a fire mage," said Mr. Talent. "Again, I thought that was common knowledge."

"So you're exceptionally talented—no pun intended—at creating intense, concentrated sources of heat. Heat that could be used in a number of different ways. Melting ores. Starting fires. Burning through things that otherwise wouldn't burn?"

Granite-face cast a fiery glare my way. "Don't patronize me, Detective...what, Daggers was it? Say what you mean to say."

"Charles, are you aware of the manner in which Reginald Powers was killed?"

"Enlighten me," he replied.

"We found him flat on his back with a six inch hole burned through his chest. Went clean through him. Melted his muscles, bones, everything. Left nothing behind."

The old man snorted. "What? And you think I killed him?"

"Your daughter, she's an only child?" I asked.

"Yes. Her mother died during labor."

"And you never remarried?"

"No."

"So, whoever marries her stands to inherit quite a fortune after your eventual passing on, correct?"

Charles Talent pressed his fingers to his temple. "Let me get this straight. You're saying Reginald was a con man, and you think he was marrying my daughter for the inheritance money. And so...what? You think I found out about that fact, and then rather than simply kicking him to the curb and forbidding him from marrying my daughter, I *killed* the man instead? That's ludicrous!"

"Is it?" I asked. "Then how do you explain the manner of Reginald's death?"

"*What?* I don't know," said Mr. Talent. "Explaining that's your job, not mine. Look, Detective, I don't know what sorts of evidence you found at Reginald's apartment, but his murder had nothing to do with my wealth. I stand by what I said. Reginald loved my daughter, and I have the paperwork to prove it."

"Excuse me?" Had the old man lost his marbles? What kind of paperwork could prove a man's love? Psychics in the city abounded, but as far as I knew they were all frauds.

The fire mage leaned to his left and opened a drawer. After leafing through some files, he produced a standard legal document with a number of signatures at the bottom of the page.

"This," he said, holding the document forth for us to inspect, "is a prenuptial agreement signed by Reginald Powers. At the bottom, you'll find his signature alongside mine and that of my banker, who's a public notary. There's an additional copy stored in a safe deposit box at my bank."

Shay, who'd started to look ashen around the moment I accused His Blazeiness of murder, took a few tentative steps forward and retrieved the printed form. "This looks legitimate," she said. "And ironclad, I might add. The money would stay in the family under any imaginable scenario."

"Which was my intention," said Mr. Talent.

Something nibbled at the back of my mind. "When was that agreement signed?"

"Um...let's see...about a month ago," said Shay.

Hmm... So the prenuptial agreement had been made before Reggie had asked Felicity to elope with her. Interesting. I pulled out my trusty spiral-bound pad and made a note.

I turned back to Mr. Talent. "Do you mind if we ask you a few more questions?"

"Yes, I do," he said. "But I don't suppose I have any choice other than to comply, do I?"

If anything, old granite-face's visage had hardened even more. He knew we had nothing on him, and he tired of us lowly public servants wasting his time.

"Where were you last night between the hours of ten and two?" I asked.

"I attended the charity ball with my daughter and Reginald until about midnight, at which point a carriage brought me home."

Despite the fact that their complaints were the primary impetus that launched the new age of human-powered transport, the city's wealthy preferred not to use the term 'rickshaw.'

"And what about this morning," I said. "Where were you at around eleven?" That would've been more or less when we found the remains of the fire at Reginald's place.

"I was taking a brisk constitutional in the neighborhood to clear my thoughts."

"Alone?"

"Yes."

"Can anyone vouch for where you were?"

"Corey keeps a dated log of everyone who comes and goes at the front. Beyond that, I'm sure some of the neighborhood watch spotted me on my walk."

I assumed Corey was the name of Mr. Dazed-and-Confused at the front gates. I'd be sure to check his logs, but it wouldn't matter. By his own admission, Chucky placed himself at the crime scene during the initial murder and claimed to be alone during the window of time in which the fire took place at Reggie's apartment. I made a few more notes in my pad and tucked it away.

My impatient silver-haired adversary noticed the action. "So, are we done here? I have a number of affairs that need to be attended to, and your unscheduled visit has pushed me behind schedule."

"We're done," I said. "Just don't leave town until we've made an arrest. Understand?"

A glare served as my only response.

I beckoned to Shay and we left.

22

Shay looked out of sorts as we reached the exit to the breezeway.

"Crotchety old badger, isn't he?" I said.

"Hmm?"

"The geezer. His Blazeiness. Charles Talent?"

"Oh...yes," said Shay. For a moment, I thought that was all she was going to offer, but she turned to me with a question in her eyes. "How do you do it?"

"Do what?" I asked.

"How do you accuse someone like Charles Talent of murder?"

"Oh, it's easy. Comes with the territory. Stick around long enough and you'll start tossing around murder accusations like they're hoops at a carnival game, too."

"I didn't mean in general," said Shay. "I meant him, personally. Someone with that much power? That much influence? How could you not be intimidated?"

The honest answer was I probably lacked some vital survival mechanism most logical beings were born with.

That, or I'd taken one too many hits to the head. Or maybe it was some sort of continuous feedback loop— the more blows to the head I took, the less I cared about my own self-preservation.

I provided a more politically correct response, however.

"People of all types and stations commit murder, and usually for the exact same reasons. The ones at the top of the heap take longer to fall. But when they land, they tend to hit the hardest. They might seem powerful, but you can't let them intimidate you. We've got the claws of justice on our side. Always remember that."

I hadn't intended to deliver a motivational speech, and part of me felt a little foolish. *Way to impress the rookie, Daggers.* But Shay hadn't rolled her eyes at me, so perhaps my words hadn't sounded as silly to her ears as they had to mine.

"Anyway," I said. "I figured you'd be comfortable around a guy like him."

"Me? Why?" Shay looked confused.

"Well, you're like two peas in a pod, aren't you? With your para-super-doopery abilities?"

Shay blushed and looked away. "Yeah, um...to compare my abilities with the sorts of powers he can unleash is exceedingly generous."

"Whatever," I said. "Magic is magic, right?"

Young Miss Steele shook her head.

My buddy, lemon-face, at the gate showed us the entry logs, but they didn't tell me anything I didn't already know.

We hailed another rickshaw and bounced our way back to the precinct.

We found Rodgers and Quinto hunched over their desks, poring over large piles of Reggie Sweatervest's personal effects. I felt a sudden outpouring of affection for the Captain who'd so generously assigned the pair to help out with the case. Without them, it would've been me and Shay on rummage detail, and the only thing keeping me from tearing out my hair at the roots would've been the never-ending flow of coffee from the break room.

I clapped Rodgers on the back. "You guys find anything useful in all that stuff?"

Rodgers lifted his head and gave me a sly grin. "Depends. What are you offering in return?"

"What's going on here?" I asked with mock seriousness. "You angling for a free beer? At my expense? I should report you to the Captain for unethical behavior."

Quinto was in on the game. "I don't know, Daggers. My throat's parched, too. If the Captain were to ask me about this here incident, I'm not sure I could properly describe what happened, given the current condition of my vocal cords."

I noticed Shay smiling. Her mood improved whenever the four of us—her, Rodgers, Quinto and me—all had a chance to interact together. Was I that much of a curmudgeon that my company alone turned her into a moody mess? Or did she just enjoy seeing *me* getting ripped on for a change? I suspected the latter.

"This is extortion, you know," I huffed. "Fine. I'll buy you guys a round later, but just one. And by one I mean a pint, not some pony keg with a handle attached." I wagged a finger at Quinto. He was clearly disappointed. "So come on, what have you got for me?"

"Lots," said Rodgers. "But I'm not sure how much of it is really useful. All of our dead guy's different identities are pulling us in separate directions. Looks like Reggie had at least a half-dozen bank accounts. All at different institutions. All in different names."

"So you're saying it's going to take a lot of legwork to sort out his financials, and even if we do, we might not get much out of it?" *Perfect.* If there was one thing I loved, it was copious amounts of low-intensity physical activity.

"The drugs and weapons might be the better route to pursue," said Quinto. "Rodgers said he knows a guy in narcotics who might be able to shed some light on these." He held up a couple of loose-leaf pages of artwork I'd noticed upon entering Reggie's apartment— the ones that held tribal-like designs.

"You think that's some sort of gang symbol?"

"My buddy Esteban should know," said Rodgers. "He's out on assignment today, but I notified the Captain. He said he'll make sure Esteban drops by first thing tomorrow to talk to us."

"For now, the weapons might be your best lead," said Quinto. "We checked the maker's marks, and they all came from a place called Drury Arms. It's on the forty-nine hundred block of East 23rd."

"That's the place Felicity said Reginald worked," said Shay. "I'm sure the owners would be eager to know their best dealmaker had a half-dozen of their finest sharp and pointy things in his apartment."

"Yeah," I said. "Arms dealers tend to be pretty persnickety when it comes to thieves. As they should be. Those who aren't tend to lose their business licenses and end up in jail."

"The forty-nine hundred block," said Shay. "That's...pretty far out on the east side."

I glanced at my partner's boots. I knew they weren't as comfortable as she'd made them out to be. One more point for me. Of course, I wasn't about to fight the notion that we should take a rickshaw either. The Captain might blow a gasket if we blew the department's weekly transportation budget in a day or two, but I could always blame it on Shay. I doubted the Captain would go ballistic on his new star recruit.

"Alright," I said. "We can hitch a ride."

"Hey, before you go," said Rodgers. "I wanted to let you know Reginald's body is down in the morgue, and Miss Talent just stopped by and identified it. We may not know if Reginald was his real name, but at least we know our dead guy is who we think he is."

"Great," I said. "Does Cairny have a report for us yet?" Cairny was our coroner, and prior to Shay's arrival, she was the only woman who I had any regular interaction with at the precinct.

"Not yet," said Rodgers. "Maybe in a few hours."

"Alright. You ready to go?" I asked Shay.

She nodded.

"Have fun on your rickshaw ride," said Quinto. I couldn't tell if he meant it as a jab at me and my partner, or if he was just plain jealous. The guy was so big most rickshaw drivers would keel over from exhaustion after dragging him a bare half-mile.

"So this should be a fun visit for you," I told Steele as we exited the precinct.

"What? Why?" she said.

"Well, you know, because smithies work mostly with steel, and your last name is Steele."

My partner looked at me blankly. "You know your last name is Daggers, right?"

I smiled. "Well, then, I guess this is going to be a rip-roaring trip down Surname Lane for both of us then, isn't it?"

Shay failed to find the same humor in that as I did.

23

The ride to Drury Arms was more eventful than I'd anticipated and not in a good way. Our rickshaw found smooth sailing up until we hit the entrance to the Bridge, at which point we became snarled in a traffic quagmire of stalled rickshaws, stationary handcarts, and impatient pedestrians.

Like most things in our city, the Bridge had a name—the East Bay Bridge—but no one had any reason to call it anything other than 'the Bridge' as it was the only decent option for traversing the Earl for ten miles north or south. I'm sure engineers got all wet in the britches whenever they set eye on it. Part suspension bridge and part bascule bridge, its weighty pylons spanned the river's wide girth while a movable section in the middle could be raised to allow passage to freighters and barges.

The Bridge was a true feat of modern engineering, with only one small caveat: the drawbridge portions in the middle were powered by a team of oxen that moved with about as much pep as a herd of dairy cows. From start to finish, the raising and lowering of the central portions of the Bridge could take nearly a half hour, and that inevitably led to traffic jams and lots of unruly foot traffic.

As luck would have it, we arrived at the Bridge right before one of its daily lift-offs. I swore. Captain wouldn't be happy about the rickshaw tab. Most of the drivers who took east-west traffic were smart. They charged by the hour.

I tried to pass the time by engaging Shay in some people watching, but she found much less enjoyment in making fun of others than I did. Apparently I was the only one she enjoyed seeing made the object of derision.

I tried not to let Miss Sourpuss ruin my crowd-watching venture. I chuckled at the massive, bulbous schnoz protruding from a heavyset laborer's face. I panted and howled when I caught sight of a sweet young piece of tail in a nearby rickshaw. And I couldn't help but stare at the unfortunate tragedy of a nearby street sweeper, who as far as I could tell was some sort of gnome-goblin hybrid. Talk about getting the short end of the stick in the gene pool lottery.

Eventually, the oxen got their hooves into gear and the Bridge reopened for traffic. Of course, we still had to fight our way through the teeming crowd of unruly barbarians who I was certain had much less of a right to be in a hurry than we did.

By the time we reached the eastern banks of the Earl, we ran right into a pile of dock traffic generated by teamsters and laborers unloading goods from the freighter that had just sailed by. I worried the Captain would skip right over Shay to blame the inflated rickshaw tab all on me. That wouldn't be good. The coffee might get confiscated again. *Oh, the horror.*

Luckily, before I drowned in a sea of self-imagined nightmare scenarios, the crowd thinned and our rickshaw driver ran double-time to get us to the forty-nine hundred block of 23rd street in a scant quarter hour.

I hopped off the cart, handed our driver some coins to cover our ride, and turned to examine our destination—Drury Arms. It stretched across half the block, and a two-story brick wall topped with barbed wire surrounded it. Behind the wall, tall smoke stacks jutted into the sky, belching black fumes that stained the neighboring rooftops as easily as the tips of the stacks themselves.

Soot was the price of progress, I suppose. In the past, outfits like Drury Arms would've used charcoal to stoke their fires, but decades of logging operations had taken their toll. Not only had local deforestation resulted in the mass immigration of elves and dark elves into the city, but it'd also driven up prices for charcoal—dramatically so. Just when it looked like businesses around town might have to close up shop, along came a budding goblin entrepreneur who offered an intriguing alternative.

As it turned out, goblins in the nearby mountain ranges had been digging foul, dirty rocks out of their tunnels for years. One day during a freak midnight torch-fighting accident, a goblin fell into the pile of discarded rocks and set the entire thing ablaze.

Can you believe it? Burning rocks. They called the stuff coal.

Anyway, the goblin entrepreneur organized a team of his cohorts to mine the stuff and sold it to local businesses. It worked out well for everyone. The goblins enjoyed rooting around in dark enclosed spaces, and the city's residents loved burning things. The only losers were the poor charcoal vendors who'd been set to make a killing during the shortage, but that's economics for you.

For the time being, the flow of coal out of the mountains was limited, but if the goblins could figure out more effective ways to mine it, the implications would be profound. If coal prices dropped enough, guys like Perspicacious Blaze might find themselves out of work.

I shuddered at the thought. As an officer of the law, I certainly didn't want to have to deal with derelict, hobo fire mages with grudges against society. Regular, run of the mill psychos and crazies were bad enough.

"You alright?" asked Shay.

"Huh?"

"You've been standing there for like a minute staring at those smoke stacks." She gave me a look that was part concern and part confusion. "Is there something about them I should know?"

"Oh. Uh, no," I said. "I was just thinking."

My partner smirked. "I see. You didn't break anything up there, did you?"

"If I did, I'd have to solve this case solely on intuition from my gut and my man parts. Don't worry. They rarely lead me astray."

Shay rolled her eyes, but I swear I caught a hint of a smile.

24

A secretary in the lobby of Drury Arms gave us a hard time about wandering in unannounced and expecting to see the owner. She badgered us with questions. Do you have an appointment? Do you have any idea how valuable Mr. Drury's time is? A quick flash of my badge and the words 'detective' and 'official police business' caused her yapper to clamp shut. Like a dog with its tail between its legs, the secretary quietly led us up a flight of grated steel stairs and into a glass-walled office that overlooked the factory floor.

The manufactory's owner, a large barrel-chested man with a short brush cut, stood with his arms crossed behind his back looking out over the blacksmiths and their forges.

"Um. Excuse me. Mr. Drury, sir?" When cowed, the secretary squeaked like a mouse. "Sorry to interrupt, but there are some, um, detectives here to see you."

Mr. Drury turned around, giving us a clean look at his face. His nose, which featured a bit of a crook under the bridge, and his wide, clean-shaven jaw gave him the look of a military man, similar to the bulldog back at the precinct.

Based on his muscular arms and chest, I wondered if he'd been a former blacksmith, perhaps while enlisted. Field smiths aren't quite as vital to an infantry unit as field medics, but a soldier without a well-honed weapon is essentially a walking bag of meat. I suspected Mr. Drury may have started his business upon returning from a tour of duty.

"Detectives, eh?" His bushy eyebrows constricted. He waved a hand at the secretary.

Once she'd ducked out of the office and closed the door behind her, Mr. Drury motioned to a couple of padded leather armchairs that faced his wide, austere desk. He sat down as we took our seats.

"So, Detectives... I didn't catch your names."

"I'm Detective Daggers," I said, "and this is, um, Detective Steele."

Shay nodded. The words still felt weird rolling off my tongue. I wondered how long it would take before calling my prep school lackey a detective would sound normal to me.

"I see. I'm Thurmond Drury, sole proprietor of Drury Arms. Now, what seems to be the problem?"

"Well, Mr. Drury, we're actually here to talk about Reginald Powers."

"Oh." Thurmond's bushy eyebrows relaxed. "Well yeah, sure, I know Reginald. What do you want to know about him?"

I pulled out my old spiral-bound. "How about you start with your relationship?"

"He's one of my employees," said Mr. Drury. "Well, not really. He's an independent contractor. Works on commission. Gets a 15% cut of any deals he strikes for my company. May not seem like much, but at the rate he's signing new customers he's doing quite well for himself."

"So he's helping expand your clientele?"

"Oh, absolutely. We've always been mostly a local distributor, but Reginald's helped us develop our inter-national profile. We've got shipments heading overseas at least every other month. Some of them quite big. And not just weapons. All kinds of stuff. He recently landed a deal for grappling hooks for the Maudrican Navy. I prefer weapons manufacturing, myself, but I've learned not to turn my nose up at free money."

I made a note in my pad.

Thurmond's eyebrows slowly came back together. "So...what's this all about, anyway? Is Reginald in some sort of trouble?"

"You could say that," I said. "He's dead."

"*DEAD!*" Thurmond's bushy eyebrows shot up in surprise before crashing back down in a fuzzy mound of consternation. "How?"

"Murdered. Someone burned a hole through his chest."

"Burned a...gods, man. That's grim. Who'd do such a thing?"

Shay piped up. "Well Mr. Drury, that's what we're trying to find out. Had Reginald shown any strange be-havior lately?"

"No. Not that I can recall."

"What about problems at work? Any disagreements with co-workers? That sort of thing?"

"What? No." Thurmond shook his head. "Reginald was a great guy. Everyone here loved him. No one ever had any problems with him despite his, well...you know."

Mr. Drury cast a glance at Shay.

"Heritage?" she offered.

"Yes."

I could've mentioned Shay was a half-elf of the regular variety, but I didn't have any interest in diving into the pot of worms that comprised Mr. Drury's personal prejudices. Most of us carried them, but we didn't need to air them in public.

Mr. Drury muttered to himself as he raked a hand through his hair. "Poor guy. And him so close to his wedding day, too."

"Well, I hate to be the bearer of more bad news," I said. Which was a lie—I really didn't mind. "But this story gets worse, I'm afraid."

Thurmond cast me a wary glance. "Worse? How could it get worse than being murdered? And in such a gruesome fashion?"

"Oh, sorry," I said. "I didn't mean for Reginald. I should've said it gets worse for you. We found a half-dozen illicit weapons in Reginald's apartment. All of them were crafted in your armory."

Mr. Drury swore and leaned back in his chair. "By the dragons' breath, you've got to be *kidding* me! Are you telling me Reginald was stealing from me?"

"That's what it looks like, Mr. Drury," said Shay.

"But why would he do that? I was paying him, wasn't I? Wasn't that enough for him?"

"Who knows," I said. "Maybe he had need of the weapons for some other reason."

Mr. Drury sighed. "You know, I've always tried to run a clean operation. The gods know I've tried. But this just goes to show you never truly know who you can trust." Thurmond swore under his breath. "I knew I never should've hired a...you know."

The prejudices reared their ugly heads again. Shay took it in stride, but I figured I'd move the conversation in a less racist direction.

"Mr. Drury, certain other things we found in Reginald's apartment lead me to believe you likely weren't aware of those weapons getting out. I'll be sure to let the Department of Commerce know that when they contact me regarding your license. For now though, we need to look into all possible leads that might direct us to Mr. Powers' murderer. The weapons he stole from you are one. The contracts he brokered for you are another. We're going to need a full list of all the deals in which Reginald was involved. I'm talking bank statements, invoices, shipping statements—you name it."

Mr. Drury groaned. Despite my assurances, the possibility of him losing his business license was starting to sink in.

"Sure, sure," he said. "Anything you need. Talk to my accountant downstairs. He'll be able to provide you with copies of everything."

I stowed my pad and nodded to Shay to go. I didn't have the heart to tell Mr. Drury that a citation and fine from the commerce guys for letting a few of his weapons leak out was probably the least of his worries. If it turned out Reginald had been involved in felony offenses, then Mr. Drury would find out fast how hot the water could really get.

25

The accountant turned out to be a squirrely little guy by the name of Walter Fry. A pair of black-rimmed spectacles sat over his smushed nose, and a bad comb-over traversed the top of his head. I wagered the guy was in his mid-to-late thirties, but the mop gods hadn't been kind to him. The line drawn by his hair was being slowly pushed back, and a small regiment of follicles staging a brave last stand on the front of his forehead was surrounded by a battalion of bare skin. The battle was lost.

"You know," I said. "You'd be better off if you owned it."

The accountant, his face stuck deep within the drawers of a filing cabinet, popped his head out and cringed. He reminded me of a skittish rabbit staring down the throat of a rabid wolf.

"E-e-excuse me, owned w-w-what, D-D-Detective?"

As if Wally's appearance didn't scream 'bookish nerd' loud enough, he also spoke with a noticeable stutter. I'm sure the presence of two inquisitive police officers in his office, one of them an attractive young female and the other a loudmouthed jerk, did little to help matters.

"The battle, man. It's lost. Time to cut ties with the soldiers and admit defeat."

Wally looked at me as if I'd jumped off the deep end and might take him with me.

"Never mind," I said.

Shay leaned against the wall of filing cabinets that took up half of Wally's cramped corner office, flipping through a shipping report by the light of a lone oil lamp. While I could appreciate that Mr. Drury valued security of his goods as well as his records, you'd think he could've put a small window in. Poor Wally looked like he was a few weeks away from developing a debilitating case of rickets, and that wouldn't be good for anyone—especially Mr. Drury. He'd be out an accountant, and his healthcare premiums would skyrocket.

Shay snapped the manila folder shut. "Well, you've sure got a lot of paperwork in here, that's for sure. How far back do you keep records?"

Walter gingerly plucked the file from Shay's fingers, handling it as if it were his firstborn. Assuming babies could be held at arm's length, that is. Those buggers are heavy.

"W-w-well, Detective Steele, the c-c-city mandates we keep records on hand for t-t-ten years. But we've got all the records from the entire b-b-business here, all t-t-twenty-three years. This is only the paperwork for the last f-f-five. The rest is in st-st-storage."

I glanced across the wall. Ten full size filing cabinets for five years of paperwork? That seemed excessive, and I worked for the government. Apparently the commerce department kept the arms manufacturers on a tight leash.

I drummed my fingers on rabbit man's desk. "Well, like I said, we're going to need to see all your files that have even the most tangential relevance to Reginald Powers. Purchase orders, bank statements, shipping receipts. Everything. If he touched it, breathed on it, or wiped his butt with it, I want to see it."

My last comment rubbed Wally the wrong way. He recoiled again. I started to wonder if his squeamishness was simply the product of our intrusion into his tightly structured environment or if the little guy was hiding something.

"Of course, D-D-Detective, of course." Wally drew a handkerchief from his pocket and wiped his moist brow. "But that's going to amount to a lot of p-p-paperwork. I'll need time to get it all to-to-together."

My verbal fertilizer sirens went off. Wally definitely knew something he wasn't sharing. I put my big boy pants on and leaned on him.

"Come on Wally, you seem like an organized guy," I said. "What's so hard about this? You find the files. You grab the files. You hand over the files."

Wally pressed on his spectacles, which were sagging on his nose. A sudden memory of grade school assaulted me, that of a know-it-all four-eyed pipsqueak who would constantly correct me every time I made a mistake in class.

With the memory fresh in my mind, my affinity for Mr. Fry dropped to a new low.

"You d-d-don't understand," stammered Wally. "These files are o-o-organized, but they're not organized by i-i-individual, they're organized by d-d-date. I'll have to comb through s-s-stacks of them before I find everything you've requested."

I leaned over and brought my face mere inches from Wally's. I could feel his breath on my cheeks. I spoke slowly in a low, measured voice.

"Listen here, Wally, and listen good. I've got a buddy at the precinct by the name of Folton Quinto. He's about six foot seven, weighs maybe three bills. If the files I've asked for aren't on my desk before we all head home for the night, I'm going to send Quinto over here to find out why. And for a point of reference, Quinto lives on the west side. He's not going to be happy if he has to come all the way out here for courier duty. Do you understand me?"

Wally swallowed heavily and nodded, sweat dripping down his face. He could barely squeak out an answer. "Y-y-yes, D-D-Detective, I un-d-d-derstand."

I turned about-face and left the office with Shay trailing.

"That was a little harsh, don't you think?" she said as we exited the factory.

I shrugged. "Eh, yeah. Maybe. I'm not actually going to sick Quinto on him. Probably not, anyway. But sometimes you get further with a stick than with a carrot."

Shay glanced back. "I think he almost fainted..."

"What can I say? He triggered some sort of...reaction in me, I guess."

Shay didn't pry. I appreciated that. I should probably learn to do the same, but what fun would that be.

26

Another long rickshaw ride later and we arrived at the precinct. The sun was working its way toward the tops of the apartment buildings across the street, sending lengthening shadows crawling from the Captain's office across the rest of the common room. Darkness had already consumed half my desk, hiding unfinished paperwork from last week. I silently thanked the impending gloom for its kind thoughts.

I lit a lamp and turned up the flame as I approached the desks, sending some much needed light cascading over Rodgers and his workspace. He looked up and gave me a nod of thanks.

"Where's Quinto?" I asked.

The big fellow was nowhere to be seen, and most of the junk that had sprawled across his and Rodgers' desks was gone.

"He's moving stuff down into the evidence lockers," said Rodgers.

"You've already got all that junk tagged?"

Rodgers gave me a snarky look. "Yeah. There was this blabbermouthed jerk here earlier who wouldn't let us get any work done, but as soon as he left our efficiency skyrocketed. Go figure."

I gave Rodgers a knowing wink. "Oh yeah. I've heard about that guy. Real pain in the ass, isn't he?" I lowered my voice to a whisper. "Word is he's angling for a promotion. Might even replace the Captain one day."

"Well...there goes the neighborhood," said Rodgers.

We both chuckled. Shay even joined in on the fun. She really did do better when there was someone else besides me around.

"So, are you and Quinto still intent on extorting that drink out of me?"

I made the statement in jest. Truth was, I hadn't gone out for a drink with the guys in some time. Seeing how well I'd fared on my last solo drinking excursion, perhaps a bit of social imbibing would do me well.

Rodgers shook his head. "No... Well, I shouldn't say that. I bet Quinto'll hound you mercilessly until you buy him that pint. But I've got to head home. Allison gets cranky when she has to deal with the rascals by herself at dinner time."

Allison was Rodgers' wife. Rodgers started dating her about five years back, and in the blink of an eye, he'd reformed his bachelor ways and gotten hitched. Now they had a couple of girls running around, one four and the other two. From what little time I'd spent around them, they made bouncing ping-pong balls seem lethargic. If I were Allison, I'd be counting down the seconds until Rodgers got home every night.

Of course, it's easy for me to see that now. Back when I was married, the same thought never wormed its way into my brain. I'd work late all the time, and then I'd wonder why my wife, Nicole, would be furious at me when I'd get home. She'd badger me about how little I helped, and remark that our son would occasionally need to lay eyes on his father in order to form lasting memories of him.

Don't get me wrong. It's not that I didn't understand what she was saying, but we never had that much to go around. If I didn't work hard, who'd put food on the table? She certainly wouldn't. So I'd yell at her. Then she'd cry, and our little slugger would wake up and start bawling, too.

I wish I could say late nights were the main reason Nicole left me, but that would be a lie. The reasons for that were too numerous for even me to remember. I bet Nicole could still rattle them off though.

"Hey, I understand," I said after a pause. "You've got to take care of your family. Give my regards to Allison, alright?"

"Sure thing, Daggers."

I moved toward my desk before I heard Rodgers give his hardwood a slap.

"Oh. I almost forgot," said Rodgers. "Cairny wanted to see you guys. Said she's got her coroner's report ready and wants to show you something interesting about the body herself."

Shay spoke in my ear, making me jump. When had she sidled up next to me like that? "Something interesting on the report, eh? I wonder what that could be?"

I waved her hot breath off my shoulder. "Probably that Reggie got blasted into the netherworld by some seriously potent magical firepower."

"Or, maybe she'll tell us just the opposite." Shay raised her eyebrows. "You remember what I told you about the threads, right?"

I smelled a wager. "What? Do you want to bet on it? Are you angling for a pint, too?"

Shay turned her nose up. "Beer? No thanks. When I drink, I prefer wine."

I gagged. "Seriously? You're a spoiled grapes girl? That explains a lot."

She ignored my jab. "I'd be willing to wager *something* though."

"Ok. I'll bite. What?"

"If I'm right and Reginald wasn't killed by magic, you have to apologize."

I scoffed. "For what?"

"Seriously?" Shay blinked and her eyes widened into saucers. "It's my first day and I've already stopped keeping track of all the things you should be sorry for. But I'd be willing to accept a simple acknowledgment that I was right and you were wrong."

I'm a man—a stubborn man with real, honest-to-goodness man parts and an ego that barely fits into my skull. Apologizing doesn't come easy, but saying no to a wager with a rookie fresh out of the ivory tower? I couldn't say no.

Besides, I was certain I was right.

27

The morgue lay in the part of the precinct we called the dungeon. Unlike the well-lit prisoner holding cells on the main floor, the morgue, which was situated about twenty or thirty feet underground, was a cold, damp, dreary place unfit for the living.

Luckily, we used it to store dead people.

For that purpose, the dungeon was ideally designed. The temperatures in the morgue remained a good twenty or thirty degrees cooler than upstairs, which helped in keeping unpleasant fragrances to a minimum. The lack of sunlight discouraged the growth of mold, mildew, and rot, and the dampness...well, I'm not sure the dampness contributed anything of use. But it did add to the morgue's ambience, and I'd yet to hear one of the morgue's patrons complain about it.

Of course, no one in their right mind would enjoy spending all day among the dungeon's cold granite walls and dark, dank passageways—especially not with the omnipresent perfume of death infusing every nook and cranny. Luckily for us, our coroner Cairny Moon-shadow was not in her right mind.

I led Shay into the main room of the charnel house where we found Cairny perched over the white sheet draped remains of our good friend, Reginald Powers.

Like so many inhabitants of our great metropolis, Cairny was only part human—a fact that spoke as equally to the diversity of our city as it did to the will-ingness of mankind to bang anything that moves. Cairny's better half came from one of the few races that were actually worth bedding—faeries.

Not to be confused with pixies who are small, winged little prats, faeries are tall, angelic beings who have much the same build and facial features as humans. As such, it can often be difficult to distinguish between humans and half-faeries. The only way I've been able to ferret out traces of fae blood in others is by looking for their aura, for lack of a better word. Faeries radiate a cerebral fragrance lacking in us regular two-legged types.

Cairny certainly emitted that aura of radiance, but in her case, it gave her the look of a fallen angel. Her huge, round eyes, long eyelashes, and ivory skin ap-peared celestial—until you noticed her hair. Arrow-straight and parted in a clean line down the middle of her skull, it cascaded over her ears and down her back in a waterfall of purest midnight. Combined with the often vacant, ethereal quality of her face, I couldn't help but wonder if she possessed the ability to commune with the dead. Perhaps that's what made her such an effective coroner.

Then again, maybe it was her dual degrees in biology and chemistry.

Today, as always, Cairny wore a jet-black, tightly fitting pantsuit that sucked in any and all errant rays of light that wandered by. She blinked at me and Shay as we joined her by the body.

"Oh... Hello, Detective Daggers." Her voice danced to its own hidden melody.

"You sound surprised to see me, Cairny."

"I am."

I scratched my head. "I'm confused. Rodgers said you wanted to see us."

"Did I say that?" Cairny gazed off into the distance. "Oh. Right. I suppose I did. Well, welcome then."

She turned her round, moon-like eyes onto Shay and stared in silence.

"Um...hi?" said Shay.

"Hello," responded Cairny.

I felt the need to intervene. "Cairny, this is Shay Steele. My new partner."

"You have a new partner?" Cairny turned her inquisitive eyes back onto me. "What happened to Griggs?"

"Hadn't you heard? He disintegrated into dust. About two weeks ago."

She didn't seem to get the joke. "Oh. Terribly sorry."

I realized I hadn't properly introduced Cairny to Shay.

"Shay," I said. "This is Cairny Moonshadow. She's our resident coroner, and she's—" How could I put it?

A mild lunatic? Half-baked? "—uniquely qualified to do her job."

"Oh," said Shay, her interest piquing. "Do you have special abilities as well?"

"Why yes," said Cairny. "I should rather think so. Mother always said I was special. I don't think she'd lie." Cairny blinked.

I wondered if Cairny's mother had experienced some premonition about her daughter prior to her birth. I mean, who in the world would name their daughter Cairny unless they somehow expected she'd spend her life poking and prodding dead people?

I drummed my fingers on the exam table as the momentary pause in conversation stalled into awkward silence.

"So, um, Cairny," I said. "You've got a report for us?"

Suddenly, the fog rose from her eyes and she stood a little taller. That tended to happen any time she was able to discuss her subjects.

"Yes, of course." Cairny peeled back the white sheet, exposing Mr. Powers from the waist up. His gaping chest cavity was much the same as we'd left it. "Based on his lividity, I'd assume Mr.—" Cairny consulted a nearby clipboard. "—Powers here died somewhere between ten and two last night. But I have a feeling you're probably more interested in what caused this rather intriguing burn wound in his torso." Cairny tapped at the edge of the gaping hole with her finger.

"You see right through us, Cairny," I said. "As a matter of fact, we've made a little wager regarding this. Haven't we, Miss Steele?"

"It's *Detective* Steele. And yes, we do have a wager. So tell us, Cairny—what, pray tell, is the cause of death?"

Coroner Moonshadow glanced between Shay and me, as if trying to decipher what sort of mystical energies bubbled between us.

I engaged my fingers in more table drumming. I was impatient. "Come on, Cairny. Spit it out. It was fire magic, wasn't it?"

28

"It wasn't magic."

"Bah!" I said, throwing my hands up in exasperation.

Shay flashed a smug smile while I dealt with having victory snatched from my jaws.

"You're sure?" I asked.

"Positive," said Cairny.

One of the good things about Miss Moonshadow was that despite her mooncalfish personality, she had quite the grasp on the hard sciences. She always provided clear explanations for her diagnoses.

"So, break it down for me," I grumbled. "If Reggie P here didn't die from a fireball to the chest, then what exactly happened to him?"

"Well," said Cairny. "A fireball to the chest is a fairly apt way to describe what occurred to Mr. Powers. But the fireball wasn't fueled by magic."

I scrunched my face up in confusion. Cairny noticed.

"Look at this," she said. She picked up a shallow glass dish that contained a number of small dust-like particles. Some were powdery and white like talc. Others had a silvery, metallic gleam.

"You're going to have to explain to me what I'm looking at here," I said.

"The powdery substance is aluminum oxide, and the small metal globules are elemental iron. I found these in the chest cavity as well as in all the small burn marks within the splash zone of the main wound."

Splash zone was an apt phrase to describe the carnage. With Reggie's shirt removed, I could easily see the hundreds of small pockmarked burns that surrounded the gaping hole in his chest. Whatever flaming disaster had hit the guy had sent off a shower of fiery sparks.

Cairny gave me a self-satisfied smile, as if to say everything should make sense now.

"Why don't you walk me through this step-by-step," I said.

"Yes," said Shay. "As if you were trying to explain things to an infant."

I gave my partner a sour look.

"Aluminum oxide and iron are byproducts of the reaction between elemental aluminum and iron oxide, more commonly known as rust," said Cairny. "When aluminum and iron oxide are exposed to intense heat, the result is a thermite reaction. It's a rather remarkable process. The iron oxide acts as a source of oxygen for the flame, and so it can't be smothered or put out once activated. Theoretically, a thermite reaction could take place underwater. More importantly, however, the reaction burns extremely hot, hot enough to melt glass or steel or even, as you can see, turn muscle and bones into nothing more than ash."

I scratched my head. Could the dead guy's death wound really have come from a chemical reaction? And more importantly, how was I going to couch my apology to Shay in a way that was both contrite and nonchalantly disrespectful at the same time?

"I see what you're thinking," said Cairny. "If the chest cavity was formed through a thermite reaction, how was it Mr. Powers sat through the entire thing without a struggle?"

That hadn't been what I was thinking at all. The thought hadn't even crossed my mind, but I played along to appear smart. "Exactly. How indeed?"

"As it turns out," said Cairny. "Mr. Powers was already dead at the time of the reaction."

That *did* raise an eyebrow. Mine, in fact.

"And how do you know that?" I asked.

Cairny grasped a set of surgical forceps and stuck them into Reggie's chest cavity. She hooked the flap of one of his internal organs and lifted.

"Look at this," she said, beckoning with a finger.

Shay swallowed hard. My salivary glands forced a similar response.

"That's alright," I said. "Just tell me what you see."

Cairny appeared to be dismayed that we didn't share her passion for day-old corpses.

"Well," she said as she straightened, "there's no scorching on the inside of the lungs. Thermite may not smoke like a regular fire, but it produces an extremely virulent reaction. If Mr. Powers had been alive and breathing at the time the thermite was ignited, he would've inhaled numerous burning particulates which would've severely burned his lungs and respiratory tract. The lack of that shows me he was already dead. Besides, if he were alive during this experience, I'm fairly sure his screams would've attracted attention."

"So if the fire didn't kill him, how did Reggie die?" I asked.

"Well," said Cairny, "it's hard to know for sure, but based on the lack of evidence of some kind of a struggle, I'd guess he was poisoned. I can run more tests if you'd like, but it'll take time."

I waved off the offer. "No need for that, Cairny. I trust you."

And I did. We could run the extra tests or petition the higher ups for authorization to bring in a real forensics mage to validate Cairny's analysis, but I didn't think it would be worthwhile. In all our years of working together, Cairny had never led me astray.

I drummed my fingers on the table again. If only I'd had a tiny banjo and a singing homunculus, I could've started my own band.

I spoke to no one in particular. "So the evidence clearly shows Reginald wasn't murdered by magic." I left out a silent 'much to my chagrin.' "But the evidence also shows Reginald was killed before the thermite fire was set? Why?"

"To set someone else up for the murder," said Shay.

I turned to my partner. I hadn't intended to bounce ideas off her, but she'd vocalized exactly what I'd been thinking myself.

"Right," I said. "Whoever killed Reggie wanted to make us think fire magic was the cause of his death, knowing it would implicate that old geezer, Perspiring Blaze."

"I think you mean Perspicacious Blaze," said Shay.

"Whatever. Same difference. The question is—who would benefit from Blaze's downfall?"

29

Quinto greeted us with a massive crooked grin as we returned to the main floor.

"Daggers," he said. "You just missed it."

"Missed what?"

"Oh, it was spectacular. Rodgers was just about to leave for the night when this little mousy guy runs in lugging a huge banker's box in his arms." Quinto patted a manila folder-filled cardboard box that sat on his desk. "He was drenched with sweat and panting like a dog. He stops Rodgers and asks about you. Wants to know where he can find you. So Rodgers tells him you're busy, but if he's got a question he can talk to me. And he points me out."

Quinto laughed.

"So this guy, I see his eyes follow Rodgers' finger. Then he sees me. And he about collapses on the spot. Somehow he gets his legs under him and walks over. He's shaking like a leaf, Daggers." Quinto picked up the cardboard box and rattled it in his arms.

"And so he says to me, 'Are you F-f-folton Qu-qu-quinto?' Papers are flying everywhere. I nod. That's when he made this sort of squeaking sound, and in one swift motion, he drops this box on the floor, turns tail, and runs. And I mean RUNS out of here. Nearly set the floor boards on fire."

Quinto's merriment grew until the entire office shook with his mirth. The big guy tucked the cardboard box under one arm so he could free a hand to wipe away tears of laughter that streamed from his eyes. "Man, I've never seen a guy in a suit run that fast. What in the world did you tell him?"

I smiled. "Oh, just if he didn't have those files here at the precinct before nightfall that I'd send *you* out after him."

Quinto took a deep breath as he wiped away the last of his tears. "Oh, that's cruel, Daggers. Real cruel. And I'm sure you neglected to emphasize my sensitive side?"

"Naturally."

"I guess I'm an easy villain, aren't I?" Quinto hitched the box of files higher up underneath his arm. "Oh well. Now, it's time to cash in. How about that brew?"

"Seriously?" I said. "You're bringing that big box of files with you to the bar?"

"No, I'm bringing it home with me to inspect it after we *leave* the bar."

I gave Quinto a sideways glance. "You're kidding me, right?"

The big lug shrugged. "Come on, Daggers. I get bored. What else am I going to do?"

"I don't know," I said. "You could take up a hobby—like needlework."

Now I was on the receiving end of a confused, sideways look. I shook my head and turned to go, but the sound of a young female half-elf clearing her throat brought me to a screeching halt.

"Aren't you forgetting something?" said Shay.

I gave myself a quick pat down. "I've got my coat, my badge, and Daisy. What else do I need?"

"Daisy? Who's—" Shay shook her head. "Never mind. I don't want to know. What I meant was, aren't you forgetting about our little wager?"

"No, but I was hoping you had," I grumbled.

"What's this?" said Quinto, suddenly curious. "Did our dear Detective Daggers lose a bet?"

Shay crossed her arms. "You could say that. Go on, Daggers. Let's hear it."

I swallowed hard.

With Quinto looming over me, there'd be no way out of apologizing. The big fellow had a chivalrous soft spot, something I'd repeatedly told him he needed to get checked out by a medical professional. So far, he'd ignored my sage advice.

"I'm, uhh, well, let's see..." I gulped. "I'm, um, I'm sorry I herber murmur derberr..."

Quinto leaned forward and cupped his ear. "What was that, Daggers? I forgot to wear my mouse ears today."

I grumbled. I needed something honest and forthright that wouldn't sound as if I were actually praising my partner for a job well done. "I'm, uhh...sorry I doubted your diagnosis. Apparently you were right about the whole fire magic thing."

"Quick, grab a pen," said Quinto. "I want somebody to record for posterity that, on this glorious day, Jake Daggers was heard in the presence of not one, but two witnesses, uttering a real, honest-to-goodness apology."

Quinto clapped me on the back with enough force to knock me over. "This is a big day, my friend. I feel like I should buy *you* a drink. But I won't. Matter of principle, you know?"

Shay smiled. Not a smirk, which I'd seen plenty of throughout the day, but a genuine smile of satisfaction with pearly, white teeth and everything. I have to admit, it looked good on her.

"I suppose that'll do," Shay said. "You gents can attend to your brews now."

"You heard the lady." I poked Quinto in the ribs to get him moving.

"Wait," said Quinto. "Detective Steele—you want to join us for a drink? Daggers is buying. He may hate wine, but I'll make sure he buys you a glass."

I started to complain, but Quinto's look silenced me.

Shay's smile flitted away, and she looked somewhat abashed. "Oh, um...thanks for the offer, Detective Quinto. Maybe some other time, ok? It's been a long day." Miss Steele grabbed a couple things from her desk, then gave me a curt nod. "Until tomorrow, Detective."

"Yeah. See you," I replied.

I watched her prance off. For not having a whole lot of curves, she did undulate well as she walked.

Then I smacked Quinto on the arm. "Say, were you hitting on my partner just now?"

Quinto gave a sheepish shrug. "One of us should."

"Seriously?"

"Shut up and buy me a beer already."

30

I took Quinto to Jjade's because it's near my apartment and I'm lazy. I expected the place to be nearly deserted on a weekday, so imagine my surprise when I pushed open the front doors and found myself staring into a sea of cherry blossom pink. Revelers clad head to toe in the pastel color packed the place like hogs at a trough, laughing and shouting and clinking glasses. Before either Quinto or I could voice any objections, we found ourselves draped with shiny, pink beads and tricorner starched paper hats.

I sicced Quinto on the crowd. He shouldered his way through to the bar where a couple of over-served partiers quickly sobered up and vacated their seats for us. A few spans down the hardwood, I spotted Jolliet Jjade.

Tonight she wore a black velvet suit jacket with an ample lapel over a white frilly lace shirt that spilled out at her cuffs. Seemingly in deference to the customers, she'd paired her outfit with a pink polka dot bow tie.

When she turned her head, I caught her eye and waved her over.

"What in the world is all this?" I asked over the din.

"Festival of St. Tabulatus. Patron saint of flooring inspectors."

I gave her the old double eyebrow raise. "You're kidding, right? There's a patron saint for that?"

"Depends on your religion," she said. "Pretty much any occupation you can think of, some sect or other has a saint for that. And if you're clever enough to come up with one nobody's thought of yet, you can christen yourself as the saint and no one'll be the wiser."

Quinto scratched his head. "Hard to believe there's that many flooring inspectors."

"There aren't, but it gives people an excuse to party." Jjade shrugged. "Hey, who am I to complain? Brings in business. Can I get you guys anything?"

I ordered Quinto and myself each a pint of Jjade's special red ale, a hoppy blend brewed with cranberries and cinnamon. I also asked Jjade what her cook recommended for the night. Gremlins gnawed at my insides, and for a lover of fried delicacies such as myself, Jjade's line cook might as well have been the world's most skilled head chef. I doubted there was a single foodstuff in Jjade's pantry that hadn't been subjected to the cruel devices of the deep fryer.

Eventually, Quinto and I settled on an extra large, coronary-inducing basket of battered, cheese-filled hot peppers that would almost certainly result in our consumption of copious amounts of Jjade's brews.

We chewed the fat as we ate and drank, plowing through more than our fair share of beers and poppers.

Quinto brought me up to speed on a couple of cases he and Rodgers had tied up while I'd been relegated to paperwork duty in the wake of Griggs' departure. After Quinto finished telling me about one case involving a sexually-deviant centaur, I started to grouse about how other guys got to have all the fun.

Quinto gave me a wide-eyed look of disbelief. "Seriously, Daggers? You're kidding me, right?"

By this point the crowds had thinned. Jjade overheard Quinto's remark. She came over and inquired. "What's Daggers complaining about this time?"

"The inherent cruelty of the universe," said Quinto. "You know. The usual."

Jjade collected our now empty basket of poppers. "You're not still bemoaning that old dust bag Griggs, are you?"

Quinto and I exchanged significant glances. So far, we'd avoided discussing the elephant in the room. Me, because I wasn't entirely sure how I felt about my new partner yet, and Quinto, because he actually possessed a measure of empathy. But Quinto probably knew some repressed part of me wanted to share the warm and squishy feelings inside. He gave me a verbal nudge.

"Well, go on. Might as well tell Jjade."

I hemmed and hawed, but once I got my mouth moving, I fell into full-on raconteur mode. I gave Jjade the full rundown on my new partner, starting with our contentious introduction and working my way from there. I related Shay's out-of-body experience at the Lawrence, shared our spectacularly awkward lunch, and finished with Shay's bold wager. I spared no expense in the detail I provided, although I may have embellished my own exploits at the expense of Shay's. Jjade was a seasoned pro at sifting through my bunkum, though. She called me out on it right away.

"So, let me get this straight," she said. "Your old partner was a wheezing, geriatric grouch. Your new partner is an attractive, intelligent young woman. Yet somehow you're complaining about this?"

Quinto expressed himself with a lips out, bug-eyed nod that screamed assent.

"No. You guys have it all wrong," I said. "Yes, she's young. And in the right light, yes, I might admit she's not all elbows and knees. But she's not some supersleuth. She's gotten lucky with a couple of predictions, that's all. Besides, you're not seeing the side of her I do. She's an elitist rich kid. She's so raw she's still mooing, and she's an estrogen-laced time bomb waiting to explode. She's infuriating, I tell you!"

As soon as the words left my lips, I knew they were false. Those had merely been my preconceptions of who I *thought* Shay would be. As it turned out, I had no real knowledge of her family's financial or social background. She was a little raw, true, but it was her first day. In our first scant few hours together she'd shown promise in her cognitive abilities. As for her temper...well, even I had to admit most of her ire was probably justified. Heck, I'd been the one who'd instigated it. Nonetheless, there *was* something about her that rubbed me the wrong way. I just couldn't put my finger on it. Not yet, anyway.

Quinto shook his head. "Daggers, I wonder about you, man. You're one of the best detectives I've ever met, yet sometimes I don't think you'd notice a white unicorn on a black sand beach even if it stumbled into you."

"Oh, I'd notice it," I said. "And I'd tell it to get the hell off my beach."

Quinto drained the last of his beer and stood to leave. "Yeah, well, anyway. I'd better get going. I want to take a look at these files before it gets too late." He hefted the cardboard box with the Drury financials under his arm.

"You're really going to go through those tonight?"

He shrugged. "I don't sleep much. See you tomorrow."

Quinto left, leaving me with an extremely leery Jjade.

"What's that look for?" I asked.

"Oh, nothing. Sometimes I think you *want* to be alone and miserable for the rest of your life."

I tossed back the last of my ale before digging some coins out of my pocket. "Misery is an old friend of mine. It's easier to hang out with him than to meet new people."

My friend the barkeep scooped up my cash. "Yes. But *easier* and *better* are not the same thing. Take care, Daggers."

"Yeah," I said. "See you 'round."

31

That night, I slept fitfully. I blamed the sleeplessness on the partner-induced turmoil that writhed inside my head, but to be fair, the combined effects of spice, grease, and alcohol may also have been to blame.

After much tossing and turning, I eventually succumbed to the inevitable. I dragged myself out of bed, dressed, and forced myself into work at an ungodly hour.

I think I arrived before 9:00.

I found Shay standing in front of our desks facing a corkboard with her arms crossed, as if deep in thought. She'd abandoned yesterday's pantsuit for a slightly more casual cream-colored blouse and slacks combination, and in place of her pointed leather boots she wore a much more sensible pair of tan cloth-bound flats.

I suppressed a smile. *My ass those boots were comfortable...*

On the board, strips of paper with names written upon them had been pinned to the cork. Reginald Powers. Felicity Talent. Charles Blaze Talent. Thurmond Drury. Other strips of paper contained place names. The Lawrence. Talent Manor. Drury Arms. Red yarn tied around the heads of the pins connected people to each other and to places of interest. Had Shay brought the yarn in herself, or had it been hiding in the supply cabinet all these years? If I'd known about it I could've made use of the corkboard long ago. You'd think after a dozen years one of the other detectives would've mentioned it. Jerks...

I snaked my way around the pin board, stripped off my coat, and draped it over the back of my wooden throne. Shay didn't so much as glance in my direction.

I sat in my chair with a thud. "Is that official police issue tracking thread?"

Shay turned around to look at me and blinked some fog away from her eyes. "Huh?"

"Oh, sorry," I said. "Didn't realize you were in one of your trances."

"What? No I wasn't." Her nostrils flared. "Why would you think that?"

I shrugged. "You had that same faraway look in your eyes, that's all."

"I was thinking. Those of us with brains are prone to do that from time to time."

"Well, it looked similar to one of your out-of-body experiences to me."

Shay rolled her eyes. "Don't tell me I need to explain how this works to you again..."

"Please don't," I said, holding up a hand. I glanced around the office. "Where are Rodgers and Quinto? Don't tell me I beat them into work."

"Rodgers—no. He was here a while ago, but he wandered off. Quinto, on the other hand, I've yet to see."

I gave Shay the old snap and point. "Hah! First time for everything, I guess. I'll have to rub it in his face when he gets in."

Shay raised an eyebrow. "Did you guys have a long night or something?"

"Not necessarily. Though the poppers might not have been such a great idea."

"I'm not going to ask."

Shay sat on the corner of her desk and turned back toward the board. I drummed my fingers on my desk.

"So...tell me what you've got here."

She glanced at me. "Really? You're a cop and you've never seen a corkboard?"

I gave her my best sneer. "Please. I meant your little red connections. Let's go through them."

"You sure?" Shay asked. "Just like that? No coffee, no kolaches? Just straight to business?"

I might've thrown up a little in my mouth. "Ugh. Don't talk to me about fried food. Although, now that you mention it..."

I wandered off without a word.

When I returned, I nursed a steaming mug of bitter caffeinated brew between my hands. I sat back down. "Alright. You may continue."

Shay snickered, but she obliged.

"Well," she said, "The two things we need to figure out are motive and opportunity. If we can discover who possessed both a motive and an opportunity to murder Reginald, that should lead us to the killer."

"Good thinking, slugger," I said. "If you hadn't read that *How to Solve Crimes* pamphlet, we'd really be up a creek with no paddle."

I got a good glare for that wisecrack, but I took it in stride. I always do.

"Look," I said. "Clearly we need to establish motive and opportunity, but as you may have noticed, we haven't found anyone with a motive yet."

"That's not entirely true," said Shay. "There was a lot of money flowing both through and around Mr. Powers' hands. We've already established Mr. Talent is wealthy. Reginald's betrothal to Felicity pretty much ensured that he was in line for a substantial windfall."

"Wait. Yesterday you were dead set against my theory that old Blazey Blaze offed Reggie. Now you've changed your mind?"

"You didn't let me finish," said Shay. "What I was going to say was perhaps someone else stood to lose from Reginald's gain—maybe a rival suitor who'd hoped to gain Felicity's hand in marriage."

"Interesting theory," I said. "We'll have to keep an eye out for lonely young mourners of the male variety who pop by the Talent estate to comfort the redhead."

Shay nodded in a smug, self-satisfied sort of way. I took a sip of joe and brought her back down to earth.

"But," I said, "even you have to admit that while we can't conceive of a motive for him to kill Reginald yet, Mr. Talent is still very much in the conversation."

Shay's eyes narrowed, and she peered at me suspiciously. "And what makes you think that?"

"Because of opportunity, my dear."

"Well, sure. Mr. Talent was at the charity ball during the time of death, but—"

"Not that kind of opportunity," I said. "Reggie was killed in a back hallway with alley access. Anyone could've killed him, whether they were at the ball or not. I'm talking about the opportunity to access our murder weapon. Something like thermite isn't sold at your neighborhood five and dime, but that old geezer Blaze could've obtained some at one of his foundries. It's the same reason Drury—" I pointed at the name on the corkboard. "—is also a prime suspect."

"But why would Mr. Drury want to kill Reginald?" said Shay. "Mr. Powers was his star player, making him rich with all those new contracts."

"Was he?" I said. "Are we really so sure of that? We know Reggie was some sort of confidence man. We just don't know what kind of con he was running. Let me tell you something I've learned about con artists over the years. They like to steal, and the thing they most often steal is money. The person at Drury Arms who happens to have the most of that particular commodity is Thurmond Drury."

"So what," said Shay. "You think Reginald was embezzling money from the company?"

"I don't know. But if he was, I'm sure we'll find out about it in the financial records. And I know just the guy to talk to about that."

"Yeah. Me," said Quinto.

32

Quinto dropped the box of files on my desk with a loud thud. I nearly jumped out of my shoes. Apparently the big guy had snuck up on me while I'd been jabbering with Shay. I reminded myself once again not to get on Quinto's bad side. A three hundred pound rock crusher was bad enough, let alone one who could get the drop on you.

"There you are," I said. "I was just about to go report you as missing to the Captain. We were going to send out a search party."

"It's not that late," said Quinto.

I hooked two thumbs at myself—a portrait of tardiness—already at work.

"You may have a point," he said. "But at least I have an excuse. I was up half the night going through these files. And you'll never believe what I found."

"A signed affidavit from Mr. Drury confessing to the murder of Reginald Powers?"

Quinto peered at me curiously. "Um...no."

I snapped my fingers. "Drat. Would've made this case a lot easier to solve."

"Are you still drunk?" asked Quinto.

"What? I was never drunk. I'm hurt that you'd—"

Shay cut me off with a loud hawk. "Why don't you tell us what you found in those documents, Detective Quinto."

"Nothing. Absolutely nothing. Everything checks out."

"Wait," I said. "I think I've got wax in my ears. Did you say you found nothing?"

"Well, nothing in the documents. But I did find something."

I tried to adopt my most befuddled look. I didn't have to try hard.

"Let me explain." My partner's desk groaned as Quinto leaned against it. "I looked through all the documents we received, and everything fit the narrative as we know it. Drury Arms cut tons of new deals—with Mr. Powers spearheading nearly all of them. Cash came in, and cash came out. Weapons were manufactured and delivered. Receipts got signed upon delivery. Taking the story as a whole, everything looked legit. But something didn't *feel* right. So I dug deeper. And I'm glad I did, because I found one slight problem. Most of the incoming payments were vapor trails."

"Huh? What do you mean?" I asked.

"I mean they disappeared, evaporated into the ether. I stopped by Mr. Drury's bank this morning—which, by the way, is the real reason I'm late—and I inquired about his accounts. Turns out, Drury Arms is almost broke. All that money from Mr. Powers' deals never got deposited."

"*What?*" I said. "How is it nobody ever noticed?"

"I don't know," said Quinto.

I stroked the fuzz growing from the tip of my chin. In my morning doldrums, I'd neglected to shave.

"If Reg stole all that contract money," I said, "nearly driving Drury Arms into bankruptcy in the process, that would be a clear motive for Thurmond Drury to want to kill him. We don't know if he was at the charity auction, but he would've certainly had access to our murder weapon—if you can call it a weapon."

"Not so fast there, hotshot," said Quinto. "I'm not so sure Mr. Drury knows about the state of his finances. These records don't smell fishy until you're so close you can feel their gills rubbing against your face. If the documents were doctored—and I'd have to assume they were—then they were doctored by someone with intimate knowledge of the business's inner workings and finances. Someone very close to the action."

"You think Walter Fry is involved?" asked Shay.

"I can't say for sure," said Quinto. "But in my experience, when you've got a case where all the money magically disappears, talking to the accountant is a good place to start."

I leaned back in my chair. "So it seems we need to have a more prolonged chat with Stutters McGee. An interrogation room would suit our needs better than his office. Quinto—you want to do the honors of bringing our little squirrel in?"

Quinto tilted his head and peered at me. "You sure that's a good idea, Daggers? I thought you wanted to interrogate the runt, not kill him."

"What are you planning, big guy? You got a vendetta against bookkeepers I don't know about?"

"No," said Quinto. "But the little dude nearly had a heart attack when he saw me yesterday while dropping a box off. Imagine what'll happen when I show up to drag his butt to the precinct for questioning."

I smiled. "Oh, I can envision it perfectly. Wally's probably going to soil himself when you show up at his doorstep. Then again, he's such a spook he'd probably do the same if it were me. I'd rather make you deal with the smell on the ride back from Drury Arms."

Quinto narrowed his eyes and set his jaw. For a moment I feared I might've gone too far in poking the bear, but then he spoke. "I get the feeling this is an elementary plan to make me do your legwork for you, Daggers."

I spread my arms out wide. "You know me too well, big guy."

"Fine." He pointed a thick finger at me. "I'll go down there. But only because you bought drinks last night. Don't get used to it."

I breathed a sigh of relief, but not too big of a sigh. My wit had helped me skirt one obligation this morning, but I spotted another approaching from the precinct's entrance.

33

Quinto stormed out the front doors as Rodgers sauntered in with an unfamiliar trench coat-clad guy in tow.

Rodgers jerked a thumb toward the door. "What's wrong with Quinto?"

"Not sure. Hemorrhoids, maybe," I said.

I heard a derisive snort emanate from the she-elf.

I nodded toward the new guy, an average height human with tan skin and dark hair. "Who's this?"

The mystery man took a step forward and extended a hand. "Detective Esteban Morales. Narcotics. You must be Detective Daggers. Rodgers has told me some interesting stories about you."

I shook the guy's hand, but before I could inquire about the lies Rodgers had filled him with he turned to Shay. "And Miss Steele. It's nice to see you again."

"Likewise, Detective. Although it's Detective Steele now."

"Oh," said Morales with a nod. "Well, congratulations then. You've come a long way in a short time if you don't mind me saying."

I busted out my best set of shifty eyes and split them between my partner and the new guy. "You two know each other?"

Morales nodded. "Miss—err, excuse me—Detective Steele interned with me a couple years back. She only spent a few days working with me, but in that short period of time it became obvious she was born to do police work. She's one of the most attentive people I've ever met. Few details escape her notice, Detective Daggers. And that prescience? Well, let's just say I'm not surprised to already find you in the position you're in, Detective Steele."

I think Shay blushed. "Thank you, Detective Morales."

Given the mental jog, I remembered the Captain mentioning something about Shay's involvement with the narcotics guys a few years back. Apparently, she knew more cops outside of the homicide unit than I did.

Rodgers shifted from side to side on the balls of his feet. "Guys, I don't mean to rush you, but I'm going to see if I can catch up to Quinto before he gets too far. Got some things to discuss with him. Detective Morales should be able to shed some light on the drug paraphernalia you found at Reginald's place."

Rodgers turned and hightailed it after his partner. I waved in the general direction of Shay's empty chair.

"Well, have a seat and share some knowledge with us," I said.

Morales glanced at Shay first. "You mind?"

"Be my guest," she said.

Morales sat. As he did so, he fished a small brown baggie out of his coat pocket. He dumped the contents onto Shay's desk. A couple syringes and the small vial of caramel-colored liquid we'd found in Reggie's apartment rolled out. He also extracted from his pocket a few billfold-sized placards drawn from Reggie's desk—the ones that had been adorned with the tribal-like designs. All three cards that Detective Morales spread before him featured the same fundamental drawing—a three-pronged radial weave of thick and fine brushstrokes, each embellished in slightly different ways.

"Rodgers gave me a little background on your investigation, but not much," said Morales. "I understand these items all came from a murdered con man. A dark elf?"

"That's right," said Shay. "One Reginald Powers."

"At least that's what we're calling him," I said. "That, or Reggie Sweatervest. Or maybe Reggie Mortis. I still like that one. Fact is, we don't know what our dead guy's real name is. We found a stack of IDs at his place."

Morales pointed at the syringes and vial. "Was this the extent of the drug paraphernalia you found in his apartment?"

I nodded.

"Well then, I can give you a couple insights into your victim. I'll start with the potentially less useful tidbit. This Powers guy probably wasn't a user." Morales picked up the brown vial. "You see this crank, here? It's low-grade stuff. You can tell by the hue and the viscosity that it's got loads of impurities in it. Not only is it incredibly dangerous—those impurities can range from the innocuous to the extremely toxic—but it takes a fair amount of this stuff to get high. If your guy was fairly well off—and from the impression Rodgers gave me, he was—he wouldn't spring for something like this. He'd buy finer quality dope. In the event he did use this low-grade crank, he'd surely have more than one tiny vial on hand. Serious users would go through this volume of dope in less than a day."

Shay leaned over her desk and picked up one of the syringes. "I'd thought that myself, Morales. And there's something else I've just now noticed. I don't think these have been used." Shay pulled back the plunger on the syringe, drawing air into the tube. "See? No residue's coming out of the tip. If these had been used, there definitely would've been some liquid remaining in the needle."

"Exactly. Good eye, Steele," said Morales.

"You were right," I said. "That wasn't a particularly useful tidbit. So what else can you tell us?"

Morales glanced at Shay.

"Don't worry about him," she snarked. "He's grumpy because he still hasn't gotten his daily infusion of fried sweet dough."

I frowned. That remark reeked of defiance. I considered taking a quick trip to Tolek's to buy a kolache so I could toss it at her head.

"Well, the more interesting information is in regards to these drawings." Morales tapped the placards with the tribal designs. "A bunch of smalltime outfits deal low-quality dope, so there's no way we could track down who sold the crank to your guy by way of the drugs alone. But we should be able to with these placards. Some of the more industrious gangs have recently started distributing these to their street teams. Gutter-snipes mostly. They hand out the cards to prospective buyers. That way the buyers know who to contact when they want to purchase product. Names are never exchanged, and the product is never specifically mentioned. Keeps the dealers from getting entrapped."

"Hold on a sec," I said. "I'm not sure I follow you. How do these cards help dope fiends find their drug dealers?"

"Oh," said Morales. "I thought that would be obvious. These designs are tattoos. Dealers have them inked onto visible body parts so buyers can identify them."

"And let me guess," said Shay. "These tattoos belong to a specific gang. I'm guessing dwarves."

Morales raised his eyebrows in surprise. "Why...yes. As a matter of fact, they do. How did you figure that out?"

Shay raised a finger. "Well, I—"

"Let me spare you her boast," I said. "Shay had a vision while at Reggie's apartment yesterday. She saw bearded men with tattoos. Obviously once she heard your take on the dope pushers, she figured we were dealing with a gang of dwarven dealers."

Shay tilted her head as she looked at me. "You remembered. I'm impressed."

"I'm not as dumb as I look. Really, I just didn't want to hear you gloat about your preternatural powers again."

"You're just jealous because you have nothing to gloat about," said Shay. "Unless you count the fact that you used the word 'preternatural' properly in a sentence for once."

"I did? Hey Morales, guess who used the word 'preternatural' correctly?"

Shay and I exchanged glares.

Morales rubbed his chin. "Should I go on?"

"Please," I said.

"Detective Steele is correct. We've traced this particular set of tattoos to a band of dwarves in the Erming. They've been in our sights for a long time now, but they only started making waves a couple months ago. Rumor has it they recently came into possession of a substantial score of illicit arms. They've been expanding their reach ever since."

The gears in my head churned. Reginald's apartment. Drug paraphernalia. The cardboard box of weapons. The Drury Arms blacksmithing operation. Dwarves with recently obtained illegal weapons.

Shay stared at me. "If you're done making the obvious connection, perhaps we should go look into this in more detail."

I blinked. "Right. Morales, what else can you tell us about these guys? Who are they? Who's in charge? Where can we find them?"

"They call themselves the Razors," said Morales. "The dude in charge is a dwarf by the name of Occam Silvervein. He—"

"Wait. Really? Occam Silvervein? Head of the Razors?" I chuckled.

"Yeah," said Morales. "Apparently the guy has a sense of humor. Anyway, they're in the Erming. I don't know where exactly. But I know a guy who might have an inkling."

"A narc?"

Morales nodded.

"Give us a name," I said.

"Mikey 'Tiny' Dulcett. You should be able to find him at a dive bar called Slippery Pete's."

I groaned and ran a hand through my hair. "Tiny? Really?"

"What? You know the guy?"

"No, but I can guess." I patted my coat pocket and felt Daisy's smooth, hard body poking out from underneath the fabric. I had a feeling I might need her.

"Grab your coat and a weapon, Steele," I said. "Papa Bear and Tenderfoot are heading to the Erming."

34

Shay and I stood outside a faded brick building with
a door that looked like it'd been pieced together
out of leftover onion crates. A sagging, moth-eaten
awning hung over the front, and a wooden sign nailed
above the door depicted a bare foot slipping in a puddle.
I figured we'd found the right place.

"You know, you still haven't told me how you know
this Tiny Dulcett character."

I turned to Shay. "I *don't* know him."

"So how come you didn't ask Detective Morales for a
description of the guy?"

"Isn't it obvious?" I said.

I pushed the door open and strode into the bar. I had
to stop for a moment as my eyes adjusted to the gloom.
A horse-faced guy armed with a dirty dishrag manned
the castle, while a number of surly, beer-saturated
goons protected the battlements.

The irregulars turned to stare as I entered. I spotted
a meaty guy with a bulbous nose, a one-eyed half-breed
with an assortment of scars crisscrossing his face, and

an old guy with a long, bushy mane and a hook for a hand. *What a welcoming party.*

The thugs snarled and went back to their brews. One guy at the end of the bar hadn't moved—a mammoth-sized pile of man meat with a wrinkled, shaved head and shoulders that could've moonlighted as traffic barricades. He loomed over the bar like a mountain, blocking out what little sunlight trickled his way.

That would be Tiny.

His stench filled the room, a mixture of onions, overripe bananas, and sweaty feet. He was chowing down on a plate of bar vittles I could only hope smelled better than he did, and a tall, empty mug of beer rested beside his plate. Foamy suds dripped down the sides onto the unlacquered wood of the bar. I contemplated a strategy.

Shay slipped in behind me as the door thudded closed. I turned to her and tipped my head toward the brute.

"See that guy over there?" I asked.

Shay looked, her eyes widening. "That's not—"

"It is."

"I see," she said. No wisecracks followed.

"Is he looking this way?"

"No," said Shay. "He's engrossed in...whatever it is he's eating."

I stole a glance over my shoulder. Big and Ugly seemed oblivious to our presence.

"So...are we going to go over there and talk to him?"

I nearly choked. "Are you kidding? And let everyone know what side he's on?"

I couldn't tell in the darkness, but I think Shay might've blushed. "Oh. Right. Sorry. So what's the plan?"

"Well," I said. "There's a Plan A and a Plan B. I'd prefer Plan A."

"Which is?"

"You pull one of your little vision thingies and figure out where Occam Silvervein is hiding."

"Sorry, Daggers. I'm not getting anything at the moment."

"Yeah, I didn't figure you would." I cracked my neck to the sides and straightened my coat.

"So what's Plan B, then?" said Shay.

"Same as it always is. I go in feet first and balls out, kicking the crap out of anything that gets in my way."

Shay looked at me with equal parts concern and disdain. "Uhh...you sure that's a good idea?"

"No, not really," I said. I reached a hand into my coat and wrapped my fingers around Daisy's cold steel. "Now stand back. The weather's looking a little murky. I'm predicting a ninety percent chance of shit storms."

I slipped Daisy out of my jacket, holding her down by my thigh as I walked past the bar. I casually waltzed over to the big fella.

"Hey Tiny!"

He turned around and responded in more or less the fashion I expected.

"Huh?" he said.

I slapped him upside the head with Daisy, but she didn't want anything to do with the big lug. She rebounded off his thick skull with a loud ring. Tiny howled and surged out of his seat, swinging at me with a giant fist.

I was prepared.

I ducked as his punch sailed over me. Tiny's momentum sent him stumbling into my outstretched leg. Leaning over, I grabbed the back of his shirt and yanked, giving him a little extra mustard.

Being as massive as he was, momentum wasn't Tiny's friend. He sailed across the bar, spinning and stumbling before crashing through a flimsy door and into a side street. I marched out after him, vaguely aware of the rest of the bar's patrons fleeing out the front. Who could blame them? Anyone stupid enough and crazy enough to mess with a guy Tiny's size deserved to be given a wide berth.

I stepped into the alley as Tiny extracted himself from a pile of tin trashcans. He pulled a knife, but I stopped him with a flash of my badge. "Hold up there, Mikey. Daggers. Homicide. I need a word."

The emotion in Tiny's eyes flashed from anger to confusion, then back to anger. "Bleeding goat sacks, man...*what the hell?*"

"Watch the language, tough guy," I said. "You're in the presence of a lady."

On cue, Shay stepped through the shattered remains of the door and into the alley at my side.

Tiny groaned, holding his head as he pulled himself to his feet. "I get it. You're fuzz. Now what in blazes do ya' want? I didn't kill nobody. Ain't so much as handed out a black eye in weeks."

"We're not here about a murder. Well, actually, we are. But that's not why we need to talk to you." I looked up and down the alley to check for stray ears. "Morales gave us your name."

Tiny sighed, letting loose a cloud of banana and feet sweat vapor. Shay gagged.

"Great...I coulda' done without the shiner."

"Sorry pal," I said. "Had to sell it, you know?"

"So what do ya' want to know?" asked Mikey.

"We're looking for a guy named Occam Silvervein. Heard of him?"

Tiny rubbed his forehead. A nice lump was sprouting there. "'Course I've heard of him. Everybody's heard of him. Can't go two skips in the Erming without stepping on a crankhead who's hopped up on his dope."

"You skip around the Erming?" I tried to envision it and failed.

"Figure o' speech," said the big lug. "Anyway, if you're looking for Occam he shouldn't be too hard to find. Just look for whatever flophouse has a bunch of his goons hanging around outside it. They're easy to spot with those ugly face tattoos of theirs."

"They have the tattoos on their faces?" Morales had failed to mention that.

"Yeah. They're a bunch o' loonies." Tiny hawked a loogie and spit. "And Occam's the worst o' the lot. You'll recognize him right away. His tattoos are the craziest of 'em all, and he's got a lazy left eye.

"Anyway, last I heard there was a gang of his guys near East 61st and Terrace. But if you're planning on going after him, you'd better get more bluecoats." He eyed Shay with a mixture of desire and contempt. "I don't think your backup is gonna' be much help in a squab."

"Duly noted," I said. "Now get the hell out of here before anyone gets suspicious."

Tiny made himself scarce.

"I can't believe that worked," said Shay.

"Which part?" I asked.

"Well...everything. I have to admit, I thought my stint with you was going to be very short-lived once you beaned him with your nightstick."

I realized I still gripped Daisy in my fist. I tucked her away in my coat, making sure she was comfortable—wouldn't want the old girl getting angry at me.

"Ehh, big dudes aren't that tough to deal with. Tiny probably weighs as much as a cart full of bricks, but his balance is too high. Makes him easy to knock over. Not like what we're going to have to deal with."

Shay crossed her arms. "You mean the dwarves?"

"Yeah. Squat with a low center of gravity. They can be real demons in a fight." I headed down the alley, motioning for Shay to follow. "We should do some quick recon. If those dwarven gangbangers are where Mikey said they'd be, we're going to have a fun morning ahead of us."

35

Tiny's intel proved accurate. A pack of short bearded
uglies with tribal face tattoos milled about at our
destination. Behind them stood a column of dull
red brick buildings plucked from the same cookie cutter
as every other hovel in the Erming.

I often wondered what sort of kickback the contractor who built the slum centuries ago received from the
bloke who was selling red bricks. Must've involved a
pile of money as tall as the clouds—or a woman with
exceptional carnal talents. The only structures con-
structed of anything other than the cinnamon-colored
clay blocks were those that had cropped up in the alleys
between buildings, and those were mostly scrap wood
lean-tos held together with rusty nails and the hopes
and dreams of the destitute.

It wasn't immediately obvious which dwelling hid
the dwarves' base of operations, but a few minutes of
reconnoitering provided the answer. Shay and I set up
base in the shade of a set of stairs leading to a split-
level home. We made awkward small talk while fending

off cutpurses and street urchins. Soon enough, I spotted a vertically-challenged tough with a tattoo around his left eye socket. He emerged from a walk-up basement three buildings from the street corner, sauntered over to the herd of dwarven loiterers, and passed out some unmarked brown paper bags. The bearded ones scattered.

"Looks like we found where Occam is hiding," I said.

My partner, bouncing back and forth on the balls of her feet, tried to steal a glance in the direction of the guy with the face art. "Please tell me you're not going to follow your last strategy here."

I scoffed. "Why not? The combination of Daisy's charm and my muscle has never let me down before. I mean, there can't be more than...what? A dozen or so dwarves in that basement? How many can you handle? Three? I don't know if I can take more than ten."

"You're kidding, right?" Shay's wide eyes spoke of disbelief and terror. "I don't want to die on my second day on the job. The Captain warned me about you before we met, but if you think—"

"Relax, Steele. I'm pulling your leg. Come on. Let's go muster up some backup."

Police stations occupied the four corners of the Erming. Slums are a lot like diseases, and police officers act as the city's immune system. Not only do they maintain the peace, but they keep the ghetto from spreading. I headed in the direction of the nearest precinct.

"Really, Daggers," said Shay. "Even with backup, are you sure this is a wise idea? Don't you think there's a reason Morales hasn't moved in on Silvervein yet?"

"Of course," I said. "It wasn't worth it to bust the guy on drug charges. But now we're knee deep in a murder investigation. One that involves large quantities of illicit weapons. If there's any chance this Occam lowlife is involved in Reggie's death, we need to get to the bottom of it. The Captain would back me up on that. Never forget what this job is about—finding the truth and delivering justice to those who deserve it, regardless of the risk."

That greased the wheels in Shay's brain. She kept quiet until we reached the local bluecoat branch.

Once there, I forced a meeting with the lieutenant in charge.

He didn't want to be my friend.

I explained to him my manpower needs and he flat-out refused. He told me I was crazy to think I could waltz into his station and request a detail of over a dozen cops for an unplanned raid on a known drug dealer and suspected arms trader. Told me quite plainly that things worked differently in the Erming than in my neck of the woods. That he wasn't going to needlessly risk his men on a mad whim from some midtown gumshoe.

Much to my own surprise, I kept a level head. I kindly informed him that while, no, I wouldn't expect his men to charge into a herd of armed dwarves simply to take down a small-to-medium-time drug dealer, that yes, I did expect them to follow me into battle when said drug dealer was now a prime person of interest in a murder investigation.

My bureaucratic nemesis held firm. I got a little sassy. I asked if it was common practice for him to let murders slide as easily as drug deals in *his* neck of the woods.

The lieutenant snarled.

I threatened to get my Captain involved.

After some back and forth, Lieutenant Protruding Broomstick Handle assigned me ten of his surliest crowd controllers, outfitted with body armor, riot shields, and lead-weighted billy clubs. Funny—he didn't offer me so much as a bandage. He did, however, give some unsolicited advice to my partner. Something along the lines of staying the hell out of the way once the fur started to fly. Despite having grabbed a baton of her own back at headquarters, Shay agreed.

With my officially sanctioned head-thumpers in tow, I led the way back toward Silvervein's hideout. The streets emptied themselves as we marched.

The folks in the Erming may be poor, but dumb they aren't. I've often thought slums are microcosms that succinctly prove the validity of evolution. In a slum, survivability trumps all other traits. Those individuals that don't possess the proper level of respect for their own hides tend to lose them fairly quickly. Folks in other neighborhoods don't understand the survival-of-the-fittest, winner-takes-all paradigm quite like slum rats do. Walk down the streets of the Pearl with a goon squad in tow, and people will come out of stores and cafés to gawk. In the Erming, people don't bother to check what side of the law a pack of toughs falls on. They just run.

Our wavefront of riot shields and living muscle attenuated in front of the building where I'd spotted my buddy with the eye socket tattoo. The street team of dealers had vanished, as had most every other living soul.

I pointed out the basement of sin and debauchery to my surly retinue. A few nodded in acknowledgement, but not a one said a word.

I couldn't blame them. The surge of adrenaline and fear that rushes through your body as you prepare for a fight tends to put the kibosh on light conversation.

I loosened my kicking foot and grabbed Daisy, caressing her as we prepared to expand our usual solo dance into a group number. I took a deep breath and headed down the stairs.

36

The door exploded off its hinges under the weight of my boot. Armored bluecoats swarmed into the cellar. I shouldered my way inside, Daisy held above my head, ready to strike anything that moved.

The basement space stretched out in front of us like a spider with rough stone passageways radiating from both sides of the main hallway. Flimsy pastel-colored drapes hung in the entryways of the corridors, adding a touch of color to the gloom. Slurred baritone shouts from deep inside the hovel mingled with the pounding of boots and the wet thuds of truncheons meeting dwarf flesh.

I only had a few seconds to orient myself before a couple of dwarven uglies came at me with pigstickers. Tweedledum and Tweedledee lunged and jabbed with their knives simultaneously, but their short arms limited their reach.

I stepped back and swept Daisy in an arc at my knees, cracking Tweedledum on the wrist. He howled in pain and dropped his knife. Tweedledee circled to my right in a defensive stance, knife held before him.

I feinted left and stutter-stepped to my right, nearly shaking Tweedledee out of his shoes. Daisy caught him in the side of the head. She whispered sweet nothings in his ear, trying to lull him to sleep, but the thick-headed blighter only dropped to his knees. I cocked a haymaker to finish him off, but before I could swing Tweedledum pounced on my back.

He'd dropped his knife in favor of the ape-like limbs that protruded from his sides. He wrapped his injured arm around my neck from behind, trying to choke the life out of me as he beat on my melon with his free fist.

Like a bronco struggling to remain unbroken, I pitched around wildly trying to free myself from Tweedledum's loving embrace. As we struggled, we fell into one of the pastel drapes which wrapped itself around our heads like an overzealous turban. In a stroke of luck, it bound my lover's arm in place, keeping him from landing further blows to my head. On the downside, it also blinded me, limiting my field of vision to a sea of mauve. With Tweedledum's chokehold still firmly in place, I began to panic.

I crashed into walls and bookshelves and cabinets, breaking glass and creating a ruckus, all the while taking pot shots at my rider with Daisy. Due to his awkward position on my back, I couldn't land any solid blows.

As darks spots danced in front of my eyes, I did the only thing I could. I threw myself into the air, arched my back, and drove the full weight of my meat, cheese, and fried dough-fed physique into the ground.

Tweedledum made a noise like air being bled out of a half-filled balloon. His choking arm went slack.

With all the speed I could muster, I rolled off him, ripped the drapes from my head, and delivered a solid kick to lover boy's skull. It wasn't a particularly sporting move, but it kept him from getting up for a while.

I gathered my bearings as I sucked in stale basement air. Much to my surprise, I'd only traveled one room over from the entryway during my battle with Sir Burlyarms. In true Jake Daggers' fashion, however, I'd managed to totally lay waste to the place. Nary a piece of furniture lay unsplintered. Captain would've thrown a fit if we'd had to pay restitution for the damages, but given that my vertically-challenged friend had been trying to kill me, I think we could argue against it.

I hitched up my pants and stepped back into the entryway. Tweedledee was sawing logs on the floor. Apparently one of my more industrious escorts had finished him off while I danced the blind hokey-pokey with Tweedledum.

A series of shouts from further on in the basement brought me to attention. My steel lady friend still clutched in my hand, I ventured further into the abyss.

After a short jog, I found the remainder of my buddies. I burst into a large open room and was nearly brought to my knees by the fumes. I blinked back tears and covered my nose with my sleeve. Enameled cast iron cauldrons spewing toxic vapors lined the side of the room to my left, while crates of raw, unfiltered opiate resin leaned against the wall at my right. My club-wielding cronies occupied the far side of the room, locked in a fierce battle with the remaining dwarves.

At the center of the melee, one particular dwarf stood out. Dark as midnight tribal tattoos crept up his neck and onto his face. They encircled his eyes before spilling onto his forehead and diving into the mass of fur that covered his cheeks. Muscles bulged from every orifice of his stained tank top. He grasped a sword as long as he was tall and swung it about with a wild, fiery rage, almost single-handedly keeping the riot cops at bay.

He also had a lazy left eye.

Using my razor-sharp deductive wit, I identified him as Occam Silvervein.

The dwarves fought well, but craziness and an opiate-induced drug haze could only get a pack of navelgazers so far. My boys were better equipped and better trained. With a few well-coordinated blocks and strikes, the tide turned in favor of the good guys.

Occam, despite the obvious milky drug film that coated his eyes, noticed the shift in the fight as soon as I did. Abandoning his remaining gangbangers, he dropped the sword and turned toward the wall.

That's when I realized why the room happened to be better lit than the rest of the basement. Lookout windows lined the top of the far wall, all of which had been propped fully open. It was a logical choice. If not for the windows, the fumes from the drug cauldrons would've proved deadly rather than merely extremely irritating.

I swore and yelled for him to stop.

With the bluecoats still engaging the remaining toughs, I raced forward and launched myself toward the middle window. Occam beat me by a hair, wriggling out the half-sized opening and into the adjoining alley.

Sucking in my gut and pinching my shoulders, I pulled myself up and out the window, flopping on the ground outside with all the grace of a dying fish. Stumbling and bumbling, I gathered my feet under me and turned after my prey.

Occam raced toward the mouth of the alley. He had a good twenty pace head start on me. Despite my own admitted lack of closing speed, I figured I had a good chance to catch him, what with his stubby legs and all. My biggest concern would be not losing him in one of the Erming's nooks and crannies. Silvervein knew the slum. I didn't. That could prove to be critical.

Occam, however, seemed to think his escape was all but inevitable. As he reached the end of the alley, he turned his head, probably to gauge the separation between us. And then the little bugger had the nerve to wink.

I growled and ran after him. There was no way I was about to let some murdering, crank-cooking dwarven gangbanger get the best of me.

Occam whipped his head back as he spilled into the street and immediately took a whistling, high-speed nightstick to the neck. He fell to the ground clutching his throat, making odd gasping sounds. Over him stood none other than my svelte, cream-colored blouse-clad partner.

I pulled up short as I reached Shay and the writhing dwarf.

"Wow. Nice shot," I said. "A guy built like him probably would've shrugged off a shot to the face, but a shot to the Adam's apple? That's cold-blooded."

Shay dropped her truncheon. She was visibly shaking. "Uh...thanks. I guess. I was actually aiming for his face, though."

"Oh. Well, nicely done anyway. Let's just hope we don't have to give him a tracheotomy. He doesn't sound so good."

Occam's gasping was turning more into a sort of gurgling noise, but I distinctly picked out the rasping sound of air coming in and out of his windpipe. Not wanting to risk losing him again, I gave him a love tap on the chin with Daisy.

Shay leaned against a brick wall and took a deep breath. I wandered over.

"You ok?" I asked.

"Um, yeah. I'm fine. It's just...It's just that..." She stared at the ground.

"You've never hit a guy before, have you?"

Shay shook her head. "Not like that."

"Don't sweat it," I said. "It'll get easier. You're a natural."

I got a raised eyebrow in response. "Seriously? You're kidding, right?"

"Nah. What you did there was no joke." I jerked a thumb at Silvervein. "Now I'm not going to lie—you'll need to put some meat on your bones so you can pack a better punch. But you did good, Steele. Which reminds me—good thinking on staking out the back exit."

"I'm starting to think I'm the one who took a blow to the skull instead of that dwarf there. Did you just give me two compliments in the same breath?"

I scratched my head. I had at that.

"Don't worry," I said. "I'm sure I'll find something disparaging to say soon enough."

Shay pushed off from the wall, stretching back to her full height. "I was sure you'd scold me for not following you into the Razors' hideout."

"No, not really," I said. "I figured you'd wait out front. I had you pegged as a pretty big coward."

My partner rolled her eyes. "And there it is. Didn't take too long, did it?"

"Told you," I said. "Now stop whining and help me gather that lump of dwarf flesh so we can question him at the station."

37

Once the riot suppressors mopped up the remaining Razors, we loaded them all in a paddy wagon and sent them off to the nearest station house. All except for my boy Occam, of course. He got an all-expenses-paid trip to the downtown precinct in a special police issue rolling lockbox.

Once there, we chained him up in a brightly lit interrogation room. It contained lots of mirrors that reflected copious amounts of lamplight directly into his face. I figured he'd find the intense light uncomfortable given his dimly lit digs and the fact that he was still strung out on his own crank.

With the pint-sized person of interest safely secured, I snagged a cup of joe, draped my coat across the back of my chair, and sat. I leaned back and propped my feet up on my desk.

Shay buzzed around me like a fly, never pausing in a single spot for more than a few seconds. "Aren't we going to interrogate the suspect?"

"Slow down there, cowgirl," I said. "There's no need to rush. Let the guy sweat a little. Trust me. A guy like Occam will need some tenderizing."

I made her wait twenty minutes or so. Shay fidgeted the entire time. Either she couldn't wait to solve the case, or she still suffered the aftereffects of endorphins released during her thrashing of Mr. Silvervein. I offered her coffee, but she turned it down. Probably a good choice. She didn't need additional stimulants.

When I finished my liquid pick-me-up, I set down my mug, gathered evidence materials we'd taken from the crime scene, and motioned for Shay to follow. "Alright, killer. Let's go have a chat with Occam."

My partner shuddered. "Please don't call me that. You know I wasn't trying to hurt him."

"You could've been trying to straighten his nose, for all I care. What matters is you laid him out good and proper."

Shay shook her head. "I'm surprised you want me along for the interrogation."

"Hey, you're the one who knocked his ass to the grass. You never know, he might be more intimidated by you than me. It won't be easy to break him, but I suspect it might be useful to have you along. Just don't pansy up the joint if I have to get rough with him."

We paused in front of the interrogation room.

"Of course," I said, "we could avoid all this if you could conjure up one of your visions right about now."

Shay sighed. "Not this again. I told you—"

"*Kidding.* Ladies first." I opened the door.

The head Razor himself sat where we'd left him, squinting into the bright lights. Shackles bound his hands and secured them to a table in front of him. A bead of sweat trickled down his forehead before losing itself in his shaggy beard.

I pulled out my chair, flipped it around, and sat. I figured an unconventional style would make me seem more of a badass. Shay took the seat to my left. She'd left her nerves at the door, her face a mask of impassiveness. I was impressed. I hadn't expected that sort of emotional control from her. It would serve us well during the questioning.

I placed a couple items on the table in front of me—the three-foot long falchion Occam had wielded while fending off the riot police and a small brown baggie with the top folded over. I opened the bag and dumped its contents out for all to see—a sticky ball of yellowish orangey-brown opium residue.

"So...Occam, is it?" I said. "Do either of these items look at all familiar to you?"

Mr. Silvervein neglected to invoke his right to free speech.

"Cat got your tongue? I understand. You may not be familiar with jurisprudence here in our fair city, so why don't I fill you in. You need special military authorization to carry a blade in these parts. Not even cops are allowed to have them. Now, if you get caught carrying a blade under four inches, that's a Class B misdemeanor. Under six inches and you've got yourself a Class A misdemeanor. Carry this thing around?" I pointed at the sword and whistled. "That's a felony, my friend."

I picked up the glob of opium resin. "The same sort of reasoning applies to dope. If we caught you lugging around an ounce of crank, we'd slap you with a misdemeanor, assess you a fine, and send you on your merry way after a few days in the pen. A chunk like this probably weighs about, say—" I hefted the glob. "—an ounce or so. So I'd estimate two dozen crates' worth, like we found in your basement, probably weighs somewhere in the range of a *giant buttload.* In case you hadn't guessed, that's a felony offense, too. As is the manufacture of dope from this stuff."

Occam finally spoke, and his voice wasn't what I expected. It flowed with warmth and sensuality—a sound that might've come out of a high-end call girl's mouth. It also had a bit of a rasp to it, but that could've been from the vicious throat slap inflicted to him by my partner.

"Those aren't mine. Never seen 'em before in my life."

I scratched my chin. "I see. And the fact that we have nearly a dozen police eye witnesses that saw you attacking them with this very blade in your crank lab surrounded by boxes of opiates wouldn't make you want to revise that statement, would it?"

Occam gave his head a single taut shake.

I hadn't expected Shay to contribute anything, so I was mildly startled when she joined the conversation.

"You know, Mr. Silvervein, much like with misdemeanors there's also different felony classes. Felony weapons possession is a Class C felony. Drug trafficking to the level of what you've been involved in would be a Class B felony. Do you know what crime qualifies as a Class A felony? *Murder.*"

That produced a reaction from the tattooed one. He squinted at Shay, his lazy left eye lagging slightly behind the right. "Murder? I haven't murdered anyone."

"No?" I said. "The name Reginald Powers ring a bell?"

Occam turned his still foggy granite-colored peepers on me. "No. It doesn't."

"Really? Tall guy. Dark hair. Dark skin. Bit of a looker. Hole in his chest."

I saw a faint hint of recognition flicker across his eyes. So...he *did* know him.

I pulled the placards we'd found at Reggie's place from my coat and spread them on the table.

"Do these look familiar to you?" I asked.

"Dope cards," said Occam. "What of 'em?"

"They're your gang's," I said, "and we found them at Reginald's apartment."

The head Razor squinted in the light. "I don't know any Reginald."

I gathered the placards and tapped them on the table a few times. Then I stared at Occam. Met him eye to eye. The light was getting to him, I could tell.

I let the silence stretch for a minute. Thankfully, my partner had the good sense to keep her mouth shut. I envisioned myself boring holes in Occam's skull with my sight similar to some sort of super-powered creature of nightmares.

"You know, it's kind of a shame, really," I said. "If you were facing Class B and C felonies, with the right word to the district attorney you could probably end up in a local penitentiary. Those aren't too bad. Heck, for a guy with some clout they can be downright cushy. But there's no leeway with Class A felonies. The magistrates send you to the federal labor camps." I turned to Shay. "You ever been to those, Detective?"

She shook her head.

"Yeah, you don't want to. They're rough. Real rough. Lots of ogres, I hear."

Occam snarled. Dwarves and ogres are about as natural enemies as cats and dogs.

"Believe it or not, though, I've heard the ogres like getting dwarves in the camps. Something to do with them being tall and you guys being short—makes it so your heads are right around groin level. And they treat you guys well—assuming you don't mind getting shaved and oiled every now and then."

The Razor bared his teeth. "What do you want, pig?"

"I want you to tell me about Reginald Powers."

Another bead of sweat dripped off the dwarf's brow. "I told you, I don't know anybody by that name."

"But you do know who I'm talking about. So quit stalling."

38

"If I tell you what I know, I get locked up local?" Occam asked.

"That's the offer," I said.

Occam chewed his lip as another drop of sweat trickled down his brow. "I also want the drug charges dropped to a Class C."

"Oh, so you're familiar with the law now?" I drummed my fingers on the table. If we did as he asked, he'd still face two Class C felony charges. He'd go away for a decade, minimum. Probably more. I couldn't imagine the district attorney would be willing to cut him any more slack than necessary.

"I can't promise anything," I said, "but I'll talk to the DA. If you're fully cooperative, we might be able to forge a compromise."

Occam blinked in the bright lights. "Alright. Deal. So what do you want to know?"

"Everything." I took out my trusty notepad and flipped it open, pencil grasped in my right hand.

"I've never met any Reginald Powers," said Occam. "But I do know who you're talking about. I've known him a long time. Don't know his real name, though. Around the Erming, we call him Snappy."

"Snappy?" I said. "Seriously?"

"Yeah, on account of him always being such a snappy dresser. Only guy I've ever met who'd risk his neck pinching a three-piece suit when he didn't even have a loaf of bread for dinner."

"Huh," I said. "Who would've guessed our dead guy's nickname would've been even dopier than his pseudonym? So you guys have some sort of history?"

Occam shrugged. "Yeah, you could say that. You could even say we were...friends—of sorts."

Shay leaned in. "So you're telling us Reginald—I mean Snappy—was your friend?"

"Of sorts."

"What does that mean?" I asked.

"It means that business comes first, no matter who you are. And that was true with Snappy, too."

I scratched my head. "You're going to have to start at the beginning."

"Fine," said Occam. "Snappy was a slum rat, born and bred, like me. I met him when he was about thirteen years old. He got caught trying to steal office supplies from an associate of mine. My friend was about to teach him a lesson he wouldn't soon forget, but I told him to wait. I figured, what kind of thirteen-year-old kid steals paper and pencils?

"So I asked Snappy what he needed 'em for. He was scared. Thought he was a goner. So, he told me. Turns out he was writing a falsified letter to a district judge.

Something about trying to get his dad released from the joint. Pretty sad story, I've gotta' admit.

"Anyway, the kid spilled his guts. Told us everything. As it turned out, he'd been stealing supplies for some time. But I figured, hey, what if instead of kill—" Occam cleared his throat. "Um, I mean, what if, instead of *punishing* the kid, we put him to work? I told him to show me what he could do. And you know what? He wasn't half bad. At forging, that is. Good at pinching, too. I had him run drugs. Swipe stuff. That sort of thing. Even ran some small time grifts.

"The kid grew on me, so I took him under my wing. Tried to keep his nose clean. Or as clean as it can be when you're doing the sort of work he was doing. But Snappy was smart. Too smart for the Erming. I always figured he'd find his way out.

"And one day, he did. Just up and disappeared. I kept my ears to the ground to see if I could find out what he was up to, but I never heard much more than whispers. Word was he was doing some sort of long con, but that's the most I heard.

"Now, like I said, I couldn't begrudge Snappy for leaving. I knew he would. We just had one small problem. Snappy never asked for my permission out of our business arrangement. And I couldn't very well let a thing like that go.

"So I kept looking. And eventually I found him. He was working at some place called Drury Arms. Hard to recognize him at first. He'd grown up a lot in the years since I'd seen him. He'd left everything from the Erming behind, or at least he'd tried. You can never totally free yourself of that place.

"Anyway, I explained our situation to Snappy and offered him a solution. He'd deliver some military grade weapons our way, like that nice little blade you see there—" Occam nodded towards the sword. "—and we'd call it a deal. Snappy hemmed and hawed, but eventually he agreed. He gave me a time and place to meet him—a warehouse not far from here. He delivered on his end of the bargain, and that's that."

"When was that?" I asked.

"About three or four months ago."

"And you hadn't seen him since?"

"No."

"Were you aware he'd been murdered?"

"Not until you insinuated as much, no," said Occam.

"You don't look surprised," I remarked.

"It's not uncommon in our line of work."

I tapped my pencil on my notepad. As interesting as Occam's story was, it didn't add a whole lot to our overarching narrative.

"Mr. Silvervein," said Shay, "can you think of anyone who'd want Snappy dead?"

"In the Erming? Nah. People knew he was with me. If they had a beef, they'd come to me first. At least they would if they had any sense."

"What about outside the Erming?" asked Shay.

"You give me too much credit, elf. The Erming's my home. Always has been, and it'll probably be my grave. I don't keep track much of what goes on outside. And I already told you, I hadn't seen Snappy in years until a few months ago. I found him. We talked. I got my weapons. That's it."

"You're not being nearly as helpful as I'd hoped," I told Occam. "You're going to have to give me something else."

"I told you, I don't know anything else," he said.

"That warehouse where you guys met. Tell me about it."

"It was a small lockup on the south side, west of the Earl. Had a half-dozen crates of weapons in it. Knives, swords, axes—the stuff you'd expect. We met Snappy there one night and cleaned the joint out."

"Where is it exactly?"

Occam delved into his brain for an address. I wrote it down.

"Better hope this leads us somewhere useful, Occam," I said. "Otherwise my recommendation to the DA might get revised."

Occam was not pleased with the addendum to our arrangement. Luckily, the chains that bound him to the table held tight.

39

I closed the door to the interrogation room behind us, drowning out Occam's shouts and threats. I headed with my partner toward the pit.

"Well, that steamed him a bit, didn't it?" I said.

"Yeah," said Shay. "He had quite a few choice words about you and your mother."

"It's a shame," I said. "I really thought we were starting to connect. Oh well. By the way—good work in there."

Shay squinted and peered at me. "Is that sarcasm?"

"Hmm? No. You left your nerves at the door. Maintained your cool. Kept your mouth shut except when needed. That's half the battle in an interrogation."

"Another compliment? Are you sure you're feeling okay?"

"You know, come to think of it, one of those dwarves back at Occam's place did treat my head like his own personal piñata. I've been feeling a little woozy ever since. You think I should check with a physician?"

Shay shook her head. "Sometimes I have a hard time telling when you're being genuine, you know that?"

"Yeah, I have the same problem myself. Could be I should see a doctor about that, too. So...what do you think?" I gave my partner a double brow raise.

"About what?"

"About Occam," I said. "Think he's involved in Reginald's murder?"

"His name was Snappy, remember?" said Shay.

"Oh, come on. Snappy's too stupid a name for us to keep tossing it back and forth like a hot potato, and it's just as made up as the one we've been calling him by. I'm going to stick with Reginald. At least that way I can continue to be rakishly deprecating by calling him things like Reggie or Reg. What could I do with a name like Snappy? Call him Snapps?" I snapped my fingers a few times. "Oh, hey, that could work..."

"See? This is what I'm talking about," said Shay.

"You didn't answer my question. What's your take on Occam?"

Shay shrugged her shoulders. "I don't know. I mean on one hand, he's clearly a violent, dangerous criminal. I wouldn't put it past him to kill someone, even someone he's known for a long time. But on the other hand, I got the impression he was being honest about Reginald. I think he actually had a sort of strange, twisted affection for the guy."

"Yeah, I had the same feeling."

"Besides," said Shay, "we don't have any evidence to indicate he had any motive to kill Reginald. I mean, he got his weapons, didn't he? From what we found in his dope lab, he had enough arms in there to equip each of his guys three times over."

"Maybe Occam wanted more weapons and Reggie wouldn't play ball," I offered. "There's lots of money to be made in illicit arms trafficking."

"That's speculation and you know it. Besides, don't you think if Occam was involved in the arms trade Detective Morales would've noticed and alerted someone? Maybe people ignore the drug trade as long as it stays in the Erming, but that's definitely not true of the weapons biz."

We approached our stations. The corkboard still stood there, making small talk with our desks. I positioned my posterior in my trusty chair and eyeballed the information on the board. We'd uncovered lots of clues, but they hadn't coalesced into anything recognizable. The puzzle of Reginald's murder still missed a vital piece. But what?

I screwed up my face and pressed my fingers to my temples.

"If it hurts that much to think, maybe you should stop."

I glared at Shay. "I take back everything nice I've said about you today. Besides, you have no right to judge. I might be concussed from all those dwarf punches I absorbed, remember?"

My elf-girl partner-in-crime rolled her eyes again, a move I was becoming very familiar with. "Right... So, what's on your mind?"

"We need to make some sense of all this." I gestured at the board.

"That's what I was trying to do this morning," said Shay.

"Yes, but clearly you were ineffective at it. Probably because you never drank any coffee. It's a well-known fact caffeine improves deductive reasoning."

"Is that so?"

"Yes," I said. "It's hard to come to brilliant conclusions when you're asleep. Ergo, it helps."

"I'm not sure that's how causation and causality work."

"You're missing the point," I said. "We should try to view things from Reggie's perspective. Approach his relations with the people on our board from his point of view."

I stood up and paced. "Let's assume Occam was telling the truth about his past with Reg. He grows up in the slums under Occam's wing. Sort of, anyway. Then one day he disappears. He finally shows up several years later working for Drury Arms. We don't know how exactly he weaseled his way in there, but we can assume his particular blend of talents had an influence. And we don't know for sure what sort of con he was running with the manufacturer, but based off what Quinto found this morning with the financials, he was up to no good.

"Then along comes Reggie's interaction with the Talent family. We can assume he met the Talents initially through a work contact, since Big Daddy Talent owns a foundry business. Logically, Reggie must've met Felicity soon after.

"Regardless of whatever con he was running at Drury Arms, he must've realized the Talent fish was the bigger catch. I mean, why settle for a slice of Drury pie when you can eat the entire Talent cake? So, he pretends to fall in love with Felicity Talent, all the while still partaking in his ongoing con with the arms manufacturers.

"Then Occam finds him and threatens him unless he can deliver a shipment of weapons—which he does. We assume that after the delivery is made Occam leaves him alone, yet a few months later, we find Reggie dead with a gaping hole in his chest."

"You kind of glossed over a few things at the end there," said Shay.

"Like what?" I asked. "We're still in the dark regarding most of the details."

"True, but what about the snags regarding Reginald's marriage. We know he signed a prenuptial agreement—"

"Which he most likely was in the process of trying to get annulled."

"Possibly," said Shay. "But he signed it nonetheless. And you forget he told Felicity he wanted to elope. That still doesn't make any sense."

"It makes sense if he knew he was in danger, which means Reggie must've known his killer. But it doesn't help us figure out who it was."

I stared at the corkboard and snapped my fingers, my mind racing through various possibilities.

"It's no use," I said. "We've still got too many holes in this piece of cheese. We need a few more tangibles before we can patch this thing together."

"Yeah? Then maybe we can help."

40

This time it was Rodgers who'd snuck up on me from behind, but Quinto didn't trail him by far. The pair must've been trading notes on how to get the drop on me.

"I need to buy you guys some clogs or something," I said.

Rodgers gave me a look.

"Never mind," I said. "You manage to find that Wally character?"

"Your accountant?" said Rodgers. "Yeah, we found him at the smithy. He about had a stroke when he saw Quinto again. He was shaking and blubbering from the get-go. When we mentioned we needed to bring him in for questioning, he literally fainted."

"I slapped him around a bit, but the guy was *out*," said Quinto. "We couldn't wake him until we got back here and administered some smelling salts."

"You slapped him around?" I asked. "You sure you didn't give the poor guy a concussion? There's a rash of those going around, apparently."

"I was gentle," said Quinto, grinning.

"So, did the little dude have anything interesting to say?"

"As a matter of fact, he did—once we were able to settle him down enough to understand him, that is." Rodgers eyed his partner. "Quinto, you want to grab some chairs?"

The big guy nodded. He brought over a pair from his and Rodgers' desks, and they both sat.

Rodgers started. "So we got Mr. Fry into one of the interrogation rooms. The dark, dreary one downstairs. *Someone* had already taken the good one upstairs."

"Don't look at me like that," I said. "There's no sign-up sheet. Those rooms are first-come, first-served."

"Yeah," said Rodgers. "Anyway. We got Mr. Fry situated—conscious but blubbering. We could barely make heads or tails of what he was saying, he was stuttering so bad. That's when Quinto accused him of doctoring his books. And wouldn't you know it? Being threatened sobered the guy up."

"To be fair," said Quinto, "I think he's one of those guys who's only comfortable in his work. Numbers make sense to him. The rest of the world doesn't. That's probably why he got so darn upset when we accused him of tampering with those records. It's *his* math."

"Yeah, you're probably right," said Rodgers. "Regardless, Walter was very defensive. Said we didn't know what we were talking about. Said we'd made a mistake. Said he'd never mess his summations up."

"So I asked him to explain the discrepancy between his own records and the bank's," said Quinto. "Wally claimed he had no idea what I was talking about. So I showed him the bank statement from this morning. The guy's eyes about popped out of his head. He was dumbfounded. Genuinely so. Wouldn't you say, Rodgers?"

His partner nodded. "Yeah. I don't think there's any question his reaction was sincere. The little guy had no idea Drury Arms was on the verge of bankruptcy."

"Hold on," said Shay. "You're sure Walter wasn't aware of the missing funds?"

"Well, about as sure as we can be going off expressions and body language," said Rodgers. "You get a pretty good feeling for who's telling the truth after doing this for as many years as we have."

"Alright," said Shay. "So if Mr. Fry wasn't involved—and I'll assume he's at least halfway competent—then how is it he never noticed Drury Arms' bank accounts were nearly dry?"

"As it turns out," said Quinto, "Mr. Drury uses a courier service to deliver shipping invoices, contracts, and other documents to and from his office. They deliver his bank statements, too. Even though Mr. Fry is the accountant for Drury Arms, he hadn't physically visited the bank in years."

"So let me guess," I said, "the bank statements Walter received via courier—they were all forged?"

"We think so," said Rodgers. "Probably every single one since Reginald started working there."

"So that cinches it, doesn't it?" said Shay. "That was Reginald's con. He orchestrated the new deals, and instead of depositing the money in the bank, he took it for himself. Then, he doctored the bank statements to make it appear as if the cash had been deposited. If Mr. Drury were to have found out..." Shay whistled.

"Hold that thought," said Quinto. "After we showed Wally the bank statements, he asked to see the rest of the files he'd brought me. I'd already gone through them and hadn't found anything, so I figured what the heck? And wouldn't you know it, the little guy noticed something on the shipping invoices.

"For legal reasons, Drury Arms can't deliver weapons shipments themselves. Not that they would for international deliveries anyway—it's too expensive. So they use an official bonded carrier. They transport the weapons to one of the bonded carrier's warehouses in the dock district, and that carrier takes it from there. But Wally said the addresses on the invoices were wrong. It was subtle. Same street, just a different number, with only two digits in the addresses swapped."

"Interesting," I said. "So those were forged, too?"

"Probably," said Rodgers. "But here's the thing. The mail that gets delivered to Drury Arms via courier is housed in a communal closet on the main floor. Anyone has access to it, so Reginald could've easily swapped forged bank statements for real ones. But the invoices are a different story. Mr. Drury writes the invoices himself, signs them, and gives them to Wally to be double-checked. This happens throughout the week as orders are processed. But the courier doesn't come by to pick them up until Friday. So Wally stores them in one of his filing cabinets until the courier arrives.

"Now, Wally claims to keep his office locked at all times, under direct orders from Thurmond Drury. We asked Wally if anyone else has a key to his office, and he claimed Mr. Drury is the only one. Also claimed he's real careful with his own key—almost to the level of paranoia. Keeps the only copy on a chain around his neck at all times."

I tapped my fingers on my temple. "So...what? Are we supposed to think Thurmond Drury's behind this? That he broke into his own accountant's office and modified his invoices? Why would Drury tamper with documents he already signed and approved?"

"It probably wasn't him," offered Shay. "Reginald was the accomplished forger, not Thurmond Drury. And we know he used to steal things for Occam Silvervein. He must've broken in and doctored the invoices."

I grunted. Something about the notion didn't sit right with me. We'd found weapons, drugs, and forgery supplies at Reggie's place—but not lock picks.

"Well," said Rodgers. "We should know who did the deed soon enough. We sent the forged bank statements and modified shipping invoices to a handwriting expert, along with the rest of the documents we found at Reginald's place and a memo from Drury to Wally. Whether it was Reginald or Thurmond Drury who doctored those files, we'll know."

"Good thinking," I said.

"We did get one more useful piece of information out of Mr. Fry, though," said Quinto. "You know all those fat contracts Reginald scored for Drury Arms? The contracts that were supposed to have been cashed into the Drury accounts, but never were? Well, they may have bankrupted Thurmond Drury, but Mr. Drury's suppliers still got paid. And for every single one of those contracts, Drury Arms used the same metals supplier—a local foundry conglomerate." Quinto raised his eyebrows at me. "Want to guess which one?"

Someone lit a candle in the dark recesses of my brain.

"That wouldn't be the one owned by Charles Talent, now would it?" I asked.

Quinto nodded.

The candle's tiny flame roared into a giant bonfire.

Shay gave me a sideways look. Maybe she noticed the smoke pouring from my ears. "Wait... You don't think that—"

"Actually, I do think that," I said. "Rodgers, go talk to the Captain. Get a warrant for Persnickety Blaze—"

"*Perspicacious* Blaze," said Shay.

"Yeah, whatever," I said. "Rodgers, get the warrant and meet us at the fire mage's place."

Rodgers gave me a look of confusion. "What? You want me to get a warrant for Charles Talent? Not Thurmond Drury?"

"That's what I said, isn't it?"

Rodgers threw up his hands. "How am I supposed to justify that to the Captain without solid evidence? Or at least a reasonable theory?"

"Use your imagination," I said. "Pretend the Captain's a young girl and charm him. Either that, or use your head and present him with a solid argument. Quinto, come with us. Before we stop at the Talent mansion, I want to make a pit stop at a warehouse a certain dwarf told me about. I want your muscle along just in case."

I used the blaze in my head as kindling to light a fire under everyone's rears. I slipped my coat on, stopping only to check for Daisy, and headed for the door.

"I hope you know what you're doing," said Shay as we left.

"You, me, and the Captain makes three," I said. "But I've got a good feeling about this. Just follow me and let's see where it goes."

Shay and Quinto exchanged looks, but I didn't let their skepticism stop me.

41

We elected to walk to the warehouse, partly because it was nearby and partly because there was no way Quinto would've fit in a rickshaw with me and my partner. The big guy was a handcart driver's worst nightmare. At least he tipped well.

The address Occam provided us with led to a commercial district southwest of the Pearl. Most of the city's manufacturing resided east of the Earl, but a good amount of more service-oriented businesses called the west side home. Within a three mile radius of the Pearl, a keen-eyed observer could find everything from banks to greengrocers to bordellos, though not all on the same block.

Rather, each neighborhood was specialized. Banks gathered on 1st, whorehouses on Flatley. Around my apartment, pipe fitters abounded. My grandmother would've said birds of a feather flock together. I tend to think more cynically. Price fixing is *so* much easier when your collusion partners are within earshot.

The warehouse we were looking for hid within a colony of drapers, although a few haberdasheries had snuck in and made themselves comfortable. Walking down the street was like navigating through a foreign bazaar. Swatches of brightly-dyed calico, tartan flannel, and thick- and fine-ridged corduroy spanned the street overhead. Vendors hawked finer fabrics such as silk and lace from the confines of their shops where those with quick fingers would be less likely to make off with the goods.

I pushed through a hanging wall of army green gabardine and found our destination. To call the place a warehouse was a bit of a reach. Four storage lockers with sheet metal roller doors, each about twice as wide as a set of outstretched arms, stared at me from the side of a four-story brick tower. I stared back. Reginald's locker, as indicated to us by the head Razor, sat third from the left. A nice fat padlock clutched the latch closed.

"Huh," I said.

Even though I'd burned shoe leather getting here, Shay and Quinto trailed me by only a few paces. Quinto held the green cloth aside for my partner before letting it fall behind him.

"What is it?" asked Shay.

I scratched my head. "Well...I was expecting something else, I guess."

"You thought it'd be bigger?" said Quinto.

"Well, yeah, for one thing," I said. I gazed toward the sky, absorbing the colorful drapery. "It's also not where I expected it to be. I mean, does this look like the sort of spot you'd hold a clandestine meeting to swap illicit arms?"

Quinto raised a finger as if to say something, but Shay beat him to the punch.

"Actually, it's perfect, isn't it?" she said. "Occam said Reginald was obsessed with fancy duds. He probably felt right at home surrounded by all these fine fabrics. Plus, it's a commercial district, so it's probably quiet at night. Not to mention all the hanging cloths obscure the place from the cross streets. I'd bet you could smuggle pretty much anything into these lockups at night without anyone being the wiser."

I stared at my partner, thumb and forefinger pinching my chin.

"Why are you giving me that look?" she said.

"Nothing. I'm tempted to give you more praise, and I'm trying to figure out what's wrong with me. You want to check me for a fever?"

Shay shrugged and held up her hands. "Really…it's not that hard to figure out."

Quinto patted her on the shoulder. "Don't worry about Daggers, Detective. He exhibits these idiot savant-like qualities sometimes. He's capable of great conclusions, but he usually doesn't have any idea how he reaches them."

"The idiot savant in me doesn't know if that's an insult or a compliment, Quinto," I said. "Now come on, help me get this padlock off."

Quinto and I crowded around the lockup's latch.

"You wouldn't happen to have a key, now, would you?" said Quinto.

"No. I was hoping you could chew it off," I said.

Quinto glared at me. "You know, if you'd given us a bit more time at the precinct, I would've grabbed bolt cutters."

"Hindsight is better than foresight—or so I've heard. You can talk to my partner to see how true that is."

Shay snorted.

"Just give me that nightstick of yours," said Quinto.

"Daisy? My one and only love? You'll treat her nicely, won't you?"

Quinto made the universal grabby hands gesture. I reluctantly handed over my hardened steel lady friend.

Quinto took a swipe at the lock, but Daisy clanged off the steel, belting out a vibrating ring.

"Come on big guy," I said. "Put some muscle into it."

"You know, that's not a bad idea..."

Quinto rammed Daisy in-between the lock and the shackle. He squatted down and gripped her hard. He then hopped and drove the full force of his body down into his grip. The lock gave, but only a smidge. Quinto repeated the dance maneuver twice more before the lock lost its will to live. It sheared in half with a grinding pop.

Quinto handed Daisy back and dusted off his hands. I inspected my love. Luckily, she'd survived with barely more than a dent. I stroked her, assuring her that evil Uncle Quinto wouldn't hurt her anymore.

Shay was giving me one of her looks again. "You're weird, you know that?"

"You're too young to understand the kind of love that can exist between a man and his truncheon."

"Right... Whatever."

"Are you lovebirds done squawking?" said Quinto. "'Cause I'm interested in seeing what's in here."

"Alright," I said. "Everyone hold onto your butts. We don't want to get knocked over by whatever's in there."

"'Hold onto your butts?'" said Shay. "Where in the world do you come up with this stuff?"

"Seriously?" I said. "You've never heard—? Oh, never mind. Quinto, open the door."

42

I braced myself for something spectacular. Quinto threw open the roller shutter, sending it clanging along its guide rail. I stepped into the lockup, expecting to find a vicious arsenal and instead found...

Nothing.

"It's empty," I said. If nothing else, I'm a master at stating the obvious.

I stepped into the storage locker, which ran about a half dozen paces back before ending in a wall of shiny metal slats. The locker enticed me about as much as an empty mug of beer and had roughly the same long-term appeal. It held nothing but a few dead leaves, a thin layer of dust, and my crushed expectations.

I crouched to inspect the dust for prints, trying to act like a supernaturally gifted detective out of a cheap dime novel, but I don't think I fooled anyone. There was nothing on the floor except for scuffs and smudges.

I stood and turned to my partner. "I don't suppose you're feeling anything coming on about now? Maybe some mystical foresight into past events or a fleeting image of the threads of time?"

Shay smushed her lips together and shrugged.

"Right now I'd settle for anything," I said. "Some déjà vu, maybe. Even a wicked case of indigestion that leads to portentous hallucinations would do the trick."

"Sorry," said Shay. "You know I can't control how it works. What exactly were you expecting to find here anyway?"

"The weapons," I said.

"What weapons? You mean the ones Occam hauled off from here? The ones we found littered all over his underground dope lab?"

"No," I said. "Not *those* weapons. The *other* weapons."

"What other weapons?" asked Quinto.

I eyed my partner and my old friend. "Really? I can't be the only one who sees this."

I got a couple blank looks in response.

"Doesn't it strike either of you as odd that Reggie, a slum rat born and bred in the Erming, was able to broker arms deals with all sorts of disparate entities, including several foreign commonwealths? That's not exactly easy. You need contacts to do that. High level contacts. Contacts that people from the Erming don't have."

I paced as I talked. "We assumed Reginald forged those bank statements to hide the fact that he stole the contract money. It made sense because that's what con men steal—money. But what if there was no money to steal? What if the contracts never existed? What if Reggie faked everything? The signed contracts, the bank statements, the shipping invoices, the receipts. Reggie's real talent was in forging, not theft. What if his con wasn't to steal money from Mr. Drury, but to steal weapons? In the right hands, weapons are as good as gold. Takes time to sell them, of course, and you have to know the right people, but coming from the Erming, those are the kinds of contacts Reggie might've had. The only problem is, he would've needed a place to store the weapons. A place like this."

Quinto scratched his head. "That's a pretty good theory, Daggers. Except for one problem—there's no weapons here."

"I know. I hate it when that happens!" I slammed my fist into the metal slats at the back of the locker.

They rattled.

"That's odd," I said. "Aren't most walls a little more...firm than that?"

I pounded again, lower on the wall, and again the wall vibrated. I searched around the seams of the metal slats looking for a handle or something to grab hold of, but I couldn't find anything.

Quinto walked over, coming shoulder to shoulder with me in the lockup.

"Here," he said. "Let's try pushing on it with our palms and lifting at the same time. I'll take this side, you take that one. On three."

He counted, and on his mark we lifted.

Wouldn't you know it—the wall slid up and back, rolling off along another guide rail like the one holding the shutter in front. Behind it stretched a cavernous, unlit room, but enough light filtered in from the street to illuminate part of its contents.

Piles of weapons, stacked to the ceiling. Hundreds of swords and daggers, axes and hatchets, maces, halberds, flails, and more. Enough to kill a man in just about every way imaginable, as long as that death somehow involved a piece of steel.

"Wow," said Quinto.

"Wow is right," I said. "Although I think you left your thought unfinished. Perhaps you meant to say, 'Wow, I can't believe how incredibly right Detective Jake Daggers was about the weapons thing.'"

Quinto turned back from the dark crevasse to speak to my partner. "In case you hadn't noticed, he likes to gloat."

"Oh, I'd noticed," said Shay. She smirked at me as she rose an eyebrow.

"Quinto, slide that door back down," I said. "We'll have to send an entire squadron of bluecoats over here later to cart off this mess. Even with your wide frame along, I doubt we'd make more than a dent in that pile by ourselves."

Quinto obliged.

"So, what now, oh master of deduction?" asked Shay.

"Now?" I said. "Now, we go dispense some justice. And maybe stop for lunch along the way. But mostly the justice part."

43

Shay thought I was kidding, but I never kid when it comes to lunch. I was hungry, gosh darn it, and I needed food.

I insisted we stop at a place called Loaders on our trip to the Talent mansion. Loaders was a sandwich shop, and true to their name, they loaded their hoagies with everything under the sun. Some of their sandwiches were so big they threatened to eat *your* face as opposed to the other way around. That suited me just fine. I was regretting my morning breakfast bypass. By the time we got our food, my stomach was grumbling worse than my ninety-year-old arthritic grandfather on the eve of a thunderstorm.

I got the Loaders version of a muffuletta, which contained no less than four distinct cured pork products, sliced thin, covered in melted cheese. Quinto ordered the special, a chicken pesto panini that tickled my nose with hints of basil, parsley, and pine nuts. Even my svelte partner partook in the feast. She ordered a hefty grinder with real, honest-to-goodness dead animal bits inside. Perhaps my particular style of gastronomy was rubbing off on her.

Quinto tore into his sub, but he still found enough free mouth space to complain. "Rodgers isn't going to be happy we made him wait."

I swallowed a hot mouthful of my delicious pig medley. "What are you talking about? He probably hasn't even left the station yet. You know how tough it is to pull a warrant out of the Captain's crevices."

Quinto shuddered at my choice of language. "Maybe you're right. Even so, he won't be happy we got lunch without him."

"I'll buy you a mint before we leave," I said. "Rodgers'll never know."

"You know," said Shay, "you still haven't explained how you intend to tie this whole mess to Mr. Talent."

"I'm saving the explanation for later when it'll have greater dramatic effect."

"Or, you're making things up as you go along," said Shay.

"Trust me," I said. "I've got a good gut feeling about this. And as far as I'm concerned, that's about as concrete a lead as one of your thread-filled visions."

Shay gave me one of those looks only women are good at, with her head cocked to one side and her lips pursed. I ignored her and wolfed down the rest of my sandwich.

After lunch, we high-tailed it to the Talent estate. We found Rodgers pacing back and forth in front of the gate, an envelope displaying the official seal of justice clutched in his left hand.

"Where the heck have you guys been?" he said. "I've been waiting here for the last half hour."

"Um..." I glanced at my partners in crime. "We got held up at the warehouse. Place was harder to find than we'd anticipated."

"Oh." Rodgers sniffed the air. "Does anybody else smell bacon?"

"Hmm?" said Shay.

"What?" said Quinto.

"I think you're losing it," I told Rodgers. "Is that our warrant?"

Rodgers lifted the envelope. "Sure is. Had to sweet-talk the Captain, but I got it. We'd better find something good here, though, otherwise the Captain's liable to flay the four of us alive. He granted this on what I'd generously refer to as shaky evidence, so it's his ass on the line if anything goes south."

"Well then, we'd better find something incriminating." I motioned toward the mansion. "Shall we?"

We pushed past the lemon-faced guard at the gate and pounded on the front door. Jeeves was none too happy to see that Shay and I had returned, or that we'd brought company for the return visit. I asked if the man of the house was in. The butler confirmed he was. Before he could object to our intrusion, I stormed off toward the fire mage's den, my personal goon squad in tow.

I burst into the elder Talent's tower office like a tornado of authority and venom and started barking orders. "Steele—search the office for any traces of thermite or other similar powders. Quinto—check the desk. See if you can find any hidden connections between Mr. Talent and Reginald. Rodgers—over there, behind that telescope...is that a safe? Let's get it open. I want to see what's inside."

The master of flames himself, old Chucky Talent, who'd been seated at his desk as we entered, stood up in a rage. Color bloomed in his cheeks, burning all the brighter next to his silvery hair. "What in the world is the meaning of this, Detective?"

Jeeves stumbled in behind us. "I'm sorry, sir. I couldn't stop them. They wouldn't listen."

I strolled over to Mr. Talent's desk, meeting him eye to eye. I handed him the envelope.

"This," I told him, "is a warrant for us to search the premises for any information regarding the death of your son-in-law-to-be, Mr. Reginald Powers. Feel free to have a look."

Charles raked his finger under the seal, flipped open the letter, and scanned his eyes across the page. If anything, the color in his cheeks reached a deeper shade of red.

"Detective Daggers, I assure you that—"

Rodgers butted in. "Mr. Talent? My apologies, but I'm going to have to see what's in this safe."

Charles shot Rodgers and me a heated glance before turning toward his strongbox with a growl. The safe was a solid, steel-bodied affair with a single dial combination lock. Mr. Talent gave the dial a few spins, cranked the lever, and cracked open the door before turning back to face me. His eyes smoldered with a fiery wrath, hinting at the untold powers swirling beneath his skin. I held my ground.

"I don't know what you're trying to accomplish here, Detective," he said with an ill-restrained fury, "but my patience with you is wearing quite thin. I tried to be as forthright with you as possible during our last meeting, yet here I am, being treated in a manner quite unbefitting of someone in my station."

"Oh, really?" I said. "And how is it that in your forthrightness you somehow forgot to mention your business arrangement with Mr. Powers? The mutual benefits you received from his contracts? Don't you think that might've been pertinent to our investigation? Let me tell you what I think, Mr. Talent. I think you know something about Mr. Powers that you're not telling us. And I intend to find out what."

"Be my guest," said Mr. Talent. "Search for something incriminating that I assure you doesn't exist. But know this. I know some very accomplished, very tenacious lawyers, and should your little warrant here prove to be unfounded, I'm sure they'll find a way to—"

"Hey, Daggers!" Rodgers spared me from learning what sort of misery awaited me if I was wrong. "Come look at this."

I eased my way around the fire mage and sidled up next to Rodgers, who stood by the safe, flipping through some papers.

"You find anything?" I asked.

"You could say that. These are all letters from Reginald. And not just any letters. Extortion letters. Reginald was blackmailing Mr. Talent."

"WHAT?" bellowed Talent. "That's preposterous!"

I hid my smirk. It seemed like a poor and potentially dangerous time to whip it out. I didn't particularly want to get burned to a crisp in a fit of rage.

"Charles Blaze Talent, the third," I said, "turn around and place your hands behind your back. You're under arrest for the murder of Reginald Powers."

Mr. Talent ground his teeth. For a moment the heat seemed to leach out of the air and flow into the stone-faced man before me. His eyes burned with a fiery passion. I sent a hasty silent prayer to the gods for mercy. I had no desire to experience what toast felt like.

Apparently, the gods heard my prayers.

Felicity Talent burst up the stairs and into the room. Her hair was wilder than before and her eyes even puffier than I remembered. She bore a look of pain, shock, and confusion, as if the sensations had been boiled together and slathered over her face with an off-set spatula.

A bare two steps behind Felicity was her beautiful friend with the frumpy name—Gretchen. She bore the same look of horror as Felicity, but it couldn't quite keep her lusty smolder at bay. I suppressed the urge to howl, but I didn't have to make quite as concerted an effort as the first time we'd met. As it turns out, the threat of being turned into a meat kebab puts a damper on my libido.

"Father!" said Felicity. "What is this? What's going on?"

Exposure to his daughter's emotional distress appeared to cool the resident fire mage, both literally and figuratively. The warmth flowed back into the space around me as he addressed his daughter.

"Now, sweetheart. Don't worry. I'm sure this is all some sort of cruel misunderstanding. I'll accompany the detectives back to their station so we can discuss what exactly it is they think they've uncovered. In the meantime, contact my lawyer. Tell him to meet me at the precinct. And for the love of the gods, take poor Gretchen home. She's a mess!"

It was true. The busty babe I'd come to know quite well in my fantasies had started to sob uncontrollably. She muttered things along the lines of 'This can't be happening...' and 'Why, gods, why?'.

Felicity wrapped her arms around her and the pair cried in tandem, belting out the world's saddest duet.

Charles Talent turned to face me. "Detective, I'd appreciate it if we could avoid handcuffs. I give you my word I won't cause any trouble. Quite honestly the cuffs wouldn't do you a whole lot of good anyway. Now, if we could please go? I'd like to settle this matter as quickly as possible."

Who was I to argue with an offer like that? I gave the geezer a nod, motioned my fellow detectives out, and got a move on.

44

"I still can't believe you went to Loaders without me. You know how much I love their sandwiches."

Rodgers glared at me from behind his desk, a limp turkey wrap clenched in his mitts.

"Every red-blooded male loves sandwiches," I said from across the office. "It comes as a package deal with the plumbing."

"Exactly," said Rodgers with a point of his index finger. "Which makes your deception that much more egregious. You owe me, bud."

"Add it to my tab. I already owe you a beer."

"That you do." Rodgers took another bite of his wrap and made a face. "Ugh. I could use one right about now to be honest."

"Don't let any of that seditious talk reach the Captain's ears," I said. "You know how he feels about drinking on the job."

"I'm pretty sure he makes an exception when the drinking is a direct response to headaches you create, Daggers." Rodgers flashed me a smile. "In fact, I'm pretty sure he has a flask in his desk earmarked specifically for days where you're particularly ornery."

"Ornery is my middle name," I said. "Would've been Sassy if I'd been born a girl."

I leaned back in my chair and turned my eyes to the documents we'd gathered at the mage's house. While I'd expected to discover some sort of incriminating evidence at the Talent palace, even I had to admit stumbling across a blackmail letter was extremely fortuitous. I scanned my eyes across the page again to be sure I'd absorbed the full meaning of the written word, as well as the unwritten intent behind it:

Charles,

You know I've always admired your shrewd business sense. You put matters of commerce above personal relationships, a fortitude many others in your position don't possess. That courage is what allowed our previous arrangement to flourish as it did, despite its somewhat dubious legal standing.

Therefore, I'm surprised you're being so steadfast in your opinion regarding the prenuptial agreement. In our last discussion, I thought I'd made it clear how dissolution of said agreement would be beneficial for both of us. For me, financially, and for you, legally.

Perhaps I wasn't clear enough. Please find enclosed a small sampling of the sorts of records that might accidentally be leaked should you fail to comply with my request.

Please do not take it personally. After all, it's just business.

—R. P.

The 'records' referred to in the letter covered the entire left half of my desk. Financial documents similar to those we'd requisitioned from Drury Arms. Collusion agreements between Reginald and Mr. Talent. Signed affidavits connecting Perspicacious Blaze to the weapons we'd uncovered in the warehouse hidden among the drapers. Some, if not most, of the documents were undoubtedly forged, but they hinted at the truth—a truth Mr. Talent had clearly not wanted revealed. A truth that had plucked Reginald from the cusp of unparalleled luxury and transported him down the river to meet his maker.

Shay and Quinto walked up as I perused the files.

"Your boy's all ready, Daggers," said Quinto.

"You've got the Talent geezer set up in an interrogation room?" I asked.

"Yeah," said Shay. "We put him in the brightly lit one. We didn't think slighting him by giving him the basement suite was a particularly smart idea."

"No kidding." We hadn't seen even a hint of Blaze's true powers, but based on the heat in his eyes when I accused him of murder, I didn't want to. "His lawyer here yet?"

"Just arrived," said Quinto.

"Great." I eyed my partner. "You ready to do this?"

Shay raised an eyebrow. "We're going in there? Just like that? No letting him sweat it out for a half hour?"

"Perspicacious Blaze isn't some small time dope dealer. He's a shrewd businessman who's used to negotiating. He won't crack under bright lights and mirrors. Besides, he's already lawyered up. Best to confront him with the facts and see what he has to say."

"So no good cop, bad cop routine this time?" Shay asked.

I shook my head. "No, we'll play it straight. Just follow my lead. You'll be fine."

Shay gave me one of those looks I'd come to associate with her suspicion.

"I'm not pulling your leg," I said as I stood. "Now come on."

Rodgers smiled from his desk as we walked by. "We'll be waiting with a fire extinguisher outside the door in case something goes wrong."

"Don't lie," I said. "You've been eyeing my desk for years. You'd love to have me gone."

"And miss out on the beers you owe me?" Rodgers called. "Hah! You can't escape me that easy, Daggers!"

I heard Shay chuckle. I couldn't help but snicker a little myself. For all their quirks, Rodgers and Quinto could always be counted on for a smile or two, but their timing in this instance wasn't ideal. My partner and I were about to question a fire mage who could convert our entire station to flaming rubble if he so wished, and greeting him with a bucketful of laughs probably wasn't the most appropriate way to engage him.

Thankfully, the gravity of the situation exerted its weight on both of us by the time we arrived at the interrogation room.

"You ready?" I asked.

Shay nodded.

I grabbed the knob to the chamber and twisted.

45

harles Talent sat at the interrogation table, hands clasped in front of him like the two halves of a vise. His jaw, like the rest of his face, appeared as if carved from stone, and his eyes smoldered with restrained anger.

A gray-suited lawyer with perfectly manicured designer stubble and a flashy pink tie sat to Talent's right, a glossy, chocolate leather briefcase propped on the table before him. The man started to lawyer me and Shay before we'd made it halfway through the door.

"Detectives Daggers? Steele?" he said. "I represent the legal council of Sir Charles Blaze Talent, the third. I'll begin by informing you that I've already fully advised my client of his judicial rights, including but not limited to his right to remain silent, his right against forcible self-incrimination, his right to due process, and your judicial mandate to present evidence and charges against him within twenty-four hours of arrest. Otherwise, he must legally be released from custody, upon which he cannot be re-apprehended for the same crime without—"

"What's your name?" I asked stubble face as I sat. Shay took the seat to my left.

"Brian Trustmont, esquire, of Merkel, Ernst, Trustmont, and Figs."

"Great," I told him. "Now why don't you invoke your own right to silence and shut the hell up. I'm not interested in what you have to say. I came to have a chat with Mr. Talent."

The lawyer stiffened like a certain male organ when presented with a firm female behind. When next he spoke, his tone was less accusatory, but also a good few degrees colder.

"You're free to talk, Detective, but I don't believe my client is feeling particularly chatty at the moment."

I swept my eyeballs back and forth between the lawyer and Mr. Talent.

"That's alright," I said. "As it turns out, I'm in more of a storytelling mood myself. Why don't I tell you a story and you listen? It's a story about a man by the name of Reginald Powers."

The lawyer rolled his eyes and snorted. I settled my eyes firmly upon the granite-faced fire mage and dove in.

"Reginald Powers was born and raised in the Erming, but he was far from your typical slum rat. He was a smart guy. Clever and calculating, but also personable. Sure, he had sticky fingers like a lot of the other urchins down there. But his fingers were good for more than just filching. His fingers had a gift. A gift...for deception.

"Reginald knew he could do better than the Erming. So he left. Looked around for the right landing spot, and eventually he found one. A local armory by the name of Drury Arms. Now, he could've worked hard—tried to climb the corporate ladder like any normal Tom, Dick, or Harry—but that wasn't Reginald's style. He had other plans.

"He landed a job where he got paid by commission negotiating contracts for arms. The money would've been good if he had the knack for it, and as it turned out, he did. Reggie scored tons of contracts. More than Mr. Drury could've hoped for. There was only one small problem.

"None of Reginald's pacts existed. They were all faked—forged with the help of Reggie's particular talent. The signed contracts? Bogus. The money to pay for them? Nonexistent. But the weapons contracted for? Well, those were real. Mr. Drury's armory was churning them out in droves. Reginald could squirrel them away in a safe place and make a killing selling them bit-by-bit on the black market. And that's where the second character in this particular tale enters. Reginald met you, Mr. Talent."

I expected some sort of reaction at that, but I got none, so I continued.

"I'm sure the meeting was probably mere happenstance. You're the largest metals supplier in the city, after all. It only makes sense you two would run across each other sooner or later. But then Reggie met your daughter—your young, single, only daughter, who was in line to inherit a very, *very* large sum of money in the not too distant future. And clever old Reginald thought to himself, 'Well, if one con is good, two must be twice as nice.' Besides, you're easily ten times as rich as Mr. Drury.

"And so he courted your daughter. Got her to fall in love with him. You, being the suspicious, cagey old geezer you are, naturally questioned his motives. So you had him sign a prenuptial agreement—which he did, but only grudgingly, to avoid suspicion. He pored over the agreement, trying to find a way out, but it was ironclad. Perhaps he asked you explicitly about annulling it, so you threatened to kick him out and expose him as a fraud to your daughter.

"Well, Reggie didn't like that, so he figured, why not combine his two cons using his natural talent for forgery. He prepared a series of documents showing in great detail how it was you, not him, who'd masterminded the actions at Drury Arms—documents that showed just how lucrative all of Mr. Drury's deals had been for you personally. And Reginald used the documents to blackmail you, all in an effort to get the prenuptial agreement dissolved.

"You refused to be intimidated. But Reginald wouldn't quit, would he? Kept threatening? And you couldn't go to the police over the whole matter because the truth fell a little too close to home, didn't it? You knew Reggie's scheme, and you willingly took part in it for financial gain. And to complicate matters, your daughter was truly in love with Reginald. Finding out the truth about him, and about you, would've crushed her—made her lose trust in you forever. So you did the only thing you could to protect yourself and your family from Mr. Powers' threats and lies. You killed him. In cold blood, the night of the charity ball, behind the stage."

The silence stretched for several seconds after I finished my soliloquy. The tension in the room hung like a fog, sticky and thick. Perspicacious Blaze hadn't so much as blinked during my speech. I wondered if rage-induced paralysis was another of his magical abilities and if he hadn't managed to infect all of us with it when eventually the lawyer cleared his throat and spoke.

"Well, that's certainly an interesting *story*, Detective. But as I'm sure you're well aware, we deal with facts and evidence in the judicial realm, not fictitious tales."

Despite my earlier instructions to avoid the good cop, bad cop dynamic, my plucky partner apparently decided I'd been too nice. She leaned forward, jaw clenched, and gave the lawyer the stink eye—a look I'd only seen levied on me. I had to admit, it was pretty effective.

"Detective Daggers was being uncommonly generous in calling it a story. By his own admission, Mr. Charles Talent was at the crime scene during the time of Reginald Powers' murder, and the blackmail documents we found in his safe provide a clear, demonstrable motive for Mr. Talent to have committed the crime. That's not a story. Those are facts. And we have the evidence to back them up."

Chucky broke his solemn vow of silence. "I'd never seen those documents before in my life until you unearthed them."

Stubble-face was quick to react. "You don't have to answer any of their questions. Don't let them provoke you."

"I know," said Mr. Talent, silencing his lawyer with his fiery gaze. "But I have a right to defend myself as well as stay silent, don't I Mr. Trustmont?"

Appropriately cowed, the lawyer sat back in his chair and shut his trap. Apparently even hard-assed, filthy rich oligarchs like Charles Talent secretly detested lawyers, too—even if they were useful to their bottom lines.

I rummaged around in my coat pocket and pulled out one of the blackmail documents we'd taken from the safe—a particularly damning piece of evidence tying together Reggie's faked contracts and Charles' own supplier's deal with Drury Arms. I laid it on the table and pushed it towards Mr. Talent with an extended index finger.

"So, let me get this straight," I said. "Your argument for why you couldn't possibly be Reginald Powers' murderer is that you've never before seen the blackmail documents we found in *your safe?*"

Charles rested his eyes on me, eyes that were fierce yet also tired. "Yes."

I sucked air in through my teeth. "Hmm. Color me unimpressed, Mr. Talent. That's the second time today I've heard the 'I've never seen that' argument, and yours is about as convincing as the one I got from the dope-addled, tattooed dwarven gangbanger." That statement raised an eyebrow but provoked little other reaction. "So you didn't place those documents in your safe yourself?"

"No."

"Who did then? Your butler? Little pixies? Fire motes dancing on the hot winds of change?"

"I don't know," said Mr. Talent.

We held each other's gazes. Surprisingly, I won the standoff.

Charles Talent sighed. "Look, Detective Daggers, I can't believe it's so difficult for you to see what's going on here."

"You have an alternative theory?" I turned to my partner, stuck out my bottom lip, and spread out my hands. "What do you think, Steele? Should we hear his grand insights?"

"Yes, let's," she said.

"Isn't it obvious?" said the fire mage. "I'm not being blackmailed. I'm being framed. I've suspected as much ever since you first revealed how Mr. Powers met his demise. Clearly someone staged his death so as to appear that a conjurer of fire magic killed him."

I raised an eyebrow at the geezer. "And how do you know dear Reginald *wasn't* killed by magic?"

"Please, Detective. If you could prove that, I suspect you would've put me in shackles the instant you discovered it. Not to mention you would've included that particular piece of evidence in your 'story,' as you called it."

"You know, it's interesting you bring that up," I said as I tapped my chin. "Do you know how Reginald actually died, Mr. Talent?"

"No, I don't," he said.

"By a thermite reaction. Do you know what thermite is?"

"Don't patronize me, Detective. Of course I do. We use thermite at the foundry in the purification of certain metal ores. My talent isn't the only intense source of heat we employ."

"So you admit you had ready access to the murder weapon?" I said.

"Anyone at any of my facilities would," said Mr. Talent. "So would anyone at any of the other foundries and smithies in the city. Access to thermite doesn't make me a murderer. Besides, as you were so quick to point out in our first encounter, I'm a fire mage. If I wished to murder Reginald by fire, why would I bother to use as crude a method as thermite?"

"Probably because you knew we'd eventually discover the true cause of his death wasn't magical in nature," I said, "and you assumed that fact would shift suspicion from you to someone else."

"That's wild speculation and you know it," said the gray-suited lawyer.

I sighed and drummed my fingers on the table, refusing to let silence fill the air. "When was the last time you opened your safe, Mr. Talent?"

"Yesterday morning, after you came by."

"And does anyone besides you have the combination to open it?"

"Only my daughter."

Interesting. I pulled on my earlobe. "So...you're going to maintain you'd never seen these documents—" I tapped the one on the table. "—before today, and when you opened your safe yesterday, they weren't there?"

"Yes," he said tersely. "I will maintain that. Because it's the truth."

Shay spoke up again, this time in a smooth, confident tone. "You know something interesting about thermite, Mr. Talent? It requires a rather intense heat source to ignite the reaction—heat that's quite difficult to provide under normal circumstances. Unless the person igniting the thermite happens to be a fire mage."

Charles Talent glared at Shay, the smolder returning to his eyes in full force. "I think I've said all I plan to, detectives. If you wish to pursue your case against me, you'll have to do so with what you currently have at your disposal."

46

After closing the door to the interrogation room, I found a couple of nearby bluecoats and gave them instructions for dealing with the fiery sorcerer. I told them to escort Mr. Talent to our most deluxe holding cell, making sure they understood exactly who they were dealing with. I would've volunteered, but I needed to finalize the casework before sending it off to the DA. I think everyone involved wanted charges filed as soon as possible.

By the time I'd finished talking to the boys, Shay had left. I found her back at her desk, staring at the corkboard's crisscrossing weave of red yarn and thumbtacks.

"You sure had some timely interjections back there." I plopped into my chair.

Shay glanced at me, blushing. "You mean that thermite bit? Sorry. I wasn't trying to get him to stop talking. I thought maybe I could squeeze something else out of him. Some other piece of information we could use."

I waved her off. "Don't sweat it. His jaw was like a steel trap on a timer—it was sure to snap shut sooner or later. You just helped him along, that's all."

Shay chewed her lip. "So, what now?"

"Now you get introduced to the most thrilling part of this profession—paperwork. We'll to need to fill out a 1053B and a 459. You ever done that before?"

Shay gave me a blank look.

"Yeah, I didn't think so. Come on, I'll show you where they are."

I rejoiced in silence. Showing my partner how to fill out the forms would mean more work for me in the short term, but once she knew what i's needed to be dotted and what t's needed to be crossed, I could foist the future paperwork on her. Delegating paperwork was one of the greatest joys of seniority—a joy Griggs had appreciated to its fullest. Now my turn to reap the rewards had finally arrived.

I took Shay on a field trip to the form office. We picked out the proper pages from a wall of wooden dispensers. As we walked back to our desks, I explained the finer points of the 1053B, specifically how it differed from a 1053 and why there wasn't a 1053A.

Shay's eyes glossed over. I couldn't blame her. It was dry stuff. But something suggested to me the bland look she sported on her face wasn't a direct response to my form blather.

"...and so that's why you need a 1053B," I said. "Now, a 1053C, on the other hand, is rare. You only need one of those if you accidentally kill a hobo in the line of duty."

Shay didn't even blink.

"Hey—you want to fill me in on what's going on up there?" I pointed at her head.

Shay startled. "Huh?"

"Were you having one of those *thingies* again?"

Shay pressed a hand to her forehead. "Not this again. I've told you, I only have visions—"

"I didn't say you were," I said. "I said you looked like it. I know you were thinking. What's on your mind?"

Shay looked at me, and I mean *really* looked at me. Her azure blues delved into my gray matter, searching my subconscious for traces of sarcasm or doubt. The look might've staggered lesser men, but I'm made of sterner stuff. Beef and fermented grain, mostly.

Regardless, the part of me that regulates interactions with women realized this was an important moment in our relationship. Shay was looking for something from me. A token of appreciation. A sign I occasionally took things seriously. An affirmation of trust.

"Look, we're partners now," I said. "For better or worse. If you need to say something, go ahead and say it. I'll listen."

Shay sat on the corner of my desk. "Ok." That one short word held more meaning than it had any right to. I'd have to chew on the implications later. "Do you really think Charles Talent is our murderer?"

I pressed my rear into my trusty throne. "The story fits. We've got motive and opportunity, not to mention plenty of evidence. I think we have a strong enough case to convict him."

"You didn't answer my question," said Shay. "Do you think he *killed* Reginald Powers?"

I took a moment to consult with my inner sense of justice. It tended to reside somewhere between my brain and gut—usually closer to the latter. "I'm not sure."

"Doesn't that bother you?" she asked.

I grunted in response. "You clearly have some thoughts nagging at you, so why don't you share?"

"Charles Talent is a smart guy. You can't become as financially successful as he is without possessing a high degree of intelligence. So how is it a guy as smart as he is left a pile of blackmail documents tying him to Reginald's murder in his own safe?"

"Smart people make stupid mistakes when they're stressed," I said. "You see that in this business all the time."

"Yes," said Shay. "I agree. But he knew he was a suspect. You basically accused him of murder yesterday afternoon. Even if he'd forgotten to cut ties with Reginald immediately after the murder, don't you think he would've destroyed the blackmail letters after our first meeting with him? Besides, what about the burnt documents we found in Reginald's apartment? Someone clearly went out of their way to destroy those. If Mr. Talent disposed of the incriminating evidence at Reginald's apartment, why would he have forgotten to do the same with his own? It doesn't make sense."

"Fair point," I said.

"There's more than that, though," said Shay. "You remember how Felicity mentioned Reginald wanted to elope?"

"How could I forget?" I said. "You've mentioned it more than once."

Shay stuck a finger up in the air before her. "Well, if Reginald was trying to blackmail Charles Talent into annulling the prenuptial agreement, why would he try to skip town and marry Felicity before the agreement was dissolved? That doesn't make any sense, either."

"Simple," I said. "He underestimated Mr. Talent. Reginald thought he'd roll over, but Charles pushed back. The encounters got passionate. Violent, maybe. He realized he never should've messed with a fire mage and tried to skip town."

"But to do so before having the agreement annulled would mean he wouldn't inherit any of Talent's money."

I shrugged. "If the choice is between money and your neck, you choose your neck every time."

"But if you're right, Daggers," said Shay, "then why ask Felicity to come along? Why bother continuing to perpetrate the ruse at that point?"

I drummed my fingers on the face of my desk. "You're right. That doesn't make sense."

Shay leaned in toward me. "I have a theory."

Her lean pulled me in like a magnet. I shifted forward in my chair. "Well, go on. Don't leave me hanging."

Shay smiled. "What if Charles Talent was telling us the truth? What if Reginald was in love with Felicity? What if the marriage wasn't a con after all?"

I raised my eyebrows. "You really think Reginald...was *in love?*"

Shay cocked her head at me. "Come on, you're not that jaded, are you? Why not?"

I stood up and threw my arms in the air. "Because it would mean this whole marriage thing was a giant red herring! And it would leave us without any clue as to who killed our dapper dark elf."

"We're not completely in the dark," said Shay.

"Oh, really? You think you know who killed Reggie?"

"Well, it's usually the obvious person, isn't it?"

I furrowed my eyebrows to the best of my ability, inviting the cream of my partner's wit. I'd be damned if I'd missed something obvious.

"You know," she said. "The guy who Rodgers, Quinto, and I all thought you were going to arrest? The other guy who had access to thermite? The guy who probably went into a rage when he found out Reginald had completely ruined him? Thurmond Drury."

"Oh. Right." I stuffed my hands in my pockets, feeling sheepish. "But what about the blackmail letters from Reginald to Talent?"

Shay twisted her lips a mite. "Yeah...that part doesn't totally jive, does it? But maybe Mr. Talent's right. Maybe someone's trying to frame him, and those documents were planted."

I paced back and forth as I mulled over my partner's thoughts. I didn't want to admit it to Shay, but I'd forgotten about Mr. Drury. In my haste to tie together the case's threads, perhaps I'd been too focused on the biggest target.

If Shay was right, and Reginald and Felicity's upcoming wedding was a thing of love and not opportunity, then Thurmond Drury was the only obvious culprit. Perhaps Drury had realized Charles Talent had been the beneficiary of his own loss, and so he'd attempted to frame him for the murder with thermite. It all seemed possible, but something about the theory nagged at the back of my mind—something that didn't fit.

Despite being deep in thought, I heard the clip-clop of approaching footsteps—for once.

47

A woman with short, spiky hair and thin rectangular bifocal glasses approached us, a brown leather attaché case in hand. She wore a mauve pantsuit over her lanky frame, and her stiletto heels knocked on the hard office floor.

"Excuse me...are you detectives Daggers and Steele?" Her voice was formal but not unpleasant.

"Yes." I eyed her. I'd already had to deal with one of Perspicacious Blaze's lawyers, and I had little interest in being badgered by another.

"I'm Annabel Clure of Zaldane and Associates. Detective Rodgers asked me to authenticate some documents for you."

"Oh." I breathed a sigh of relief. "You're the handwriting expert. Rodgers had you looking at the bank statements and shipping invoices, didn't he?"

"That's correct." Ms. Clure set her attaché case down on my desk and snapped the case's clasps open with a pop. She extracted two bank statements and set them on my desk. Next to them she placed a letter of some sort.

"I'm sure your time is as valuable as mine, detectives, so I'll try to be brief. On the right is one of the bank statements you suspect of having been forged. In the center is the official statement obtained by Detective Quinto this morning, and on the left is a reference document from your suspected tamperer, Mr. Powers.

"Given the full spectrum of evidence, I can say with confidence the bank statements represented by the specimen here on the right were, in fact, forged by Mr. Powers. The signals are subtle, as Mr. Powers was clearly an expert at symbolic mimicry, but the weight of the script is identical in the forged statements and in the control."

I wasn't sure I understood everything she said, but I got the gist of it. "Well, that's not really a surprise. What about the invoices?"

Ms. Clure extracted one of the shipping invoices and a memo from Mr. Drury from her attaché case, laying them over the bank statements on the desk.

"Good question." The graphologist pointed at the memo. "If I could draw your attention to this numeral here—the number four. See how the line that composes the upper left quadrant of the number curves in?"

I leaned over the page to look. Shay did the same.

"That's how Mr. Drury scripts his fours. Now take a look at the shipping invoice." Annabel pointed at the address that had been modified. "This number four features a much straighter line in the same quadrant. To the lay eye, it seems a trivial difference, but line curvature is an important trait of writing. This portion of the document was clearly rewritten.

"Now, if we turn our attention to Mr. Powers' handiwork—" Ms. Clure pointed at the reference page. "—we also find a number four. You'll notice how the nose of the four has a slight curl to it, right at the tip. That's a distinctly different feature than seen in the other two documents.

"From analyzing Mr. Powers' work on the bank statements, I can tell he was a highly trained forger. If he'd wanted to match his script to Mr. Drury's, he would've. On the other hand, Mr. Drury's handwriting would have no reason to fluctuate between the memo and the invoice. Overall, the evidence is clear."

I scratched my chin. I hated it when people left things unsaid. "So…"

"The invoices were tampered with, but not by Mr. Powers or Mr. Drury."

"*Say what?*" I peered at Shay. "Does that make any sense to you?"

My partner crossed her arms. "No. If neither Reginald nor Thurmond modified those shipping invoices, then who did?"

Ms. Clure snapped her attaché case shut. "I'm sorry, detectives, but that I don't know. I can guarantee you, however, that it was a third party. If there's nothing else you need of me, I'll be on my way."

"Wait…actually there is one more thing." I dug around in my coat and pulled out the blackmail letter I'd presented to Charles Talent. I unfolded it and handed it over to Ms. Clure. "Is there any chance you can tell us who wrote this letter?"

Annabel scrunched her nose, peering through the bottom portion of her bifocals, scanning her eyes across the page. After a minute she set it on the desk.

"Well, after a cursory examination I can see some telltale stylistic elements of this writing that stand out. For example, the curvature of the crossed portion of the t's and the slope of the f's. I'm working off a limited data set you understand, but upon first glance, I'd hazard to guess this document was written by the same individual who doctored the shipping invoices."

I felt like someone had taken a sledgehammer to the support beams of our case's foundation. The graphologist's testimony was supposed to have confirmed our suspicions, not thrown all of our previous conclusions into question.

I funneled my frustrations into a fierce grumble. "Well, that's just great."

"Pardon?" said Annabel.

"Nothing," I said. "That'll be all. Thanks for your time."

Shay scratched her head as Ms. Clure walked away. "So...if Reginald didn't write those blackmail letters, then I was right—Mr. Talent *is* being framed. But the letters aren't in Mr. Drury's handwriting. So who wrote them?"

Answers eluded me. I desperately needed to mortar the cracks before our entire case collapsed into dust.

"I don't know," I said. "But everything you said about Thurmond Drury still applies. He's the most likely suspect. He had motive to kill Reginald and access to thermite. Just because he didn't fake the blackmail documents himself doesn't mean he didn't commission someone else to do so. I'm going to take a run at him."

"With what?" said Shay. "Even though he seems like an obvious suspect, we don't have any evidence that ties him to the crime."

"Yeah," I said. "But he doesn't know that. I'll go at him hard and see if he breaks. Let's gather up Rodgers and Quinto. They'll want to be a part of this."

48

We found Rodgers and Quinto in the break room. Rodgers swilled coffee while Quinto nursed some horrible, weak concoction I could only assume was tea. Rodgers was still miffed about being left out of the Loaders brigade, so he hemmed and hawed when I asked him and Quinto to tag along to the Drury establishment. He whined about his limp turkey wrap and made vague references to chopped liver. I offered to buy him a nice palate-cleansing kolache, and he changed his tune.

Outside the precinct, we flagged down a herd of rickshaws and rolled our way across the Bridge to the city's east side. A cool breeze wafted off the river and into the cart I shared with Shay, bringing with it brackish smells and hints of coming rains. For the time being though, the afternoon sun held the showers at bay, beating back oncoming clouds with its potent rays.

Most days, I would've appreciated the rickshaw ride for what it was—a chance to decompress and let my mind wander. But my stubborn brain refused to cooperate. Something about Reginald and Mr. Drury picked at the back of my skull like a raccoon stuck between the walls of a house, trying to scratch his way out through the drywall. It drove me bonkers, rendering me less chatty and effervescent than usual.

When we arrived, Drury Arms looked much the same as we'd left it the previous day, with its barbed wire-topped brick wall and jutting smokestacks. Unlike yesterday, however, the chimneys stood calm and quiet. Nary a hint of black smoke emanated from their stacks.

I led my consorts into the lobby where I found the same surly secretary as before sitting behind her desk. She stood as we approached, but I cut her off before she could spout off any sass.

"Thurmond Drury. Where is he?"

"He's in his office," she said. "But—"

"No buts," I said. I whisked past her and pounced onto the grated steel stairs, taking them two at a time. In a grand act of self-control, I held back from kicking down the office door, though I did throw it open hard enough to cause it to fly into the wall with a bang.

Thurmond Drury, seated at his desk, startled at the crash. He lifted his head in alarm, exposing bleary, bloodshot eyes. A nearly empty fifth of whiskey leaned against a single shot glass, its walls still slick with the caramel-colored liquid.

Mr. Drury was a big man, but the amount of sauce he'd consumed would've affected even the stoutest of fellows. His inebriety was a boon I wouldn't reject. I'd take any edge I could get to try and break him.

"Huh?" he said. "Oh. It's you. The detective. Wonderful. Just the sort of person I'd want to share my misery with. Although..." He eyed the bottle's dregs. "It doesn't look as if I have much left to share, does it? I don't suppose you've brought some with you?"

"Some what?" I asked. "Whiskey? Or misery?"

"Either. Although brandy would do in a pinch."

My coworkers filtered in behind me, fanning out to my sides like police-issue doppelgangers.

Thurmond Drury raised a bushy eyebrow. "Eh? What's this? You've brought friends? Well, I guess it's a party then. Too bad I didn't think to bring any streamers."

"Don't play dumb, Thurmond," I said. "You know what this is about. It's the same reason you're drinking yourself into oblivion."

"Oh, so you've come to help me cope with my impending financial ruin? Well, that's thoughtful. I would've assumed you boys had grief counselors for that sort of thing, but apparently they've got you and your friends doing double duty. I guess your police department balance sheets are only slightly less desperate than my own."

"Cut the crap, Drury. We're here about Reginald."

Mr. Drury's jaw clenched. "Oh. Yes. Certainly. Let's talk about that backstabbing bastard, shall we?"

"Let's," I said. "Specifically, let's talk about how you murdered him."

The big man paused for a moment as he stared at me, his eyes narrowing nearly to slits. Then he pounded the table with a clenched fist and broke into a hearty, belly-shaking laugh. It filled the room with his forced mirth.

"Hah! Oh, that's a good one, Detective. You almost had me there. Now, don't get me wrong—I probably *should've* killed him, or at least thrashed him within an inch of his life. But it seems someone beat me to it, didn't they? Oh well...I suppose it's karmic justice, isn't it? He screwed me into oblivion and then that cold bitch karma screwed him right back." He poured himself the last shot of whiskey. "A toast then? To dark humor?"

I didn't say a word. Neither did any of my companions. I'd instructed them to stay quiet before we left the station.

Drury raised the glass to his lips and held it there. He passed his eyes back and forth, from me to Shay to Quinto and back to me. The spirits untouched, he slowly lowered the glass back to the table.

"Wait," he said. "You're serious. You think I killed Reginald, don't you?"

"It all points to you, Drury," I said. "You're the only person he well and truly screwed over. Just admit it. You found out about his theft, and your passions got the best of you. You killed him. But you needed to hide your tracks, and who better to frame than your old pal Charles Talent who made out like a bandit from your loss. All you needed was thermite and some faked blackmail letters."

The blacksmith looked as if he'd swallowed a fly. "What? *Blackmail?*"

Now was the time to grab hold of Mr. Drury, to shake him and squeeze until a confession spurted out of him. But conjecture and hearsay wouldn't break him. I needed evidence, and I didn't have any. I could feel the case slipping away, like sand between my fingers. I swore under my breath.

"Rodgers, Quinto," I said. "Cuff him and take him back to base. We'll sort through this in interrogation." At least I hoped we would.

"I can't believe this." Mr. Drury wiped a meaty hand down his face. "First Reginald ruined me, and now he's working to imprison me."

Quinto and Rodgers approached the blacksmith and helped him to his feet. He wobbled as he stood, but he didn't resist as Rodgers fitted him with a set of irons. Quinto led him by the arm toward the door.

As he passed me, Thurmond paused. "A word of advice, Detective, since it seems it might apply to you. Beware your business partnerships. Apparently they can follow you to their graves."

Ever since we'd entered the arms factory, the nagging feeling at the back of my mind had been pushed aside by my machismo-fueled sense of justice, but suddenly, there it was again. I could almost see its little raccoon face and hear the scratching within my skull.

"Hold on a sec," I said to Quinto. "Mr. Drury, there's something bugging me. Why did you hire Reginald in the first place?"

"I told you before," said Thurmond. "He wasn't an employee. He was an independent contractor."

"Whatever. He may have fooled you into thinking otherwise, but Reginald was just a street rat from the Erming. He didn't have any contacts that would've helped him land the sorts of foreign arms deals you'd covet. So what gave you any confidence he'd land new contracts for you? Did he play you like a fiddle? Provide you with fake references? A forged resume? What?"

In his liquor-soaked state, it took a moment for my question to sink in. Thurmond's eyebrows furrowed in thought. "Well, no. It wasn't anything like that, actually. He came highly recommended, that's all."

"Recommended?" I doubt I hid the obvious incredulity from my voice. "By who?"

"Walter."

"Your accountant?"

"Yes."

Finally. There it was. The piece I'd been missing. I turned to Quinto. "Is Wally still back at the precinct?"

The big guy shook his head. "No. We cut him loose after the interrogation. Figured he didn't have anything else useful to offer."

"Damn it," I said. "We need to find him, pronto. Thurmond, is he here?"

The businessman similarly gave his head a shake. "No. But he stopped by about an hour ago."

"And?"

"And I promptly canned him," said Mr. Drury. "Any fool accountant who could miss the kind of gross negligence that occurred under his watch deserves to be prosecuted, let alone fired."

"Thurmond, we need to find him. Think. Where would he have gone after you delivered the news? Does he have any haunts? A bar, a club, anything like that?"

Mr. Drury snorted. "Walter? Are you serious? The man's a recluse. He probably went home to cry in his ledgers."

"You have an address?"

"I don't know," Thurmond said. "Check with my secretary."

I pursed my lips. "Quinto. Rodgers. Take Thurmond back to the precinct for safekeeping. Shay and I have an accountant to catch."

Quinto nodded and escorted Mr. Drury out.

Rodgers paused at the door and gave me a look. "If I miss anything fun while babysitting your suspect, Daggers, you know I'm going to come calling for more than beers and a kolache."

"I thought you didn't want to be here," I said.

Rodgers shrugged.

"Look," I said, "if I end up in an epic battle of wits with an accountant who's the best damn method actor you and your partner have ever met, then Shay can recount the experience to you for posterity—and I'll buy you a steak dinner."

Rodgers smiled and winked as he left.

"So," said Shay as she walked up from behind. "Walter, of all people. You really think he did it? You think he's a murderer?"

"This case still feels like it's one card short of a full deck," I said. "Walter may or may not be our killer, but I'd bet the odds he's involved. Let's go see if we can shake some acorns from the squirrely man's tree."

49

The secretary stared, mouth agape, as Quinto and Rodgers escorted Mr. Drury from the premises. When I asked for Walter Fry's address, she held her lip and complied without the slightest hint of resistance. She flipped through a rolodex numbly until she found the proper card.

I felt bad for the gal. Con men invariably target the rich because they're the ones with money, but it's also easy to get wrapped up in the notion that rich people are inherently evil and that stealing from them is akin to righting some cosmic injustice. Maybe that's true. Only the gods know—but one thing's for certain. When rich guys go down, everyone else gets trampled underfoot, too. I wondered if Reggie knew that by conning Thurmond, he'd end up putting every working stiff at Drury Arms out of a job.

Address in hand, I exited the compound. Luckily enough, our rickshaw driver was still parked in front. He was no dummy. He knew waiting for our return fare was a safer bet than trying to find a new one in the factory district. Rickshaw fares may be cheap, but they're still out of the price range of day laborers.

The rolodex address listed a place back on the west side, not too far from Reginald's apartment. Shay and I hopped into the cart and our driver hoofed it.

Buildings flew past in a blur as my mind raced in lockstep with the driver. Could mousy, stammering Wally Fry really be the murderer? He didn't seem the type. Then again, I couldn't discount the possibility Wally was enacting his own con—an all-consuming piece of performance art where he pretended to be a bumbling, introverted schmuck to avoid suspicion. If so, then well done, sir.

Or perhaps Wally wasn't the murderer but merely an accomplice of Reginald's. His recommendation of Reggie as a suitable contract negotiator for Drury Arms suggested something along those lines, but the possibility raised more questions. How did Reginald and Wally know each other? Where had they met? The Erming would've chewed up and spit out a guy like Wally in about fifteen minutes.

Eventually, our driver dropped us off at a five-story stonework building a half-dozen blocks or so from the edge of the Pearl. It wasn't quite swanky enough to merit a doorman, but it did have a communal first floor lounge with a couple of red velvet sofa chairs by the windows. The real mark of class was the lack of hobos inside. The building tenants probably pitched in to keep a rent-a-cop on retainer, and judging by the distinct lack of urine smell in the lounge, the hired thug treated loiterers poorly.

Wally's place was on the third floor. I led the way, Shay close at my heels. When we found the apartment door, I stepped back, gathered my weight, and readied my foot.

"Wait," said Shay. "You're not going to kick the door down, are you? Didn't we go through this yesterday?"

"That was Reginald's place," I said. "He's dead. Walter, to the best of our knowledge, is very much alive. I doubt he left his door unlocked."

"Yeah, but there's a good chance he's in his apartment right now. You could knock, you know."

"And give him an opportunity to shimmy out a window and down a fire escape?"

Shay tilted her head at me. "Really?"

"Come on," I said. "Kicking down doors is one of my greatest joys in life. You'd really deny me that?"

My partner sighed. "Fine. If the Captain asks, I'll say you heard a noise inside—a screech that carried a note of distress on its wings."

I smiled. Women didn't understand the ecstasy of kicking down a door. That was a joy the gods only blessed men with, like the thrill of throwing rocks into a lake or the appeal of a spitting contest.

My itchy foot spurred me to action.

"Police! Open Up!"

My boot blasted the door from its hinges with a resounding crash. I stormed into the apartment—a compact studio affair. A rumpled quilt with a garish flowery print covered a convertible futon bed, and a flimsy particleboard desk soaked up the afternoon sun from under a lonely window. A couple tumblers sat on a glass-topped coffee table next to an unidentifiable bottle of hooch.

I ventured further inside. The studio had an L-shape construction, with the kitchenette tucked around a corner. I popped my head into the food prep area, but instead of Wally I only found a stack of boxes of half-eaten takeout food and a pile of dirty dishes.

"Damn," I said. "I guess Wally's not—"

Shay stood in the middle of the apartment, eyes glossed over, hands held out to her sides tickling the air and pulling at invisible strings.

"Oh, wonderful," I grumbled.

I took another glance around the apartment. Clutter abounded, from the takeout containers to clothes thrown haphazardly across the futon to books sprawled over shelves. I shook my head. Apparently Wally valued his personal tidiness less strongly than his professional.

A squeaking hinge interrupted my musings.

I snatched Daisy from my coat and spun, ready to pound any oncoming threat into oblivion, but I failed to encounter any fang-toothed monsters or fiery demons. Instead, I found Wally emerging from his bathroom. His face was pale and his hands shook.

"M-m-my door!" he said. He eyed the prone piece of pine on the floor that used to usher guests into his studio.

"Wally!" I stashed my truncheon and approached him. His head barely scraped my chin. I snarled as he stared at me, his spectacles slipping on his sweat-slicked nose. "What in blazes are you doing? When a cop comes crashing into your place, you're supposed to come out with your hands up!"

"I-I-I..." Wally swallowed back a lump in his throat. "I was u-u-using the b-b-bathroom."

I couldn't contest that argument. Little in life trumps the needs of a man's bowels. Normally I would've cut Wally some slack, but I was tired of the wild goose chase on which we'd been led. I wanted answers, damn it!

I puffed myself up to look more intimidating, although next to Wally even a declawed housecat would've seemed a hulking jaguar.

"Let's cut to the chase, Wally," I said. "You lied about your relationship with Reginald. You knew him much better than you let on."

"W-w-what?"

"You were in cahoots with him, weren't you? You helped him get a foot in the Drury Arms door, and you knew what he was up to. You helped him doctor the files, but why? What's your beef with Thurmond Drury? Did years of squirming under your boss's thumb finally get to you? Figured it was time for payback?"

"I-I-I—"

"I swear to the gods, Wally, if that stammering of yours is a ploy I'll throw the book at you so hard it'll leave your eyes crossed for weeks. Now spit it out, man! How did you know Reginald? Did you meet him on the street? Did he con you? Blackmail you? Did you know him from the Erming? Were you friends? Enemies? Were you...romantically involved?"

That last idea blossomed in my mind. Perhaps Reginald fancied the less fair of the sexes. If he did, though, you'd think a stunner like Reggie could've done better than a drip like Wally.

Small Fry looked at me, confusion and fear waging a losing battle with dignity across his face.

I grabbed Walter roughly by the front of his shirt and slammed him against the wall. He squeaked in terror. If he hadn't just visited the little boy's room, we might've both had to deal with the olfactory consequences.

"Cut the crap, Wally! You know who killed Reginald. Either you did it, or it was someone you know, so spill the beans! Who did it? WHO?"

I shook Wally as I demanded answers, and with every shake another pint of blood drained from his face. He opened his mouth and tried to speak. His tongue moved, but no sound came out. I raised a hand to slap him when a voice caught me from behind in mid windup.

"Who is she, Wally?"

I turned. Shay stood with her hands on her hips, a fierce look of authority radiating from her.

"Wha-wha-wha—"

"Your girlfriend, Wally. Who is she?"

"Girlfriend?" I looked back at Wally. "*Girlfriend? You?* You have *a girlfriend?* You've got to be kidding me."

Shay pushed on, undeterred by my incredulity. "Don't lie to us, Wally. Slim. Pretty. Who is she?"

"Whoa, whoa. Wait a second," I said, throwing my hands up. "You can't be serious."

"I saw it, Daggers," said Shay. "In the vision. And she's involved. I know it."

Free from my clutches, Wally tried to force out a response, but his nerves were sabotaging his vocal cords. "Her n-n-n...her n-n-nay—"

Wally's stammering filled my ears, but the noise felt like nothing more than a gnat's buzzing. I tried to process what Shay had said. Wally? A girlfriend? And not just any girlfriend, but a pretty one? That made no sense at all. How in the world could a schmuck like Walter Fry land a pretty girl? I could barely get one to look at me as if I wasn't some sort of mutant human-cockroach hybrid. It's not as if the guy was rich. His apartment was tiny, and a dump at that. Why, the only way him having a girlfriend made any sense at all was if...

And then it hit me like a ton of bricks. It was obvious in retrospect.

Wally was still trying to force out a name. "Her n-n-name i-i-i—"

"Save it, Wally," I said. "We don't need a name. I know who murdered Reginald Powers."

Shay turned to me, her eyebrows furrowed. "What? Really? You do?"

"Yes," I said. "And we'd better move fast before someone else gets hurt. Reginald may be dead, but his cons are still very much alive."

"Cons?" asked Shay. "As in plural?"

I turned to leave, giving Shay no choice but to follow.

50

Shay peppered me with questions as our rickshaw bounced along the cobblestone streets, but she soon became surly at my lack of verbosity.

"Seriously?" she said. "You're not going to tell me your theory?"

"It's not a theory," I replied. "The word 'theory' implies a lack of observational evidence to support a notion. This time, I know for a fact who killed Reginald Powers."

"And you're not going to enlighten me?"

"Not yet. It's more fun this way. Plus it makes me look super smart when I make the final reveal."

Shay rolled her eyes.

Eventually, our driver pulled up and dropped us off in front of the Talent mansion. I waved to my good friend lemon-face at the gate and pushed on through to the front door.

Furious pounding on my part eventually brought about a response. The door opened, manned by the Talent's manservant. He eyed me and my partner with a look most people reserved for dogs that pass gas at the dinner table.

"Ahh, detectives," the butler said dryly. "What a pleasant surprise. And to what can we attribute this particular honor?"

"Nice to see you too, Jeeves," I said. "We're looking for Felicity Talent? She home?"

"Regrettably not, sir."

"And would you know where she is?"

"To my knowledge, Detective, she's at the place of business of both her and her father's legal representation. As you may recall, her father is currently in police custody under suspicion of murder. She requires legal representation to help defend her father against the accusations of a pompous, overzealous windbag."

Dealing with a passive-aggressive butler wasn't on my to-do list when I'd gotten up in the morning, but I took his snarkiness in stride. I had bigger fish to fry, and the afternoon was starting to wear.

"Right," I said. "And I'm sure arranging her father's legal representation is *all* she's doing there."

Jeeves looked at me blankly.

"So what was the name of those guys?" I asked. "Mackerel, Angst, Crustfont, and Pigs?"

"Merkel, Ernst, Trustmont, and Figs."

"Close enough. You got an address?"

"1118 Riverview. Suite 110. In uptown. If memory serves me correct, sir."

"Thanks, Jeeves," I said. "Stay out of trouble. Wouldn't want to piss off the wrong people."

He closed the door without so much as a goodbye.

Shay accompanied me back toward the street. "What did you mean by that comment?"

Gravel from the Talent's walkway crunched underfoot as we walked. "Which one?"

"The one about Felicity's legal representation."

"Let me ask you something," I said. "Are you familiar with inheritance law?"

"Not in particular," said Shay.

"Well, as it turns out, if someone is convicted of murder they lose their right to property and their entire estate passes on to their next of kin. From a legal standpoint, it's as if they suddenly died."

I saw a light flicker behind Shay's eyes. "Are you saying what I think you're saying? Why would Felicity frame her own father? She's already the heir to his fortune."

"You're close, but not quite there," I said. "Just hang with me a little longer. We're about to finally unravel this thing, and I know how much you like your threads."

51

I craned my neck up to look at the building that stood at 1118 Riverview, a five-story tower with polished marble columns and grotesque gargoyles perched on top. Much like a lawyer, the building was both intimidating and monstrous—or it would've been if the fool landlord had let the structure be. In an attempt to conform to more modern architectural sensibilities, the ground floor of the tower had been gutted and filled with glass and polished steel.

I'd blame the lawyers for the structural defacement, but I'm fairly sure they were only tenants, not owners. As much as I'd like to blame lawyers for all of society's ills, there are limits to their deplorability.

A chill breeze whipped up the street and worked its way into the gap between my neck and collar. The rain clouds that had been threatening earlier had now fully committed to their domination of the sky, and with them they brought abnormally cool temperatures.

"What are we waiting for?" Goosebumps prickled on Shay's forearms as another gust of wind flitted down the street. She rubbed her skin.

"Sorry," I said. "Got lost in thought."

I pushed into the palace of glass and steel and found my way to the law offices of the four stooges. A heavily painted secretary wearing a tight ivory blouse greeted us from behind a cherry wood desk. Exotic potted trees with gnarled trunks and tightly manicured foliage stood at attention flanking each side.

"Can I help you?" said the secretary in a high-pitched tone.

I flashed my badge. "Detective Daggers. This is Detective Steele. I need to see Miss Felicity Talent."

"Oh, I'm sorry, Detective," said the secretary. "Miss Talent is currently in session with one of our attorneys regarding her father's ongoing case. As I'm sure you're well aware, attorney client privilege dictates that all conversations between clients, their families, and their legal representation remain private. If you wish to see Miss Talent, I'm sure you'll be able to find her at her residence at a later time."

The secretary offered me an insincere, prefabricated smile.

I smiled back and leaned over the desk. I meant it as a faux gesture of geniality—a riposte to the secretary's jab—but it also afforded me a better view of her not unsubstantial cleavage. I may have leered a little.

"You misunderstand me," I said. "I'm not here to talk. I'm here to make an arrest."

The secretary scrunched her eyebrows in confusion. "Excuse me?"

"Show me where Miss Talent is," I said, "or I'm liable to start kicking down doors until I find her."

The secretary glanced at my partner, who nodded in agreement. "You think he's kidding, but it's his third favorite pastime—behind snarking and overeating."

I would've leered at Shay, but my leering skills were still fully occupied by the prominently displayed knockers in front of me.

The secretary humphed and led us down a corridor.

As it turned out, my threat to kick down doors turned out to be unnecessary. The interior of the suite held as much glass as the exterior lobby, all meticulously cleaned and free of smudges. Part of me longed to wipe a hand across my forehead and trail it along the translucent paneling just for kicks.

Soon enough, the conference room that held Miss Talent popped into view. Felicity sat with her back to the glass facing another smarmy member of the gray suit brigade—a middle-aged man with a beak nose and salt and pepper hair. Felicity's ever-present, ravishing friend Gretchen sat at her left, her arm draped around Felicity's shoulders in a comforting embrace.

I waved the secretary away and let myself into the meeting room.

The lawyer looked up from the documents that covered the conference table. "Excuse me, but this is a private consultation. Now if you'll kindly—"

"Detective Daggers. Detective Steele." Felicity turned around in her chair to face us. "What are you doing here?"

Felicity's eyes were redder and puffier than they'd been on our last encounter, if such a thing was possible.

She looked as if she hadn't slept in at least two days. Her friend Gretchen, however, looked alert, well-rested, and as radiant as ever. Her bronze-colored hair shone with a glossy sheen, and her rosy cheeks radiated good health. Only her eyes betrayed any hint of distress.

The lawyer stood. "Ahh. So you're from the police department. Well then, detectives, I'm sure you're well aware of the impropriety of your actions in coming here. Not only are you breaking the covenant of our attorney-client relationship, but you're causing undue distress and emotional turmoil to my client and her family—a point I'll be sure to make to your superiors in the form of an official, written complaint."

"Sit down and shut up, poindexter," I said. "We didn't come here to create a headache for the department. We're here to make an arrest."

That perked everyone's ears.

"What?" said the lawyer.

"Huh?" said Felicity.

Gretchen stared at me, a look of pained confusion on her face.

"You know," I said, "on our way here I was discussing an interesting point with Detective Steele. As it turns out, if someone is convicted of murder their entire estate passes to their next of kin, or whoever is listed as the beneficiary in their will if they have one. Isn't that right, Mr...what's your name?" I eyeballed the lawyer.

"Marshall Figs," he said. "And yes, that's correct."

I turned to Felicity. "Now don't you find that interesting, Miss Talent? If your father does, in fact, get convicted for the murder of your fiancé, you'd instantly inherit all your family's wealth. I wonder who that could benefit?"

Felicity's eyes widened, a wildness creeping into them from the corners. "Wha... What are you implying? Are you saying you think I murdered my own fiancé, and then I framed my father for the murder so I could access our family's wealth!? Why...you MONSTER!"

Felicity jumped out of her chair and whipped an open-handed blow at my face, but years of getting slapped by women who'd been provoked had sharpened my reflexes. I blocked the slap with ease.

"Word to the wise, Miss Talent," I said. "Never attempt to strike a police officer. And to answer your question—no, I don't think you killed your fiancé. I know you loved him, and beyond that I believe he loved you, too. I think he loved you more than anything. More than his career. More than money. And that, actually, is why your friend Gretchen killed him."

"What? *Gretchen?*" Felicity pulled back, turning her puffy eyes on her friend.

"I...I'm sorry, Detective," said Gretchen. "I must've misheard you. It sounded like you said I killed Reginald."

I set my eyes firmly on the bombshell. "That's exactly what I said."

Gretchen scoffed. "And...why would I kill Reginald? What possible reason could I have for murdering my best friend's fiancé?"

"Oh, I don't know," I said. "Probably because he ruined years' worth of planning when he fell in love with your mark—the wealthy, single, and before you came along, friendless Felicity Talent."

Felicity stepped away from the table, clutching the folds of her blouse near her chest. "What? What are you saying? Gretchen, what's he talking about?"

Gretchen looked me in the eyes, color darkening her cheeks. "I have no idea what he's talking about, Felicity."

"Oh, really?" I said. "So I don't suppose there's anything in these legal documents Miss Talent's been signing that would transfer any of her wealth over to you in the event of her father's imprisonment, would there?"

I snatched a stack of papers from the conference table. The lawyer tried to snatch them back.

"Hey! Put those down," Figs said. "Those are private documents between my client and her legal team. You need a warrant to look at them."

"Not so. I happened to see evidence of coercion in this document right on top. That makes the whole stack admissible evidence."

That was a lie of course. I had no idea what the legal documents contained—I'm not much of a speed reader—but I suspected if I looked closely, I'd find documents signed by Miss Talent that had nothing to do with her father's case. Documents that likely cut Gretchen Winters into a substantial share of her family's fortune.

I made a show of flipping through the papers before stuffing them into my interior coat pocket where they could keep Daisy company.

The lawyer blustered and tossed around threats and insults in legalese. Gretchen sat there, gritting her teeth and staring at me. I could see the daggers forming in her irises.

"Gretchen Winters," I said. "You're under arrest for the murder of Reginald Powers, as well as multiple counts of forgery, impersonation, trespassing, and felony blackmail. Stand up and put your hands behind your back."

Like the good girl she wasn't, Gretchen obeyed orders. The lawyer tried to interfere, but his gentlemanly protection of Miss Winters quickly turned to panicked self-preservation when I told Shay to cuff him for conspiracy to commit fraud. While Shay bent Mr. Figs over the table, I slipped a pair of cold steel shackles over Gretchen's slender wrists.

As I did so, Gretchen turned on the charm. She batted her eyelashes at me. "Really, Detective? Handcuffs? You can't possibly see me as a threat, can you?"

"Sweetheart," I said, "yesterday, I would've fallen head over heels for your damsel-in-distress routine. But I've already got a mistress, and her name's Lady Justice. Good luck trumping her."

And with that, I led my captive out the door and on a journey toward my mistress's cold embrace.

52

Shay accompanied me from the interrogation room back to our desks. Despite what they say about beauty and brains being an either-or proposition in the fairer sex, Gretchen Winters was no dummy. She kept her mouth shut for the most part, but the evidence spoke for itself. The documents I'd seized at the law offices contained a few outliers—notably a form signed by Miss Talent that gave Gretchen power of attorney over Talent's entire estate. In addition, our forensics team had revisited the blackmail documents we'd found in Charles Talent's safe.

They'd found Gretchen's prints on more than one page.

"I still don't see why you needed to give Gretchen a thorough pat down," said Shay as we walked down the hallway. "That seemed unnecessary."

"Better safe than sorry," I said. "You never know what sorts of concealed weapons she might've had on her, or what evidence she might've hidden on her person."

"Under pants as tight as hers? Right..." Shay rolled her eyes.

"Come on, you know I'm a one woman man." I patted the pocket that held Daisy.

"One at a time maybe..."

I smiled in response.

We found Rodgers and Quinto loitering near our desks. I'd tasked them with interviewing the gray suit.

"You guys are done already?" I said. "Get anything out of that Figs character?"

"Not much," said Rodgers. "Claimed he's madly in love with Gretchen. Thought she was 'the one.' Went so far as to allege a 'fog of love' kept him from seeing and thinking clearly. Claimed he had no idea the extent of the documents he'd asked Miss Talent to sign."

"Right. I'm sure," I said. "And how long have he and Miss Winters been an item?"

"A week or so," said Quinto. "Said Gretchen came on to him hard, and he responded in kind."

"Heh, well, at least part of him responded in kind." Rodgers sniggered. Quinto joined in the mirth. As long as men walked the earth, dick jokes would never get old.

"To be fair, though, Daggers," said Quinto. "I'd probably be foggy, too, if I'd been doing the dirty deed as often as Figs said he and Gretchen were."

I glanced at Shay. "Poor Wally. He's going to be heartbroken. Losing his job and his girlfriend in the same fell blow."

My partner shrugged. "Such is life."

Rodgers and Quinto eyed us with a certain level of curiosity. They still hadn't been filled in on everything.

"So," said Rodgers as he sat on the corner of my desk, "is it true? Was it the Talent girl's friend the whole time? How'd you figure it out?"

"Yes, oh wise sage," said Quinto, crossing his arms. "Regale us with a tale of your deductive wisdom."

The boys knew me well. I secretly itched to crow about how I'd deftly unraveled the case, but they fluffed my ego nonetheless.

I sat in my chair. "Well, the key was the marriage between Reginald and Felicity. Detective Steele made a good point about the prenuptial agreement. It didn't make sense that Reginald would've considered eloping with Felicity if he was after her money. So their marriage had to have been based in mutual love. But at the same time, I couldn't accept the marriage was proceeding for all the right reasons."

"Probably because you're old and jaded and have a lump of coal for a heart," said Shay.

I poked the air with my finger. "I prefer the alternative explanation that I have experience with people and their motives, and you don't. Don't worry, we'll take your training wheels off once you've learned how to steer."

Shay grinned. "And there's the Daggers I know. Praising me for a good point one moment, throwing me under the carriage the next."

I gave Shay the old single eyebrow raise. She smirked back at me.

"Are you going to get on with it?" said Rodgers.

"Right," I said. "Anyway, we were at Wally's place when Shay had one of her out-of-body experiences, and this time her insight actually proved to be useful."

"*This* time?" said Shay incredulously. "It's been useful every time!"

"But this time it was particularly useful because it helped *me* solve the case. Detective Steele saw evidence of Wally's girlfriend. A stunner by all accounts."

"That guy was dating someone?" said Rodgers.

"That was my reaction," I said. "I couldn't make sense of it, either. Wally? With an attractive girl? That's when I put the pieces together. The girl had to be Gretchen, and she and Reginald had to be partners. They were running two separate undercover lover cons."

Rodgers and Quinto made noises of agreement and nodded their heads.

Shay cast a confused look my way. "An undercover lover con?"

"A classic gambit," I said. "The undercover lover con is where one member of a team goes in and seduces someone on the inside of an operation in order to gain access for another member. In this case, Reginald and Gretchen pulled two slightly different variations of the same con.

"In the first case, Gretchen seduced Walter Fry and used her influence to get Reginald a position at Drury Arms, despite the fact that he had no experience acquiring and negotiating contracts. While Reginald worked his con to steal illicit arms from the Drurys, Gretchen continued to work her angle on Wally. Why? Because she needed access to his office key so she could doctor the Drury Arms shipping invoices. She must've borrowed the key at night while Wally slept and returned it before he realized anything was amiss.

"Then, while Gretchen and Reginald were working their first con, one of them came into contact with Felicity and saw the opportunity to swindle her. So they pulled another iteration of the same con. In this case, Gretchen befriended the lonely Felicity and got to know everything she could about her so Reginald could come in and seduce her. And it worked. The only problem was, Reginald actually fell for Felicity. It's the only thing that explains his willingness to sign the prenuptial agreement.

"Of course, Gretchen must've found out about Reginald's true feelings for Felicity. Angry over it, she must've threatened him. That's why Reginald wanted to elope. He wanted to leave Gretchen and his old life behind and run off with Felicity.

"Unfortunately for him, Gretchen figured out a way to finish the con without his assistance. She killed Reginald and framed Charles Talent for his murder, knowing that once convicted Mr. Talent's wealth would pass on to Felicity. Given that Felicity was overcome with grief from her fiancé's murder and her father's imprisonment, Gretchen figured she could coerce Felicity into making some rather dubious financial decisions—which is exactly what we found.

"As if that wasn't a sure enough thing, it appears Gretchen decided to double down by bedding one of the lawyers, too. It wouldn't surprise me if she planned to work multiple legal angles. Gretchen probably thought she could scuttle Mr. Talent's case from the inside to ensure his conviction."

Rodgers rubbed his chin. "So...I guess it's a done deal, isn't it?"

"Pretty much," I said. "We're sending a sample of Gretchen's penmanship to the handwriting expert to confirm she's the one who wrote the blackmail letters, but with all the other evidence we've got, this case is as good as closed. Which reminds me—" I glanced at my partner. "I never finished showing you how to fill out the post-case paperwork, did I?"

Shay shook her head.

"Alright," I said. "Let's get it done before it gets too late. Rodgers, Quinto. You guys mind releasing Mr. Drury and Mr. Talent? I'd rather not face the latter. Not that I think he's liable to turn me into a crisp for setting him free and figuring out who framed him, but still..."

Quinto gave me a knowing nod. "No worries, Daggers. We'll take care of it."

53

While we filled out and filed the proper forms, the heavens opened up and unleashed the full force of their fury on our fair city. Raindrops battered the police building, but the deluge only lasted a half hour or so. As we finished our work, the rain abruptly stopped. From through the windows that lined the Captain's office, I could see the clouds begin to part.

It was late. The sun had already set, but its rays still curved over the horizon to light portions of the sky. Gaps between clouds shone with the choicest colors of an artist's arsenal—bright oranges, pale yellows, and deep purples.

Shay cleared and stored the corkboard while I gazed at the skies.

Rodgers and Quinto sometimes give me crap for not possessing an artistically discerning bone in my body— which is true. I can't stand art. But I can appreciate the beauty of nature, and not just certain aspects of nature that walk around wearing tight skirts.

As I stared into the mixed palate of colors that blossomed above the buildings, I couldn't help but think about cycles. Cycles of heat and cold that gathered moisture from the earth and brought it crashing back down in sheets of rain. Cycles of life and death and decay that sprouted saplings from the bodies of the dead. And cycles of human nature, like those where old, grizzled partners got replaced by fresh-faced new ones.

Would I be like Griggs one day? Would I hang up my badge and vanish into the night, leaving a partner to scramble in my wake, never having uncovered the hopes and dreams and feelings that churned underneath my hard exterior? Or could I finally take down the walls I'd erected, the ones I'd forged out of humor and indifference to protect me when someone I cared about rejected or left me? And could the person to help me through that monumental task possibly be my new slender, half-elf partner?

"Something on your mind, Daggers?" Shay had returned and was gathering her things.

"Huh? Me? Nah. Just glad I won't have to walk to Jjade's in the rain."

"You really like that place, huh?"

"What can I say. I don't cook much."

Shay gave her head a slight shake and smiled.

"You leaving?" I asked. "I'll walk you out."

Shay didn't explicitly sanction my gentlemanly gesture, but neither did she put up a stink.

We walked to the front and out the precinct's wide, double doors. I took a deep breath of the cool evening air, cherishing the clean, moist smell. While I never fancied getting spat on by the gods, I did appreciate the rain's ability to wash away the scents of garbage and urine that usually infused the city streets.

"You know, I've been thinking about our case," said Shay, pausing on the station's front steps.

"Yeah? What about it?" I said.

"Knowing what we now know, do you think Gretchen killed Reginald just to keep their con alive?"

"What do you mean?" I asked.

"Well, think about it," said Shay. "Gretchen and Reginald worked together, but what was their relationship like? Were they partners in crime, or partners in life? What if, unbeknownst to Reginald, Gretchen was madly in love with him, and when she found out that Reginald had fallen for Felicity, she lost it and killed him."

I scratched my chin. "Huh. You know, that theory makes a lot of sense—a lover's con ruined by a lover's triangle. It's poetic, in a murderous, twisted sort of way." I shrugged. "I guess we'll never know for sure, though. Not unless Gretchen decides to open up her heart to the judicial system, and I don't think the chances of that are particularly good."

"Yeah, me neither," said Shay.

I stood there for a moment, my hands in my pockets, as the cool breeze pressed against my back. "Well... goodnight."

I turned to go.

"Wait... Detective Daggers?"

I stopped and turned back. "Yes?"

Shay scratched at the back of her neck. "Look, I just wanted to say...I mean...how do I put this?"

"What is it?"

"Well... I know we got off to a bit of a rough start yesterday. Part of that was my fault. Part of it clearly was yours. Regardless of the blame, though, I went home last night feeling kind of...*confused*, for lack of a better word. And that feeling lasted throughout the night and into the morning. I didn't know what today would hold. When I came to work this morning, I was apprehensive to say the least. But I have to admit—today's events were stimulating. And more than that, I felt a lot more at ease with you today than I did yesterday."

I wasn't sure how to respond. "That's...good to hear, I guess."

"I think what I'm trying to say is...I think we can make this partnership work. We might both have to adapt a little, but between my abilities and your deductive sense, not to mention your somewhat *unorthodox* methodologies, I think we'll make a good team."

Something about what she said festered at the back of my mind—a piece of cud I'd been chewing on for a while but hadn't yet swallowed. I scratched my head as I considered my options.

"Cons are fun, aren't they?" I said. "Not all cases are this entertaining. Most are pretty cut and dry. Usually someone sticks a knife in somebody else and they die. And most murderers are pretty dumb. It feels like half the time we find the killer with his hand still on the hilt. At least most con artists have half a brain. Makes the chase more fun, wouldn't you say?"

"Well, I don't have a lot of experience," said Shay, "but yes, this case was fun—as much fun as a murder investigation can be, I suppose."

"When you think about it though, most cons are pretty straight forward. The con man is almost invariably after money, but some differ. Some are after love—maybe even prestige." I paused and looked at Shay. "So, the question is...what are you after?"

My partner raised an eyebrow. "Excuse me?"

"The con you're running. What's the point?"

"I...don't follow," said Shay.

I gave Shay a smile. Not a snarky, insincere smile, but a genuine one. "Come now, Miss Steele. I know I look dumb. I swear it's not my mother's fault. It's a by-product of taking too many hits to the face. And to be fair, I act the part my face advertises for the most part. But give me some credit. I know a con when I see one."

To Shay's credit, she continued to play the role she'd undertaken. "Daggers, if this is some sort of weird joke, or a hazing ritual, then—"

"Am I going to have to spell it out for you?" I asked. "Very well. I'm always happy to oblige. In Wally's apartment, you had a vision of his attractive girlfriend. Well, it was pretty obvious someone else had been living there besides Wally. The amount of food in the kitchen. The pair of glasses on the coffee table. Not to mention the mess. A guy like Wally wouldn't have lived like that on his own. I'm guessing you saw something that gave it away. Maybe a brassiere or a pair of panties. Maybe you even guessed it belonged to Gretchen. I know I spared a few glances at her bosom. Picking out her bra from a pile wouldn't have been that hard.

"Your vision at Reginald's place had two components. The fire part was easy to guess. You were in his room before I was, and you're a half-elf, so I'm willing to bet your sense of smell is better than mine. You simply sniffed out the fire in the wastebasket before I did. The part about you predicting that dangerous, tattooed short guys were involved had me stumped for a while—until we met Detective Morales, that is. When I found out you interned with him it all made sense. You must've spotted the calligraphed tattoo designs on the calling cards in Reginald's room and connected the dots. Maybe you didn't remember the exact gang that sported those tattoos, but you were clever enough to recall the designs were dwarven.

"The one vision I still can't completely explain is the first one. I'm not sure how you knew Reggie didn't die by magic. My best guess is you noticed there weren't any burn marks on the walls of the corridor. If Reginald had taken a fireball to the chest—a fireball potent enough to burn right through him—it should've kept going and left its mark somewhere. Instead, the only burn mark was right underneath Reggie on the floor. So you must've surmised Reginald was already dead at the time of the murder, and why would a fire mage knock a guy out and hit him with a fireball afterward? Or maybe you noticed some pattern to the spray marks on the floor that I didn't. That's my best guess, anyway, but I'm all ears if you have a different explanation."

54

hay's cheeks blossomed a bright red, and her eyes resembled those of a fox cornered by slobbering, baying hounds. She opened her mouth, but no sound came out. She ran her tongue across her lips, swallowed, and tried again.

"Actually," she said, "my father's a chemist. I recognized the silvery-gray residue on Reginald's chest as the remains of a thermite reaction."

"Oh," I said. "Well, I guess that makes sense, too."

We both stood there in silence, partaking in the deepening evening gloom. Lamplighters crawled over the streets, trying to stay ahead of the sun's withdrawal. One of them stopped nearby and lit the lamps that flanked the police station doors with his long wick-ended pole. As he left, a stray breeze—a remnant of the afternoon's storms—flitted past. It raised the hackles on my arms.

Shay seemed oblivious to it.

"You must think me the worst kind of fraud," she said after what seemed like an eternity.

"No. Certainly not the worst kind," I said. "You forget—I've met a lot of unsavory characters in my day. Lying about having supernatural powers doesn't automatically place you among them. I'm just trying to figure out why you did it. Why the façade?"

Shay forced out a bitter laugh. "Really, Daggers? You may be excellent at piecing together evidence, but you're not particularly observant, are you? The clues are right in front of your face, day in and day out, and you don't even notice them."

That sounded like an insult. I responded defiantly. "Huh?"

Shay shook her head, then settled her eyes on me. "Look at me, Daggers. What do you see?"

I took a good look. I saw a young half-elf woman with long, dark brown hair. A looker who downplayed her own sexuality either because she didn't know how to use it, or because she didn't want to. A woman who lacked a certain measure of confidence, despite the fact that she'd picked up on things even a seasoned veteran like myself had missed. And in her first two days on the job, no less.

I wasn't entirely sure how I was supposed to respond to her question, though. I went with the literal route.

"Well, I see a woman in a cream-colored blouse and slacks. She's got long hair, slender arms, and a pair of perky br—"

"A *woman*, Daggers," said Shay. "The answer I was looking for was *a woman*. Honestly, look around you. What do you see? Or more accurately, what don't you see? The answer to that question is the same as before.

Women. There's not a single woman in a position of authority in the entire precinct.

"When I showed up yesterday morning, you thought I was a secretary. Do you know why I got so mad? It's not because you acted like a chauvinist jerk—which you did, by the way. It's because that's the same sort of response I've been getting my entire life. I've wanted to be a detective since I was a little girl. To be able to solve mysteries and make the world a safer place at the same time—it's a thrilling feeling. You know how it feels. I've seen it in your eyes over the last two days.

"But the difference between us, I'd be willing to wager, is no one ever told *you* to forget about your passion and pursue something else—something that would be more suited to your sex. Not your *skills*, mind you, but your gender.

"I realized pretty early on I'd never be taken seriously in this field. Unless...I did something drastic. And so I pretended I had a gift—a gift for seeing things. Past events. Bits of crimes. Threads, I decided to call them. It seemed like as good a description as any. Certainly it convinced my teachers at school. From there, I ran with it. Created a whole routine to go along with my visions. Once I got started, it took on a life of its own. And eventually it brought me here—where I've always dreamed of being."

I ran my tongue across my teeth. "What I don't get is, how is it nobody ever noticed you were making it all up?"

Shay shrugged. "I don't know. I'm observant. I pick up on little things other people tend to ignore. But how

I was able to fool so many people for so long? Well...people see what they want to see, I guess."

I nodded. I'd seen the truth of that statement time and time again. Part of the reason I succeeded at my job was because I often took note of what other people were perfectly willing to ignore.

Shay took a deep breath and sighed. "Well, it was good while it lasted, I suppose. Even if it only lasted two days."

"What are you talking about?" I asked.

"This job. I'll have to hand in my resignation now."

"*What*? Why?"

My partner looked at me as if I were denser than lead. "Because I lied, that's why."

"So what," I said. "Everybody lies about something or other. You lied about your abilities, but only because you craved the job. That's not a crime."

"But—"

"But nothing. So what if you don't have supernatural abilities to see into the past? What you have is better. You have a keen sense of observation. In this line of work, that's far more useful. And in a sense, it lets you see into the past as well as some psychic ability would've. Trust me, I'd much rather have someone with your eyes and brain at my side—somebody with the passion you exhibit—than some dope who got here simply because she was gifted with a sixth sense from the gods."

Shay peered at me through squinting eyes, as if she couldn't believe what she was hearing. "So you're serious, then? You don't want me to resign?"

"Are you kidding?" I said. "I'm finally starting to like you. Besides, if you left, the old bulldog would probably try to convince Griggs to come out of retirement. I don't think that's a scenario any of us wants to endure."

"But...what'll we tell the captain?"

"As far as I'm concerned, we don't have to tell him anything. It doesn't matter how you do your job as long as you do it well. If Captain or Rodgers or Quinto is along for a case, maybe you can pretend to have one of your visions every now and then, but other than that, we'll pretend nothing's changed."

Shay took a few slow breaths, then nodded. "Umm...well. Ok, then. I'm still trying to process all of this, but...thanks for the vote of confidence, Daggers." She stuck out a hand.

I shook it. "No problem. It's what partners do."

Shay pulled her hand back. "So...see you tomorrow?"

"Yup," I said. "See you tomorrow—*Detective* Steele."

It was the first time I'd called her a detective to her face without anyone else around to impress. The meaning wasn't lost on her. She smiled, her eyes twinkling with confidence, before turning to walk away.

I hitched up my coat and headed off toward Jjade's, my boots squelching in puddles as I walked. I let my brain wander, free to ponder the day's events, everything from the case to Shay's revelation to our newly fortified partnership.

Detectives Daggers and Steele, homicide.

A grin slowly spread across my face. I had to admit, it had a nice ring to it.

ABOUT THE AUTHOR

Alex P. Berg is a mystery, fantasy, and science fiction author, a scientist, and a heavy metal aficionado. Connect with him at www.alexpberg.com. If you'd like to be notified when new books are released, please sign up for his mailing list on his website. You will only be contacted when new books come out, your address will never be shared, and you can unsubscribe at any time.

Word of mouth is critical to author success. If you enjoyed this novel, please consider leaving a positive review on Amazon. Even if it's only a line or two, it would be a *huge* help. Thanks!

92688424R00178

Made in the USA
Lexington, KY
07 July 2018